CRIME DOESN'T PAY

The McCrory ship *Crystal* fled Shann system, bearing three human looters of its ancient civilization. The ship's nimble engines had outrun the pursuit, though the Guild-ship's detectors still tracked them inexorably.

"Crystal," the radio demanded, "Return to port."

As before, *Crystal* ignored it.

"They've lost us. Guild beacon receding."

Lume scowled at his brother-in-law. "I still think we should go back, return the Light to . . ."

"Let it go, little brother. You're outvoted."

The flight board chimed a warning and Roycrai promptly swiveled back to the controls. "New contact," he told them. "Out here? Where in the hell did it come from?"

Lume scowled again. "Maybe the Guild keeps a ship out here, waiting for types like you, Roycrai."

"Shut up."

The overhead visual screen flicked on automatically, activated by the approaching ship . . .

Lume had a flashing impression of a huge black hull hurtling past them, blanking the stars. The alien cruiser swept past, raking *Crystal* with the piercing light of high-power lasers, stabbing, enshrouding, killing. The control boards exploded in a shower of sparks and blue-arced fire. Roycrai screamed thinly, his hands pinned to the controls by the electricity coursing through his body.

"Roycrai!"

Lume heard his sister's despairing cry and grabbed her as she lunged toward her husband. She struggled wildly against Lume, crying out again and again as Roycrai's body jerked convulsively, his hands blackening as flesh burned.

"No! No, no, no, no . . ."

PAULA KING

MAD ROY'S LIGHT

A Baen Books Original

Baen Publishing Enterprises
260 Fifth Avenue
New York, N.Y. 10001

ISBN: 0-671-72015-5

Cover art by Donald Clavette

First printing, September 1990

Distributed by
SIMON & SCHUSTER
1230 Avenue of the Americas
New York, N.Y. 10020

Printed in the United States of America

DEDICATION

This book is dedicated to my husband and fellow writer, T. Jackson King, whom I love in all the ways; and to my parents, Duane and Elaine Downing.

Acknowledgements

My special thanks to C.J. Cherryh and Andre Norton for their many years of inspiration and wonderful books; to Jacqueline Lichtenberg for her encouragement and enthusiasm; to Marti Steussy, Lana James, and Kathleen Woodbury for their friendship and help with *Mad Roy's Light*; to Toni Weisskopf and Josepha Sherman of Baen Books; to Bev Carter, Susan Hastings, Claudia Ingram, and Roy Dwyer; and to Tom Sr. and Sarah King.

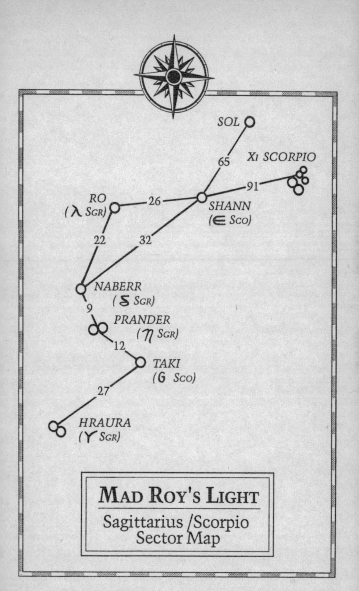

SOL

XI SCORPIO

65

RO
(λ Sgr) ——26—— SHANN
(∈ Sco)

91

22   32

NABERR
(Ƨ Sgr)

9

PRANDER
(η Sgr)

12

TAKI
(6 Sco)

27

HRAURA
(Υ Sgr)

MAD ROY'S LIGHT

Sagittarius/Scorpio
Sector Map

Prologue

The Shenda voyager-ship, *Tavendor*, approached
Shann home-planet after a long journey, its weary
crew grateful to be home. Madringa Station grew
steadily larger in the command-deck screens, showing its crisscross pattern of habitats, fusion plants,
and industrial parks. A dozen interstellar clanships
lay in their port cradles, their bulk diminished by
distance. In the background loomed the ruddy cra-
tered bulk of Shann's single moon, Madringa, about
which the station orbited, and, beyond Madringa
and its busy commerce, the soft blueness of Shann
itself, now in quarter-eclipse. Someday other ships
might come to this place, should Shann's outrunner
ships find other folk in their long constant search
among the nearby stars.

For centuries, the Shenda had searched, finding
only a few primitives, near-animal races who thought
but did not understand, who could not yet build,
who lived from day to day, hunting their food. *Someone must be the eldest,* the wise said, but the young
among the Shenda wished otherwise and continued
the search, constructing new devices to power their

ships, finding new means to slip faster and farther through non-space. A few warned against the newer devices, doubting a ship-drive that progressively tampered with the strange fabric of space-time, but still the ships went outward, searching.

And stretched too far. Deep in the bowels of *Tavendor,* the new drive-component shuddered and bent suddenly into non-space, dragging at its connecting parts. The ship lurched violently as an explosion ripped through the engine room, destroying other essential controls. *Tavendor* rolled helplessly on its axis, then spun out of control, falling inexorably towards Madringa.

On the control deck, a tall and flickering shape emerged through the deck-plate from the engine room below, stretching upwards with tendril hands. At its head, a single ruby eye flashed a waxing flame, an eerie counterpart of the drive-pivot that had malfunctioned. The thing shuddered in the ecstasy of its creation. *I AM THE LIGHT!* it cried without voice, without sound, and took the Shenda crew into its substance. *Die with me,* it crooned, then reached outward for others.

Its hull flickering with a reddish light, *Tavendor* plunged through Madringa Station, ripping aside ships and girders, breaching the fragile containment of nuclear power-stations, feeding the creature's strength. *I AM THE LIGHT!* it cried in its thousand dead voices, and hungrily reached to Madringa itself. A ruby light suffused the dusty plains and craters, leaping forward in ruddy shadows to engulf a world, then, unable to absorb more, shattered all in a cataclysm of self-destruction.

On Shann, the Shenda watched helplessly as Madringa slowly dismembered before their eyes, disbelieving until the deadly bombardment began. Over the course of days, the fragments of Madringa smashed into Shann, leveling cities, killing the millions, ending all hopes.

It was the death of youth, and the beginning of insanity.

Chapter 1

The McCrory ship *Crystal* fled Shann system, bearing three human looters of its ancient civilization. The ship's nimble engines had outrun the pursuit, though the Guild-ship's detectors still tracked them inexorably. *Crystal* skipped through the outer tumbling fragments of dark comets and ice, using Shann's Oort cloud to shake off that last slender hold of the alien Daruma who guarded Shann.

"*Crystal*," the radio demanded, the Daruma captain's voice high with outrage. "You will return to port."

As before, *Crystal* ignored him.

Sitting idly by *Crystal's* comm-panel, Lume Tanner turned the madringal in his hand, watching the ruby shift of reflected light across its battered surface. It was a slender statuette, barely two handsbreadths high, topped by a cracked ruby jewel. The Shenda made them by the thousands to display in their bazaars, multiplying deity beyond all reason in their mad fervency. Fifteen millenia ago, the Daruma said, the Shenda culture had collapsed in disaster, a cataclysm remembered only in religious

4

myths and the strange Shenda compulsion of the madringals.

Why? he wondered, guessing at the truth and wishing he could ask someone, especially a Guildsman. The Daruma of Naberr, the golden sun Terra called Delta Sagittarii, had lived among the other five Sagittarian races for centuries, binding them together in the economic and cultural web of their Guild-mediated trade, long ago taking up the guardianship of the senile Shenda. A Guildsman might know, once he had the key Lume now held in his hand.

He watched the ship lights glimmer in the madringal's metal surface, and knew he'd never have the chance to ask, not after this. "Damn," he muttered furiously.

"They've lost us. Guild beacon receding." Roycrai leaned back from his pilot controls and stretched, a satisfied smile on his saturnine face.

Lume scowled at his brother-in-law. "I still think we should go back, return the Light to . . ."

"Let it go, little brother." Roycrai stretched again. "You're outvoted. Right, Tayna?"

Lume's sister, seated in the chair beyond Roycrai, nodded unhappily and glanced an appeal at Lume. "Lume . . ."

Lume tightened his lips, refusing to unbend even to her. He stood up abruptly and snapped open a nearby cabinet, then shoved the statuette within. The cabinet door slammed like a pistol shot. He turned back to the others.

"We at least should have told the McCrory chief. Maybe he could talk to the Guildsmen. . . ."

"And let *him* take a share? Where's your business sense, Lume?" Roycrai smirked, then waved magnanimously at the tach-radio. "But there—why don't you call big-brother Vaughn and ask him? He's probably still at Ro, mucking out petty contracts for the Ro lizard-men. He'd tell you the same: it's about time McCrory tweaked a few Daruma noses."

"Vaughn isn't here—and he would never be stupid enough to steal from the Shenda, not with the Guild watching. He plays by the rules, and no place in Sagittarius-sector has more rules than Shann. How many ships do the Daruma have to shoot up to convince you?"

Roycrai shrugged him off. "That was a long time ago."

"*And* the last time a Terran trader tried to steal from the Shenda. But what do you care? You'll sell the Light to that private Centauri lab and get Terra booted out of Sagittarius. What happens then, Roy?"

"So? We'll be rich."

Lume snorted. "That's what I thought. Tayna, can't you see . . ."

The flight board chimed a warning and Roycrai promptly swiveled back to the controls. "New contact," he told them. "Out here? Where in the hell did it come from?"

Lume scowled. "Maybe the Guild keeps a ship out here, waiting for types like you, Roycrai."

"Shut up."

The visual board displayed a tiny light-point arcing towards them, a tracer-light matching the graceful curve. Roycrai tapped the keys on his board, then glanced at the side-display. "Big sucker, Class-Four cruiser at least."

"Guild?" Tayna asked.

"Who else could it be?" Roycrai swore. "Jesus, it's moving fast. Prepare for jump."

Tayna's mouth dropped. "Here? We're still ten AU from jump-point. You can't jump inside a gravity well."

"I said prepare for jump!" Roycrai snarled and reached for the jump-control.

"No!" Tayna's hand slapped down on the damper switch. "We're too close to Shann. You want to get to Centauri as a sine-wave?"

The overhead visual screen flicked on automatically, activated by the approaching ship, distracting Lume's attention. In the star-pointed blackness, Shann's sun glowed a distant orange, its light a shimmering reflection on the sleek silvery-black sides of the approaching ship. *God, it's big!* Lume thought, awed. *Do the Daruma have anything that big?*

"Stop that!" Tayna said irritably, pushing at Roycrai. She again slapped her palm on the jump-damper, and Roycrai knocked her hand away.

"Goddamn it, Roy!" Tayna yelled as Roycrai again reached for the jump-control. Furious, she grabbed his arm and pulled him half from his chair.

"Hey! Wait a minute!" Lume yelled, sensing an imminent fight inches from the ship controls. Neither listened. Roycrai swung angrily at Tayna, missing as she ducked. She stumbled backward from the boards and lost her balance, lurching hard against Lume. They both fell in a tangle of arms and legs.

"No, Roy!" Tayna shrieked and gathered herself to leap for Roycrai. Lume had a flashing impression of a huge black hull hurtling past them, blanking the stars. The alien cruiser swept past, raking *Crystal* with the piercing light of high-power lasers, stabbing, enshrouding, killing. The control boards exploded in a shower of sparks and blue-arced fire. Roycrai screamed thinly and writhed, his head thrown backwards, his hands pinned to the controls by the electricity coursing through his body.

"Roycrai!"

Lume heard Tayna's despairing cry and grabbed her as she lunged toward Roycrai. She struggled wildly against him, crying out again and again, her eyes staring, her mouth an "O" of horror, as Roycrai's body jerked convulsively, his hands blackening as flesh burned.

"Noooo! No, no, no, no. . . ."

The alien ship swept by again, adding to its destruction. Lume heard the whistle of escaping atmosphere as plates buckled to open space. With a groan, he wrapped his arms around the weeping Tayna and held her close. The view-screen flickered as the flames at the control boards flared out abruptly, extinguished by the automatic dampers. Roycrai's body slumped slowly forward, his eyes staring in dead surprise, and the stench of his burned flesh filled the cabin, tainting the fast-escaping air.

"They didn't even give a warning," Tayna sobbed. "Why?"

Lume lacked breath for an answer. His lungs ached from the falling pressure, making him gasp for the air no longer there. Black spots wavered uneasily across his vision as he slipped into anoxia. Dimly he felt Tayna slump loosely against him. One of the spots swelled in the view-screen, its bay doors gaping. He saw the brilliant lights within the bay, a glimpse of shadowed lean figures moving quickly, then nothing.

He lost time then, to awaken as the aliens boarded *Crystal*. Fresh air flooded through the small cabin, strangely scented but breathable. As Lume lifted his head groggily, two figures pushed into the cabin— not the stumpy, dwarfish figures of Daruma, dressed in the beige uniforms of the Trade Guild, but tall, lean, unnaturally-attenuated figures in smooth gray vacuum-suits. One leaned over to grasp him roughly, and he saw the gleam of crimson eyes through the faceplate.

"You!" it croaked. "Come!"

"Who . . . ?" Lume asked, dazed. Then he gaped as the second alien removed its helmet and gazed at him coldly. Lume stared at the stiff feathered crest and mottled pale skin, the rudimentary beak of an avian ancestry, the facial planes lengthened like a distorted reflection. With a sudden chill, he realized the race was utterly unknown to him. Not Shenda, not Daruma, not any other alien race he knew.

Outsider.

And two feet away, hidden behind a thin cabinet panel, was the Light, a Shenda thing that had tempted Roycrai and Tayna into betraying every loyalty they had.

"Who!" he demanded.

The pale thin lips twisted into a mockery of a human smile. "Who?" the alien taunted. "Maybe you find out, human." It lifted a narrow-bore metal object in its three-fingered hand and jerked it towards the door. "Out now. You go out."

Lume hesitated, to be answered by a warning growl from their captor. He pressed his lips against Tayna's hair for a moment, then carefully lowered her unconscious body to the deck.

"Out!"

Lume numbly moved to obey. Thus began a hard captivity among the ruthless aliens who called themselves Li Fawn.

Chapter 2

The Hleri was large and orange and had stopped traffic for three city blocks. It stood in the middle of the intersection, its short amphibian legs splayed wide, its wattled jaw protruding, as it swore at the glowing figure of a Vang two yards away. The Vang snooted back with a few words of its own, and the Hleri shook its fist. Horns blared from all directions.

Guildswoman Jennan Bartlett, four autocabs back in traffic, cracked the roof of her cab and stood up. She flipped back her sun goggles, squinting against the harsh ultraviolet of Naberr's summer sky. She was late, and obviously she wouldn't get any earlier. She echoed one of the Hleri's choicest cuss-words, punched a return command on the console, and climbed out. The autocab hood slid shut, the control lights blinking busily as the cab considered its problem. She wished it luck getting home anytime soon.

She hiked past the argument and moved quickly into the shadows of the nearby buildings. Foot traffic was light in the commercial quarter, and she strode along on her long legs, enshrouded in her protective burnoose, its billowy folds flapping behind her.

Shadows were infrequent in the noon sun, and the light beat down upon her in a steady glare.

A half-kilometer later, she took an improper short-cut across the lawn and climbed the stone steps of the Guild Hall. As she stepped through the wide portal of the Hall, she sighed in relief. The ultraviolet of Naberr's summer might be basking-weather for the native Daruma, but it slow-baked a human, especially when that human had to stalk the streets swathed in anti-solar gear. Jennan stripped off her burnoose and goggles, fluffed her short dark hair, then tugged at her Guild uniform to straighten the sweat-dampened wrinkles. The cool and capacious Hall was an oasis to her overheated body. She stepped to one side of the doorway and sat down on a cushioned bench, her head swimming unpleasantly.

The wide Hall bustled with late-afternoon activity, as dozens of Guildsmen and merchants bid for the latest sector business. The assignment board high on the far wall flashed its information in slow-pace time, while harried Guild clerks in a half-dozen cubicles stamped endless papers. Naberr's Guild Hall was the nexus of the Guild's heavy chore of mediating Sagittarian trade. For centuries the Daruma Guild had bound together the sector's six local races in a tightly-woven economy of mutual cooperation; now it struggled to assimilate a seventh as Terra came to trade.

And perhaps an eighth, if the Li Fawn ever unbent their odd paranoia and explained their reasons. The Li Fawn cruiser had appeared in Sagittarius from nowhere a dozen years before, large and black and heavily weaponed, but fled whenever approached by a Guild ship. Aside from a few nasty incidents here and there, each yielding another snippet of information, the Li Fawn still kept their distance. In time, the Guild chose to ignore them, wisely or not.

Lately some Daruma had wished they could ignore Terra, too. Terran merchants had put a finger in every Sagittarian pie, and the Guild higher-ups still argued about the handful of humans, now journeymen, admitted to the Guild five years before. Despite the centuries of association, none of the local races had ever shown an interest in joining the Guild; even the Vang, the most advanced of the other Sagittarian races, contented themselves with the fancy star-piloting to which they were so supremely suited. In a moment of largesse, mostly promoted by the current Guildmaster, the Guild had opened its ranks to the newcomer Terrans—and now had second thoughts. The ongoing debate had effectively stalled Jennan's Guild career in boring and minor Naberrian trades.

She watched a pair of Daruma merchants talking near the door, their fluted ears moving in graceful counterpoint to their conversation. A Vang pilot, resplendent in admiral maroon and gold lace, stalked sedately across the stone floor and joined the nearest line, followed by a group of senior Guildsmen, two wearing out-system insignia. Each stirred a faint breeze as they passed, an unconscious courtesy Jennan appreciated.

Sweat dripped into her eyes and she wiped her face with the soft material of her burnoose, annoyed by the salty sting. One simply did not play games with heat stroke, and she was wary of her light headache that danced spots before her eyes. She stretched out her long legs, slumping comfortably against the cool polished stone of the wall, and closed her eyes. The spots waltzed unpleasantly across the darkness.

"You're late," she heard Morgen rumble, and felt the cushion shift as her team-second sat down.

"You're early," she retorted, loathe to move as the faint breeze of another arrival wafted across her face.

"Jennan?" She heard the faint anxiety in his voice, and opened her eyes to smile at him.

Morgen was short and wide-bodied like all Daruma, with wrinkled grayish skin and large dark eyes in a broad humanoid face. Large delicate ears rose several centimeters above his naked skull, the faint ridges of their musculature apparent through the skin. It was a combination Jennan associated with her childhood nurse and her Daruma playmates in Narena's clan-house, now reinforced by the constant associations of her years in the Guild. In some ways she thought herself more Daruma than human, a process that continued.

"I'm just a little hot," she assured him. "What's on the board today?"

"A little hot, she says," Morgen grumbled. "Why didn't you take a cab?"

"I did, partway. Then a Hleri got into an argument with a Vang and snarled traffic for three blocks, so I hiked. Why don't you fix that sun of yours?"

Morgen snorted. "I'll mention it at the next World Council. I'm sure they'll be aghast at the oversight. Breathe deeply and close your eyes." He relieved her of the burnoose and folded it neatly in his lap.

"Yes, effrendi." She closed her eyes obediently and sagged against the wall. "What's on the board today?" she repeated.

"How would you like an out-system trade?"

Jennan sat up abruptly. "Out-system? Are you serious?"

"Of course I'm serious," Morgen grumped, "so settle yourself to listen." He consulted his pocket-tablet. "First: a Terran trader wants to sell luxury goods to a Hleri combine. Luminescent salts. Want to go back to Hrauru?"

Jennan wrinkled her nose. She had spent fourteen months on Hrauru as an apprentice—the year had been thirteen months too long. But she frowned, considering the trade. "Salts? For what purpose?"

"To decorate their swamps, maybe. How would I know? Explain to me a Hleri's mind."

"Oh, sure." She thought another moment. "It occurs to me," she said, "that two or three of Terra's salts are salts on Terra and narcotics on Hrauru. Could the combine be a D'rasshua front?"

Morgen grunted. "You hang out in the wrong bars. I hadn't made that connection, and apparently the assignment clerk hasn't, either." His stylus scratched on the pad. "The D'rasshua are getting damn bold to start shipping dope through Guild channels."

"They're creative. That's how they make all that illegal money. What else?"

"The Vang want to sell light-mode equipment to Shann. Think of the possibilities."

"Oh, Lord." She could just imagine what the manic Shenda would do with Vang body holograms. "And the Guild's agreeable?"

"Shenda fads have launched with far less, and a Shenda fad is megabucks for the consignee while it lasts. It's not a bad idea; I don't know why the Vang hadn't thought of it sooner." He paused and waggled his ears. "And us with Chandra to model, too."

"Oh, no, he won't. I'm just getting used to the Green Elf." Their pilot's latest creation was eight feet tall, neon green, and fanged. Ship life of late hadn't been easy. "What else?"

"Not so fast, Jennan," Morgen reproved. "Shann has possibilities. Schizophrenic or not, the Shenda are still the oldest race in the sector, a starfaring people when you and I were still trying to connect the idea of seed and plant. However much they've lost, most of their ancient culture still survives—that is," he added, "as much as the Guild can keep Terra from carting away."

"Has the Guild caught *Crystal* yet?"

"No, but we will," Morgen said, his dark eyes glinting.

Jennan glanced away and sighed. The Guild Hall was still reverberating with the outrage about *Crystal*, generating stiff meetings with Terran officials, angry charges and countercharges, and other significant noise. A few of Jennan's Daruma opponents had already informed her they held her personally responsible for *Crystal's* theft of whatever-it-was. Sometimes being human didn't seem worth getting up in the morning.

"Thanks, but no thanks," she said firmly. "Shann isn't a great place for Terrans right now. We'd never get past the preliminaries of me." She raised an eyebrow.

"I suppose you're right." He shrugged a little wistfully. "Ah, well. Taki foodstuffs to the Raome?"

"Hmmm. Setha's house?"

"Yes. He's asked for you, by the way. The intermediary is a human trader named Vaughn Tanner. Factor for the McCrory Line, and with a rare touch for the Takinaki, I hear. They don't take often to offworlders, especially Terrans. Humans smell funny."

"Thanks."

"Is nothing. Taki has asked for you, too, because of T'wing, and so it's double-marked for our attention. It's a big trade, Jennan. Taki contracts aren't easy even with an intermediary."

"Hmmm."

"The Guildmaster also adds his request."

"You're joking. What's so special to get *his* attention?"

"I told you. It's an important contract."

"Maybe, maybe." Jennan wiped irritably at her face with her sleeve, then caught Morgen's disappointed expression. "I'm sorry, Morgen. You're right: it's a good trade. Go tell the desk about the salts and accept the fact-tapes for the Taki trade. Then you can load me into a cab and we can go home."

"Gladly. I hate seeing you melt into your boots like that." Jennan grinned at him, and Morgen flipped his ears in disgust. "A team-second," he said severely, "has more important things to do than babysit team-first, but you persist in this stupid behavior."

"Yes, Morgen."

"I will nag you relentlessly about this."

"Yes, Morgen. Go get the fact-tapes."

He handed her the burnoose and left her. Jennan remained slumped against the wall, burnoose held loosely in her lap, until he returned several minutes later, a tape-pack in his hand.

Morgen loaded her into a autocab outside the Hall and settled next to her on the seat, pointedly darkening the polarized shield overhead to near twilight. As promised, he fussed over her all the way to Portside. Jennan responded absently as she watched the downtown buildings change to the burnished-white stucco of a wide residential area, then abruptly to the warehouses and ship-support docks of Portside.

Beyond them the spaceport field stretched nearly to the horizon, a wide squared grid with a forest of ships of all sizes and description. Naberr Field was the major spaceport of the sector, ever busy, always crowded. As the autocab rolled smoothly onto the tarmac, they passed a Terran cargo-lander, a half-dozen human figures busy at its base.

"Hmmm," Morgen said, peering at the ship. "Ling-Choi?"

Jennan craned her head backward to see the ship's prow symbols and caught a glimpse before the auto-cab bore them onward.

"Yes. They have some kind of new consignment to Sorema House." She glanced at him. "Why do you ask?"

"Oh, just noticing. I notice everything."

"I've noticed," she murmured.

"Oh? With your head swimming like that? How?"

She ignored him. After several minutes, they glimpsed the distant shape of *Ariel,* a small jump-ship squeezed between a Daruma cargo-lander and the sleek needle of a Guild courier. As the autocar rolled steadily towards her, Jennan admired *Ariel*'s slim lines yet again, never tiring of the looking. There had been times, as the politics and racial bias of her alien Guild swirled around her, when she thought a team-first assignment forever beyond her reach. But *Ariel* was hers now, to possess and to lead. The Guild could prudently assign a senior Guildsman as her team-second as it had assigned Morgen, but the rank and authority remained hers— and with it, *Ariel.* She had renamed the ship to honor an ancient Terran spirit of light and air, not caring that the extra paperwork intensely annoyed the Ship Records bureaucrats—that, too, was part of her privilege.

The autocab rolled to a stop at *Ariel*'s air lock and Morgen promptly trundled Jennan aboard to a wait-ing sling-chair in the lounge. She sighed dramatically and winked up at him. T'wing, picking up her mood, flapped to Jennan's shoulder and waggled her long tufted ears in random enthusiasm. Morgen glared at the Taki pseudobat.

"Now, Morgen," Jennan said, answering the look. "You know she doesn't know what she's saying."

"Oh? Most of those swear words I taught you in that Hrauru bar. An amazing coincidence."

"Really?" Jennan looked with surprise at the still-oscillating pseudobat. Morgen waggled a trenchant remark of his own, and T'wing semaphored back gleefully. Morgen threw up his hands, collected Jennan's burnoose, and stamped into the elevator. The elevator whine stopped two levels below with a decided thud.

"Ah, sweet T'wing," she murmured, stroking the pseudobat's soft fur. "I don't think he likes your humor. You must remember to not use those words around other Daruma. They might cook you into a stew." T'wing rustled her wings and sang a song into Jennan's mind, a playful song with fillips and trills and loving contentment.

"Yes, I'm glad to be home again. I was gone only a few hours. I was here this morning—don't you remember?"

She detached T'wing from her shoulder and gently upended her in her lap, stroking the soft belly fur and smoothing the long, frilled wings. T'wing batted at her hands with her hind feet, squeaking in protest. Jennan released her and T'wing promptly crawled back to her former perch. She chirruped, then began busily grooming herself. Jennan relaxed, basking in the filtered light from the lounge windows.

The *Ariel* was a standard Class D jumpship, small and nimble and easily crewed by a Guild team. The four levels of engine room, living quarters, flight deck, and observation lounge were each pierced by a central well five meters wide. Although the ship was equipped with both elevator and intercom, *Ariel*'s crew preferred the shorter route of the well ladder and halloos up the shaft. Even now she could hear Morgen's indignant clatter below.

Nonverbal communication, she thought wryly, as

Morgen slammed a cabinet door. She wondered how upset he really was. Daruma lived and breathed their propriety, and, however much he unbent to Jennan, Morgen could be unaccountably touchy sometimes. T'wing had been anything but discreet.

"You have no manners," she told the pseudobat.

T'wing sang her a smile, unrepentant, and Jennan smiled in response. "All right, I'll make your apologies for you one more time. But you still don't have any manners."

Her headache had quite disappeared. She leaned forward and picked up the tape-pack from the sidetable. T'wing squawked at the sudden change of attitude and clung with needle-sharp claws to Jennan's shoulder.

"Ouch, T'wing! You *are* a pest today." T'wing shrieked in protest, her voice spiraling up into ultrasonics. Jennan winced at the double assault on her flesh and ears. "Well, I'm going below, so get on board if you're coming." She waited until T'wing had her balance, then went over the well railing, tape in hand.

Like the lounge, the common-room level centered on the open interior well. A dining area, an automated kitchen, and the crew's individual work areas clustered around the circular rail. A narrow walkway separated the tables and equipment from several doors lining the outer wall, each crew suite bracketed by storage compartments and more seating. Morgen sat at his computer console, studying the printouts of the ship's supplies.

Jennan glanced at the darkened doorway of Chandra's suite. "Where's Chandra?" she asked.

"Signing forms at the Port office. He'll be in a great mood when he gets back—he hates forms."

"Did he wear the Elf?"

"Naturally. You can imagine what remarks he'll

get, too. Port-office types have no sense of the heroic."

"The bonds of diversity," Jennan said ironically, quoting the Guild motto. She paused awkwardly. "Morgen, I apologize for T'wing's behavior. I didn't put her up to it."

Morgen swiveled in his chair, ears canted in surprise. "I never thought you did; I was only worried about your stupid flirting with sunstroke. As for that creature of yours, I stopped paying attention to her long ago." He spread his fingers in a gesture of peace and smiled. "My dear Jennan, I thought we agreed at the start that we would compromise. I would accept your regrettable human informality and you would admit Daruma propriety is the highest social order." He shrugged magnanimously. "Forget it."

Jennan scowled at him. "I'm almost sorry I apologized. 'Regrettable informality'?"

"A regrettable choice of words."

"Most regrettable. 'Highest social order'?"

"Also regrettable. Perhaps I misunderstood what we agreed."

"You sure did. How are we on supplies?"

"Low on a few items, but nothing important. We can raise ship tomorrow if you like."

Jennan looked at the inscription on the tape-pack cover. "I'll check the flight time with Chandra. We probably have a few days leeway."

She left Morgen to his printouts and walked the half-circle to her own suite. The narrow bedroom contained her bed, a storage locker at its foot, a small desk with a tape-viewer and chair, and shelves littered with tapes and papers. A door to the right led to a small bathroom and shower, a second door to the left to personal storage built into the hull. A Taki sculpture and Daruma prints softened the utilitarian effect of the metal walls, and a bright Terran fabric covered her bed, its splash of color reflected in the polished metal of her desk and chair.

The burnoose lay on her bed where Morgan had stowed it earlier. As Jennan set the tapes on her desk, T'wing made a demanding *queert* and Jennan obligingly dumped her on the burnoose. T'wing stretched out ecstatically, humming, and rolled herself into the soft fabric until not an inch of pseudobat showed. Jennan looked down at the lump in the burnoose with some disgust. She sincerely hoped T'wing's intelligent Taki cousins lacked similar instincts. It could play hell with the contract definitions.

"I wish I knew why you do that." The lump burbled happily. "Be helpful, T'wing," Jennan added impulsively, "tell me what you know about Taki."

T'wing responded. Her song flared into Jennan's mind, and Jennan stiffened, surprised into immobility.

> *the deep forest glades*
> *firelight, oh see the stars*
> *my people of youth and fire,*
> *measured rhythm of ageless wisdom*
> *life-song*
> *sunlight*
> *windsong*
> *water and green glades*
> *the forest paths of the ages*
> *oh hear the mindsong of Taki!*

The song faded slowly from Jennan's mind, a flickering of after-images of sunlight on water, the soft shirring of green leaves in a high canopy. She stood transfixed for some moments. Finally T'wing chirped in concern and poked her head out of the burnoose folds. Jennan shook herself slightly and smiled at the tiny creature.

"Thank you, dear one," she said. She looked into

T'wing's dark eyes, trying clumsily to reach the little mind, but T'wing's empathic touch darted away into irrelevancies, as always. Jennan sighed.

Despite all the years of their association, her contact with T'wing was at T'wing's discretion, the touch of their minds often beyond T'wing's ability to communicate, hampered by the mismatch of their alien minds. T'wing "sang" to her, obviously picked up her emotions, behaved sometimes quite unlike the semi-intelligent pet she supposedly was, but Jennan always felt they missed the greater of the whole.

"I wish we could really talk, T'wing," Jennan murmured.

T'wing ducked back into the burnoose and wriggled comfortably. Jennan patted her gently, and then sat down at her console with the fact-tapes, a small jab of worry pricking at her. She knew her own abilities, but she also knew the unswerving opposition of certain masters at the Hall, conservative Daruma of powerful families who still loudly objected to the taint of six humans within Naberr's ancient Guild.

How had she, of all the Guildsmen, earned this out-system trade?

Chapter 3

A clatter beyond her closed door distracted her. When she heard the low rumble of Chandra's angry voice, she reluctantly put the tape-pack on the top of the console. *Ariel*'s pilot did not sound pleased.

"Damn Elf," she muttered and patted the sleeping T'wing as she left the room.

The Green Elf was standing near the air lock door, his tentacled hands grasping a sheaf of faxes. Whatever mechanism powered the Vang light-modes inevitably affected the wearer's mood and the Elf was on another rampage. Jennan leaned on the corner of her desk and listened to Chandra's arm-swinging tirade. When the pilot had exhausted the topics of Port-side officialdom, Morgen's lack of sympathy and worthlessness of person, and most of the state of the universe, he finally got around to his team-first.

"And you just stand there and simper," he said to her angrily.

"I am not simpering. I am smiling affectionately."

"Nuts."

"I really wish you'd get rid of that Elf, Chandra,"

she said, her own temper rising. "Why don't you
wear something else—anything else? It's affecting
your mind."

The Vang glared at her with red-rimmed eyes,
then quieted a bit. He sucked his teeth reflectively,
a particularly disgusting sight. "You really think so?"
he said, interested.

Jennan tightened her lips, trying to control her
temper. The Vang held their light-modes above criticism, however they paraded for horrified stares. And
Vang reactions were always unpredictable—not even
the Daruma had figured out all the rules. For that
reason she had tolerated the past weeks with the Elf.
But no more.

"You're the expert," she said with asperity. "I
don't wear light-modes. Right now I'm glad I don't
and sorry you do. Especially that Elf."

"I had not realized," the Vang rumbled. A tentacled fist smacked to the Elf's forehead in despair. "I
have been a burden."

"Oh, Lord," Jennan sighed.

Morgen chuckled quietly and earned himself an
Elfish glare. Chandra disdainfully tossed the Port
faxes on Morgen's desk.

"The Elf," he announced loftily, "dines on Daruma." And, with that, he stalked off towards his
suite.

Morgen watched him go, scowling. "Damn Elf,"
he muttered as Chandra's door swished shut.

"Agreed."

Morgen sighed. "I don't know how you do that,
Jennan. A Vang would never take that from a
Daruma."

"Has the Guild ever figured out why the Vang
wear those things?"

"No, except that they're never seen without them.
There've been incidents, but you're probably the

only one who ever got close to a naked Vang. They
suicide first. By the time anyone comes close, the
body's disintegrated." Morgen looked uneasily at
Chandra's door. "Chandra accepted your interference on Hrauru, but I'm not sure how he resolved
it."

"Neither am I, but at least he's still with us. Did
the Guild ever find out why the Li Fawn ambushed
him?"

"No. Maybe they were plotting with the D'rasshua—though I can't believe the D'rasshua would
attack a Vang, whatever their morals. They use Vang
to pilot their ships like everybody else, and Prander
takes such things personally."

"Right," Jennan said absently. She frowned.

Three years before, Chandra had affably run an
errand for Palani, Jennan's pilot, and had stumbled
into a late-night meeting between a Li Fawn and
several D'rasshua bigshots. After the Hleri fled the
scene, the Li Fawn had stripped Chandra of his
light-mode, tortured him, then dumped him in a
corner of the warehouse. Jennan and Morgen had
found him there, cowering behind a stack of bales.

He had whimpered as she approached him, then
tried to crawl under the heavy bales at his back,
scrabbling with his claws at the sacking. She had
finally coaxed the hysterical Vang to her, wrapped
him in her cloak, and carried him back to his ship,
uncaring about the venomous sting that reflexively
prodded her ribs at every step. Morgen had carefully
averted his eyes and kept his distance behind her,
watching the shadows.

Only later had Jennan learned from Palani how
her rescue had startled every Vang in port—and created for Jennan a reputation that had echoed all the
way to Prander, the Vang homeworld. When Jennan
got *Ariel* a year later, Chandra had demanded the

pilot's berth and apparently had the Guild connections to get it. It had been a good partnership, Elf notwithstanding.

Morgen raised his eyebrows questioningly. She shrugged. "Puzzling. Well, maybe someday all questions will have answers. Let's hope the Elf just died."

"Seconded, fervently. How are the tapes?"

"I still have to read them. Let me know if Chandra makes any more trouble."

"Oh, I'm sure you'll hear." Morgen sounded aggrieved. Jennan laughed and returned to her suite. As she reentered her room, a faint whistling snore came from the burnoose on the bed. At least somebody hadn't a care.

She sat down at her desk and unwrapped the packet of tapes to read the individual inscriptions. Then she read them again, enjoying the slight weight of the tapes in her hand, her own out-system trade. She smiled at herself for her ceremony, knowing the act was very Daruma. With a contented sigh, she slipped the alpha tape into her viewer.

She quickly reviewed the proposed terms of the trade, sited on Ro with Tanner as the Taki representative. It was a trans-sector trade, one of the niches successfully exploited by the McCrory trading line. The Raome prized the delicate Taki foods, and the Takinaki liked certain sparkly minerals from Ro's mines. Since both races rarely left their homeworlds, arranging such a minor trade was a laborious and expensive business. Sometimes several Raome families would combine to pay a Guild negotiator to shuttle back and forth across the sector, but Guild ship fees could rise alarmingly if either side got technical. And, even with a settled agreement, the parties had to arrange transport. Few local merchants had the time or interest for such long haulage and marginal profit.

And so McCrory found an opportunity. The trade now proposed was the third factored by Tanner within the past year. McCrory not only provided Tanner as intermediary but handled transport of the goods. Jennan whistled when she saw the fire-sale prices. The combine obviously counted on later volume to cover its present losses.

Perhaps, the tape opined, McCrory had long-range plans for a wider interest in either or both local worlds; the line had the wealth and ships to be patient. Neither the conservative Raome nor the skittish Takinaki could be pushed, and McCrory's success in Sagittarian trade was founded on a patient study of the local markets. The clerk seemed a bit bemused at McCrory's circumspection: some early Terran behavior had enriched the local languages with some new and unfortunate metaphors.

Jennan's father had said as much about McCrory, on those rare occasions when he felt affable with his alien-happy daughter. "Nothing impresses like success," he'd say, and began assiduously courting any McCrory big shots who visited the legation. Had the McCrory big shots been less bent on their business or her father more impressive in his sycophancy, Jennan might now be a McCrory brat rising fast in the combine hierarchy.

But McCrory had been indifferent, and her father had remained a second-string official in the legation bureaucracy, doomed to attendance at the lower social functions, the most routine of legation duties. Two years after Jennan had entered the Guild, he had returned to Earth, a much disappointed man.

Only later did she realize that she had been his last hope. She fingered the Guild insignia on her sleeve and remembered the several lavish legation dinners during her apprenticeship. She had been courted and praised, while her father beamed at her side, nodding deferentially at her, almost basking in her presence. She had marveled at his change of attitude, naively believed his compliments.

Only belatedly did she realize the gradual drift of the questions. When she smilingly refused to break Guild confidences, the atmosphere turned chilly. Her father retreated into his usual cold reserve. There was a bitter argument, with emotions bared that were best left hidden. To leave the legation for an alien Guild was infuriating, but to tempt Lane Bartlett's ambition was unforgivable. And he had not forgiven. Never that.

She had heard that he had remarried at last, twenty years after her mother's death. He disliked the crowded cities on Earth, had settled on Luna as a minor trade official with his new bride. Jennan had never answered the letter.

She fingered the sleeve insignia, and realized she did not have one Terran friend. Guild discretion had created a gulf; time and conflicting duties had done the rest. She had grown up among the children at the legation, though she spent most of her time with her Daruma nurse's family at the clan-house. Even as a child she had preferred the Daruma to her own kind, fascinated by their clicking speech and gentle manners, their incomprehensible rules, their unfailing kindness to a lonely Terran child. Now the legation children had grown up and passed into Terran trade; few remained on Naberr, even if she were interested in resuming an association.

Her Guild emblem stood on the shelf above her desk, the token she had received when she entered the Guild. It gleamed in the muted room-light, a tiny golden ship emblazoned with her name in Daruma script. Her stubbornness had won her that emblem, patience had won her the *Ariel*. She had realistically expected nothing more for several years— and had prepared for the possibility of losing all.

How had she won this offworld trade?

She scanned the remainder of the alpha tape, then quickly scanned beta and gamma, the standard cultural descriptions of the parties. The Raome she knew well through her Ro apprenticeship with Nadashi, the Takinaki through her scrupulous Guild education and T'wing's occasional tutoring-by-example. The delta tape, strangely, discussed Tanner himself. She turned the fourth tape over in her hand, wondering why the Guild would emphasize Tanner in that fashion. As the Takinaki's factor, he was considered part of the Taki party, not a separate component in the trade. She frowned, puzzled, then loaded the tape into her viewer.

The tape scanned through a minimal biography, a fax of the Taki authorization, a psychological profile. She frowned more deeply, then keyed the tape onward. House name, company rank, and number of support staff may define a Daruma, but it said little about a Terran. Humans were too individualistic to reflect the group psychology so typical of the Daruma. This summary told her practically nothing.

More importantly, the tape omitted the Guildsman's synopsis of Tanner's previous trades, standard information easily available from the Guild archives. Nadashi still stood as local factor on Ro, and likely he had mediated both trades. She would have appreciated her old tutor's assessments. Probably Nadashi had a conflicting obligation, and thus the change to another Guildsman—but the tape made no mention of him. She dialed through the rest of the tape, noting other omissions.

The tape clicked on the ending runner, preparing to rewind, when her console suddenly beeped for attention. A highlighted script flashed onto the screen.

CONFIDENTIAL TO TEAM-FIRST

Vaughn Tanner has been seen in the company of a suspected D'rasshua sub-chief.

Loru crystals, a component of the Hleri drug dhumar, are similar in appearance and specific weight to crain light-stones. Taki has recently reported shortages in Tanner's shipments.

You will accordingly block agreement without arousing the parties' suspicions. No discretion.

You will keep this information confidential from all other persons, including team personnel. No discretion.

Larovi Soran
Guildmaster

Jennan had barely enough time to read through the text before it flared and vanished. She immediately tried to retrieve it, without success, then removed the tape to examine it visually. Nothing. Her fingers shaking, she slowly wound the tape back into the cartridge, then sat unmoving at her desk. To sabotage a trade! It was unbelievable.

No Guildsman ever sabotaged a trade. The strength of the Guild—and thus the foundation of Daruma influence in the sector—was its absolute impartiality. The Guild made no judgments, took no sides. It refused only the most blatantly illegal of trades, and, even then, never reported the trade to the authorities. Impartiality was a tenet of Guild honor, never broken, never compromised. Even a whisper of suspicion would break a Guildsman's career.

Why?

A "suspected sub-chief?" Not even the Hrauru police knew all the twistings and false-trails of D'rasshua organization. Were light-stones really a

component of a drug named dhumar? Dhumar?
She'd never heard of it. Word of a new drug quickly
circled through port gossip to Guild ears, and she'd
not seen any ship-fax about it. And why target
McCrory?

It made no sense at all.

So, she thought, *I'm told to keep a secret I can't
keep, about (maybe) shipments of (maybe) a nonexistent drug, arranged by a McCrory factor who
(maybe) had lunch with a pug-ugly Hleri somebody
thinks (maybe) is a hood.*

"Well," she said aloud, "the Hleri was ugly. I'll
take bets either way on the rest."

She stacked the delta tape on the others and
regarded it gloomily. Could this be a test of some
kind, some little puzzle for J. Bartlett to solve? Test
of what? That she wouldn't sabotage trades? Or
maybe a test of her human loyalties? The Guild knew
all about her arguments with her father, even knew
about those rotten banquets. The Guild knew everything about her.

Or maybe she was just plain expendable. The con-
servatives had finally won and now used this trade
as a convenient way to kick Jennan out of the Guild.
What plots did they plan for the others?

*I'm paranoid. The Guild likes Terra—they let me
and Anitra and Rolf and the others in, didn't they?
The Guild does not make moral judgments, does not
seek its own gain. Or so I've been told. . . .*

She had thought she did well, that *Ariel* was truly
hers on merit. Yet they ordered her to destroy her
own honor within the honor-conscious Guild, to
prove herself an alien to all their ways. They asked
such a thing. *He* asked such a thing.

Faces imaged in her mind—comrades, teachers,
the Guildmaster himself. Master Larovi had given
her the Guild emblem with his own hands. He had

championed her admission to the Guild since she
had first accosted him at the Hall, a gawky adoles-
cent girl ignorant of the meaning of the rank badges.
He wasn't Guildmaster then, but if she had known
who he really was, she would never have dared
approach him. They had talked of many things in
those early days, both arranging to meet "by chance"
on those days she could run away to the Hall, he
listening as she waved her arms in enthusiasm, she
talking as if the time available could not hold half
her words.

They had not talked as much later. Rank finally
intervened, but she had always believed he cared
for her best interests, as her own father had not.

He had ordered this. No Guild clerk would dare
include such an order in her instructions without
his express approval. Likely he had set the security
erasure himself. *Why?* she thought in anguish, and
abruptly stifled the pain. She would find the answer,
one way or another, and learn what was truth. She
stood up in her agitation, then slowly sat down again
to think.

She had to talk to Morgen, whatever the order.
Approaching her team-second about a direct order
not to divulge would be tricky. For all his tolerance
of her human habits, Morgen was as much a stickler
as any Daruma about his propriety, with the inevitable problems of his seeing little difference in degree.
A Guild order is a Guild order, he would say, and
roll up his ears.

They had known each other for three years, ever
since she had dragged him out of a Portside bar to
find a lost pilot. Although senior in rank, he had
accepted the post of *Ariel's* team-second to help with
her training. Others may have reservations about her
abilities, but Morgen did not. It was a web of mutual

respect, even love, built from three years of friendship. But would he listen?

She set her jaw and stood up.

Morgen was seated at his study table in the common-room, busy with his current project for the
Guild Historical Office. Morgen delighted in end-
lessly tedious tasks of collating material, cross-index-
ing and sorting and classifying, and the Historical
Office had benignly dumped on him a few thousand
trade summaries to survey. As Jennan sat down near
his table, he twitched his ears in polite acknowledgement of her presence. She waited patiently, glad of
the chance to order her emotions.

Morgen finished his sequence and tapped the data
into his recorder, then leaned back to stretch his
shoulder muscles.

"How's the project going?" she asked.

"Ably. Have you finished the tapes already?"

"I have a hypothetical for you, Morgen. Are you
at a stopping point, or should we talk later?"

"A hypothetical?" Morgen asked, puzzled. "Like
in wishy-washy ways to ask if something's proper
without offending my proper self?"

Jennan wrinkled her nose at him. "Yes, like
that. You worry me sometimes, the way you read
minds."

"I'm merely a student of Terran behavior," Morgen said reprovingly. "One Terran in particular,
whom I serve with devotion and zeal. It also saves
shocks to my poor system. What's your hypothetical?"

She hesitated. "Let me wash some other wishes
first. Before you took up my care and were still con-
ducting your own trades, did you have eyes-only
orders, kept back even from your own team?"

Morgen's brows climbed. "The tapes have a team-
out order?"

"This is a hypothetical, Morgen."

"Ah, yes. My apologies. Let me see." He thought a moment. "Once. It was an intra-system trade between two Daruma parties. My team-second was distantly related to one of the merchants, and it was felt unwise to conflict his loyalties that way. He concurred, and spent the time catching up on his gambling or somesuch. Does that help?"

"Maybe. Here's the first plank of the hypothetical. Assume you have such an order to exclude your team from certain information, but the tape gives no reason for the exclusion."

"The context might suggest the reason."

"It does not. Or, rather, the trade doesn't provide the reason; the confidential information does, in a sense. Maybe." She shifted in her chair uneasily. "I'm getting ahead of myself. Given that one has such an order without reasons, and that one feels intensely uneasy about the content of the confidential information . . ."

She paused, wiping her sweaty palms on her thighs. The banter had faded from Morgen's eyes, replaced by an expression she could not read. She opened her mouth, shut it, then finished in a rush: "Can one properly disclose the information to the team, despite the order not to?"

"No," Morgen said flatly. Jennan flushed and looked away. She started to rise from her chair, to murmur an awkward apology, but Morgen caught quickly at her sleeve to detain her. "It definitely is not proper," he continued quietly, "but tell me, anyway. What has so disturbed you?"

She looked at him in bewilderment. "What?"

Morgen smiled at her and ear-twitched a comment about her obtuseness. "I said tell me, anyway." He released her sleeve, and she sank back into her chair. "My dear Jennan, I know you well enough to know you would never consider asking if you hadn't cause. Propriety governs the predictable, when everyone knows the rules—and reasons. It defines honor, binds persons, gives meaning to the social order. But it is not the answer to all possible situations. Someday we Daruma will collect all those possibles and have rules for everything, but we haven't managed that yet. What was on the tape?"

"A security order, erased after first reading. It suggested Tanner is substituting light-stones for Taki's crystals and passing them to the D'rasshua to make some new drug. I'm supposed to collect the dirt on Tanner while I sabotage the trade."

"Sabotage the trade?" Morgen looked stunned. Then his broad face suffused with anger. "Sabotage the trade?" he repeated, his voice rising. He stood up, then abruptly sat down, an unconscious echo of her own reaction. Morgen drummed his fingers on the fax-sheets on the table, then grimaced at her, plainly upset.

"I'll say you felt uneasy. Whatever has got into the Guild office's mind? Assuming they have a mind. I can't believe it."

"It was the Guildmaster's express order," Jennan said unhappily.

Morgen looked at her with sudden compassion. "He must have his reasons, Jennan, though for the life of me I can't imagine what they are. Don't doubt him yet." He scowled.

"What's the drug?" he asked after a moment.

"Dhumar."

"The component again?"

"Crain light-stones. They're supposed to look like the crystals, easily substituted."

"I've heard of the light-stones, but not the drug. Why does the Guild think Tanner's diverting to Hrauru?"

"He was seen with a 'suspected sub-chief.' "

"Hmmph. That doesn't prove anything. In fact, it doesn't add up at all. The Takinaki trust Tanner. You can't deceive telepaths that way."

"Telepaths?" Jennan asked in surprise.

"Hush. That's a secret. Ultimate unpropriety even to suspect it. They're really not, but you've had enough experience with T'wing to know Taki creatures know things in weird ways. The Takinaki certainly do. Tanner has to be bona fide." He snorted at her expression. "You look relieved."

Jennan laughed ruefully. "Race loyalty, I guess. I can accept arrogance and bumbles—at least Terra's learning. But I'd hate to think a Terran was subverting the local races. That's more Li Fawn style."

The same thought occurred to them simultaneously, and they regarded each other solemnly. Morgen finally grunted. "The problem with paranoia is that it drapes plots over every bush. Aside from the attack on Chandra and some minor incidents, all they've done is act antisocial."

"I've heard other stories."

"None of that was ever proven. The Li Fawn can't be responsible for everything, as hard as they try. And I haven't yet heard that they have hooks into the Guildmaster." He drummed his fingers again. "But it is a very interesting idea. They've meddled by rumor-mongering before. But how could they have arranged this? Who's the target?"

Jennan smiled, relief bubbling up inside her. Then she laughed and jumped to her feet. Morgen raised a cautioning hand.

"It's hardly certain, not even likely."

"But it's more than I had before. It's something to consider, to work with. All I had was a tangle of nonsensical details and a wrecked career." She spread her hands. "Thanks, Morgen!"

"You are graciously welcome, if you have cause

for thanks, that is. You may not. We'll have to look at all the possibilities."

"Yes, all kinds of fascinating possibilities. And a truth to find at the end of the tangle!"

Chapter 4

A week later, *Ariel* emerged into normal space a full light-day from Ro, well beyond the debris of the Raome's gravity-skewed system. Five massive gas-giants had scattered the fragments of would-be planetary sisters into broad fragmented rings. The asteroids provided millions of ore-rich chunks for the taking, making the Raome wealthy and their system a navigational menace. Guild beacons marked the largest of the out-system perils, but piloting inward from jump-point was a wary business. As they approached the first of the out-system rings, Jennan took second-pilot station to spare Chandra the more routine acknowledgements.

The Vang, abstractly dressed in globular neon, barely noticed her presence as he focused every sense on his screens. Half the controls on *Ariel's* deck were adapted for Vang handling, drawing heavily on the Vang's unique ability to sense gravity waves. With that sense, a Vang pilot could actually *see* the minute spatial disturbances of the warp points and the curves of the *not-when* and *not-here* of hyperspace. Other control designs exploited a

Vang's faster reflexes and certain subsidary controls in his light-mode. Lesser mortals could still fly the ship from other controls, but Daruma ship design had inevitably bent itself toward the Vang's special abilities. Chandra flew *Ariel* with the natural elegance of his breed: Jennan never tired of watching him.

Ro itself was the largest moon of the innermost gas-giant, Sarn—close enough to Ro's sun to be habitable, far enough from its massive companion to avoid the worst of tectonic disruption. As *Ariel* decelerated into orbit, a temporary moonlet among Sarn's six dozen satellites, a Raome controller directed their approach, his voice distorted by the magnetic stresses of the system. Chandra chased Ro in its orbit for more than an hour, then began *Ariel*'s descent to Portside.

After they landed, the Vang promptly left the ship to begin battle with Raome officialdom. The Raome always tried to gouge the Guild for fuel and Port charges, sensing a bottomless pit of moneyed opportunity. Fortunately, the Guild's Vang pilots were more than a match for any bureaucrat, even the Raome variety. Still the Raome kept trying, scenting vast profit should they ever chink the wall.

Jennan stood at the lounge window and watched Chandra's glowing figure emerge from the air lock twenty meters below. He hailed a scurrying ground-car and climbed aboard, winking and flashing in neon glory. As the driver whizzed him away toward Portside Control, Jennan wished him luck.

The squat profile of Ro's Portside skirted the landing field in a vast semicircle, each warren separated by a wide municipal walkway like spokes on a wheel. Arc-lights burned at random across the city, winking jewels in the twilight. At one end of the semicircle, the tower of Port Control rose eighty meters above

the plain, ablaze with light and activity. To the far
right, beyond the silhouettes of other ships, stretched
a barren waste of rock and sand washed by the pale
light of Sarn now rising in the west. The huge planet
seemed to rush down on Ro, inexorable in its turbu-
lence and mass. Jennan shivered.

T'wing fluttered to her shoulder and chirped for
attention, unimpressed by scenery. Jennan scratched
her pet's ear absently, then turned away from the
window. Morgen sat curled in one of the lounge
chairs, watching her, his large ears half-folded as he
relaxed.

"I like this place," she remarked. "No surface
water, lots of sand, low air, but it's not half-bad for
skywatching."

"I can think of better things than watching a planet
fall on me," he said.

"You're a small-souled type." She took the chair
next to him and stretched out her legs. They sat in
a companionable silence. Far below, the night wind
shirred sand against the ship's hull, an undercurrent
whisper to the familiar sounds of *Ariel* at rest. A
counter on the flight deck kept its measured time to
the faint rhythm of working machinery. Air sighed
through the ship's ventilators. A faint rattle of crock-
ery drifted upward as the ground vibrated to the lift-
off of a nearby ship. She stirred.

"Maybe they're waiting for us to call them."

"The Raome can't be hurried. Setha has his dignity to maintain—he always has the other males in
mind, sometimes so much that he reacts more to
them than to you."

"But Setha's one of the wealthiest males on Ro.
Why should he worry about prestige?"

"You're talking about trade and politics; I'm talking about sex."

"Oh." Morgen snickered at her expression. She flipped her hand at him.

"Remember, Jennan, the females don't count at all. They stay in the harem with the hatchlings. But the male's sexual partners, the anorphs, are a ferment of politics and intrigue. You must consider them because it's they, not the males, who impose the rules. And all without having an ounce of status in Raome society."

"I guess I'm not used to thinking in terms of three sexes."

"Who is?"

"So who makes the first move?"

"That depends. Here you're a dominant male just like Setha and Tanner, though hardly as weighty as Setha. You have to think of your own prestige. Take it from your faithful anorph." Morgen made a mock bow from his chair. "I do wish the Raome would admit that other species have other arrangements, but even an anorph has a few freedoms. But you've been here before. Didn't you work team-second to Nadashi during your apprenticeship?"

"Yes, but I missed the opening formalities. Nadashi never did explain things much, and then Setha got embroiled in that battle with Terga House. And then the ship nearly got blown over in a sandstorm. It was a treat." She frowned. "I guess what I want to ask is your best guess about Setha's reaction—as a Raome male—to an approach I have in mind. Do you think Setha or Tanner has any inkling about the Guild's suspicions?"

"If they do, you can't ask them during the trade. The formalities don't permit it."

"If the trade failed, could we ask them then?"

"You mean follow the Guild order? Sabotage the trade?"

"Not exactly. Call it a cooperative sabotage. Raome

sexuality aside, would a direct appeal to Setha have any influence? The Guild saved his skin once."

"Raome understand gratitude in a different way. Don't count on it."

"But if I told him . . . Maybe the Li Fawn picked Setha, if they did, because of his troubles before. Or maybe Tanner's the target because he's human and McCrory is making mega-credits in the sector now. Or maybe . . . hmmm."

Morgen flipped his ears at her and stretched. "It sure beats me. What would we ever do if the Li Fawn weren't around to spice things?"

"If it is Li Fawn," she said gloomily. "Do you think Setha would know?"

"Be careful, Jennan. You're playing with more than that sabotage order. Guildsmen don't interest themselves in racial politics, even Li Fawn misbehavior against merchant houses."

"Officially, that is."

"Guild Hall would never admit it—and if you get caught meddling, they'll disown you, secret orders or not."

"I know, I know. Just follow my lead at the trade, Morgen."

"Always."

The ship's comm chimed on the flight deck below. Jennan got up, deposited T'wing in Morgen's lap, and climbed down the ladder. As she stepped onto the flight deck, she quickly checked the instrument banks that formed the three enclosed walls of the deck; everything seemed operational. Behind her, the fourth wall stretched upward past the lounge balcony to a curved ceiling thirty meters overhead, creating an open airy space two levels tall—not exactly designed for pseudobat exercise but employed for that purpose aboard *Ariel*. T'wing swooped down in mock attack, screeching.

"Can it, T'wing. I'm busy."

"Message incoming," the computer intoned. "Display or print?"

"Print, please." *Ariel* blinked her control lights busily.

The machine chattered and Jennan ripped the fax from the dispenser. The message—not from Setha as she had expected, but from McCrory—invited her to appear at Setha's home-house forty minutes ago. The top script read in the original English, with a labored translation in Daruma Trade below. No doubt this Lenart had given the message to Port Control well in advance but hadn't bothered to translate it for the clerk. Maybe he even thought himself prudent for the omission, not realizing that no self-deserving anorph would ever let a message out of his hands until he knew what he said. Thus the delay, and thus she was already an hour late.

"Wonderful," she muttered. "Computer, ask Port Control to send us a groundcar."

"Acknowledged."

Ten minutes later, a groundcar whirled up to the base of the ship, shedding sand in twin whorls behind its turbos. Jennan and Morgen climbed into the comfortable rear seat, ignoring the cowled anorph at the wheel. The Raome waited deferentially until they were seated, then neatly backed his machine and sped them away towards Portside.

The groundcar whispered across the tarmac, accelerating to an almost uncomfortable velocity. Jennan squinted against the sharp breeze. The anorph neatly dodged the massive fins of Raome ore freighters and smaller offworlder jumpships, then scarcely slowed as they swung in a wide turn around a hulking ore-carrier. Jennan smiled, delighted with the speed and rush of the air.

As they neared the warren, the car slowed to

jockey around groundcars and pedestrians, then dropped to walking pace as they entered the warren proper, bumping over the cobblestones. The car turned into a narrow alley and rolled to a stop in front of a squat one-storied building illuminated by the reddish glare of Ro's infra-red lamps. The two alighted, and Morgen retrieved her case from the seat. As they set foot on the flight of short steps to the doorway, the anorph guards edged aside with just the right blend of deference for the Guild and disdain for their offworlder persons.

Setha's chief steward, Ba Crai, met them at the door. With lowered eyes, he silently signaled his abasement, his long tongue nervously flicking his snout. He bowed again, then preceded them into the long anteroom. Dark glittering eyes watched their progress as they passed the single-file ranks of anorphs lining the walls, each servant as short and squat as his master, each as swathed in drab gray robes, a single pattern seemingly repeated in unbroken series. After a quick glance down the defile, Jennan kept her eyes on the back of Crai's head. She felt a strange menace in the immobile lines, an emotion quite different from her previous experience on Ro. Imagination, perhaps, but the feeling remained, heavy on the air.

Crai bowed them through a curtained door, and Jennan heard the patter of bare feet as several anorphs slid into the room after them. She repressed an instinctive glance behind her. One never looked casually at an anorph. As Morgen had warned her, the third Raome sex were nothing yet everything, ruled yet ruling in their relationship to the patriarchal male. And nothing suited better as a weathervane of their master's mood. Setha must be having a fit.

The apparent objects of Setha's ire sat at the table

in room center, two human traders lounging on pillows in standard patriarchal style, quite oblivious to the anorph displeasure which surrounded them. McCrory insignia winked at their collar tabs and cuffs, and several rank slashes decorated the sleeve of the older man. Tanner was a handsome man in his mid-thirties, dark-haired, compactly built, completely at ease in the alien surroundings. His companion, pinched-faced and sandy-haired, clutched a dispatch case as if its contents were too valuable to risk even on the cushion beside him. Jennan could think of no better way to convince the anorphs to take a look-see into that case. Already two were circling the room to sneak up from the rear.

As she and Morgen entered, Tanner rose smoothly to his feet and bowed. The other trader merely glared, and Jennan's stomach sank as the look told on the anorphs.

"Gods, an amateur," Morgen muttered. "Just what we need."

"Watch me squash him the first time he tries." She donned her best Guild smile and approached the table.

"Gentlemen," she said. "Excuse my delay."

"Good evening," Tanner replied pleasantly. "I am Vaughn Tanner, factor for Taki in this trade." He gestured towards his companion. "Although courtesy offends, my aide, Jay Lenart." Lenart shifted his glare, outraged at the style of Tanner's introduction. But Lenart was an anorph here, and glances spoke words in the byzantine world of the anorphs. Jennan felt rather than heard another stir around the room.

"Ser Tanner," she said, ignoring Lenart completely. "Shall we be seated to await the other party? I formally remind you that all parties must be present for conversation of any kind."

"I am aware of the restriction, Guildswoman,"

Tanner replied smoothly. He resumed his seat. Jennan arranged herself on another cushion and took her case from Morgen. Morgen deferentially handed her a pen, and Jennan rustled papers for some useful noise.

"You had better get your aide under control," she murmured, "or you've got problems like you wouldn't believe."

Tanner gave her a startled glance but otherwise didn't twitch an ear. After a few moments, he stretched, drummed his fingers on the table, then smothered a yawn behind his fist. A smooth one, this Tanner. Jennan studied her papers, watching both Terrans and anorphs with her peripheral vision.

"This waiting is a bit tedious, Guildswoman," Tanner said finally. "May I excuse myself for a space of evening air?"

"Of course."

"Come along, Jay. *Now.*" The two traders made their way out of the room, Lenart still clutching that dratted case. Morgen raised an eyebrow, but she shook her head slightly at him. The Daruma contented himself with commenting by ear, to all but her, she hoped, an idle fanning of Morgen's fluted ears.

Better to squash him yourself, he suggested.

"I hear Tanner is an able trader," she said firmly. She tapped her papers. "An interesting trade, twice successful. Taki must be pleased with him." Neither missed the immediate rise of tension among the anorphs.

So—it's the trade itself, Morgen said. *Ro's heard about the missing shipments.*

"Like I said," Jennan remarked to the open air, "an interesting trade."

She focused on the papers in her hands, biting her lip. Missing shipments would explain much.

Four years before, a rival male had managed to subvert one of Setha's anorphs and short Setha's ore
deliveries. Jennan's team-first had uncovered the
machinations, and only Nadashi's distaste for the
hoodwinking of Guild-brokered contracts had saved
Setha's fortune. She frowned.

What was Tanner up to, if anything? Guildsman
as she was, with all that implied about human loyalties, she did not want Terra in trouble with the
Guild. Humans had stepped on enough toes in the
sector already, merely by acting typically human,
and McCrory would drag down other Terran houses
with it. And what then? What would Terra do if
the Guild banned humanity from Sagittarius? She
shuddered. She knew quite well what Terra could
do.

She heard the returning footsteps of the McCrory
traders and slipped her papers back into their case.
After the Terrans had reseated themselves, the four
sat several more minutes, politely ignoring each
other, watched closely by Setha's anorphs.

Finally a flurry of anorphs near the door signaled
Setha's arrival, and the Raome patriarch waddled
briskly into the room. He was dressed in heavy
robes, his tiny hands clasped on his rounded paunch,
his small clawed feet winking in and out beneath the
hem of his robe. Broad vestigial scales on his forehead were cruelly tattooed with symbols of house
and rank, and shadowed a pair of shrewd black eyes
set deep into their sockets. His tongue flickered on
his narrow snout, tasting the air. As Setha marched
towards their table, Crai and another anorph scurried ahead to plump a seat cushion, then withdrew
with deeply deferential bows.

Tanner stood up and began to murmur introduc-
tions, but Setha cut him off. "I have no interest in
your courtesy," he said. "I appear here only for the

Guildswoman Bartlett." He spared Jennan a disdainful glance. "That being accomplished," he added loftily, "I go." He whirled and stamped towards the
door, scattering his anorphs like a ship breasting the
wave.

Jennan leaped to her feet.

"Setha!" she shouted.

The Raome turned, startled, and a growl went up
from the anorphs. Jennan swept the room with a
furious glare, stilling it.

"There was a trade proposed here. You insult the
Guild with your conduct!"

Morgen's jaw dropped. She glanced at him, throwing him the ball, and he responded instinctively. He
snatched up her case with an imperious sweep of his
hand, closed it with a snap and swung it to his side,
the picture of incipient departure in a huff. Then he
looked at her, awaiting her command.

Your turn.

Right, she thought, and cast about wildly for some
ideas.

Setha swelled with rage, drawing himself up in
offended dignity. His finger stabbed at Jennan. "You!
You human! You're in it with him! Only you could
arrange this farce. I spit on you!"

"Farce?" Lenart yelled. "You little wart. . . ."

Tanner backhanded Lenart like a pistol shot, sending him heels over backward off the cushions. Lenart's case skidded out of his hands across the stone
floor, and an anorph promptly pounced on it.

"Down!" Jennan shouted. "Put that down!" The
anorph dropped the case hastily and backed away,
teeth bared. Panting a little, Jennan turned back to
Setha. Then she took a deep breath, showed her
teeth, and clasped her hands over her stomach.
Patriarch to patriarch, you old lizard. Setha eyed
her warily, his snout twitching.

"By what conduct have I merited this abuse?" Jennan asked, rattling her voice in an ominous croon. "The Guild saved your property, your reputation, and your skin. It had no duty to do so—the Guild doesn't care about the fortunes of one merchant." She flicked her fingers, and dropped her voice into a naked threat. "Nor does it care for unprovoked insult. Do you wish to lose its services?"

Morgen rolled his eyes upward, a gesture Jennan hoped the Raome thought ominous. The problem with improvising was keeping it up or all your plates dropped in a crash.

She allowed a silence to take hold, pressuring Setha to respond. Tanner and Lenart had the good sense to freeze. Setha stirred uneasily, eyeing his anorphs. She dangerously risked his position with this tack, something she definitely did not want. She changed tactics and made a placating gesture to moderate her challenge, hoping the body language translated.

"Return to the table, Ser Setha. May I suggest your servants withdraw so that we may discuss matters in privacy?"

The steward Crai jerked in outrage. "Ba Crai," she added hastily. "I breach propriety with direct speech, but deep plots are at work here and your master is in danger. Your presence constrains him from the action he must take. I ask your concurrence, devoted steward."

Crai's eyes sidled to his master, and Setha dismissed him with a flick of his hand. Crai barked harshly at the other anorphs. Jennan waited until all the anorphs had started towards the door, then turned to Tanner. "I suggest, trader, that our aides remove themselves as well. We have enough stresses in the room." It was a sop to Setha, but she got a

puzzled look from Morgen, another glare from
Lenart.

What the hell?

"As you wish, Guildswoman," Tanner said.

Tanner helped Lenart to his feet and pointed at
the door. When the two were gone, Jennan put her
hands on her hips and glared at the Raome. "And
just how much of that outrage was real, Setha?"

Setha flicked dust from his sleeve. "Not much.
But I have a position to maintain—and no patience
for worthless humans who've cheated me!" His finger jabbed at Tanner.

"Cheated!" Tanner said, astounded. Setha sniffed
disparagingly and she saw a dangerous glint come
into Tanner's dark eyes. She waved him down.

"Hush, Tanner," Jennan said. "Don't rattle my
bean-jar. And put your finger away, Setha; there are
no anorphs here. Shall we sit down, gentlemen?"
Setha and Tanner exchanged a glance, none too
friendly, and nodded. Jennan reseated herself and
took a deep breath. *Now . . . some cooperative sabotage,* she thought grimly, and wondered what exactly
she risked.

Chapter 5

The two merchants arranged themselves on cushions, and Setha picked up a wine glass, waving it
lazily under his nose.

"All right, Setha, what farce?"

Setha continued sniffing the wine, eyes half closed,
and flicked his snout with his quick tongue, sampling
the air for more than the wine's aroma. She waited
patiently, willing her pores to release the right mix-
ture of emotional threat. Setha's tongue flicked
again, and he looked at her from the side of his eye.
Then he slammed his glass on the table with a report
that rang through the room.

"Farce? A veritable comedy. He shorted my crystal shipments!"

"Shorted?" Tanner exploded, half rising from his seat.

"Sit down, Tanner!"

Tanner subsided, barely, his eyes again flashing.
Setha looked impressed—if only by Tanner's acting
ability. Jennan thought it no act, and felt something
uncoil within her in relief—Tanner hadn't known.
Now to persuade the Raome merchant, if she could
get him back to reality.

She turned to Setha. "How did you learn this information, if I may ask?" Tanner made a half-strangled noise but controlled himself.

Setha preened a bit, his glance darting to the fuming Tanner. "I've heard rumors, and so asked for verification from Taki. The message arrived only today by subspace radio. A warehouse inventory shows a thirty percent shortage, a shortage *he* arranged!" Setha's finger jabbed out again at Tanner, and Tanner jumped to his feet, scattering cushions in every direction.

"Tanner, sit down! Setha, put your finger away. Great gods, you two! Must I clong your heads together?" She took a deep breath and glared them down. "Ser Setha, it is my considered judgment, for which I have no proof at all except Tanner's reaction, that he had nothing to do with the shortages on Taki. You are assuming that the crystals disappeared in transit to Taki, not after delivery. Is not the latter more likely? Do the Takinaki bother to weigh the boxes?"

"Might not have weighed them," the Raome replied grumpily. "Could have lead-lined the boxes for fake-weight even if they did."

"Or might have delivered whole, with later thefts from storage. Let us consider all the possibilities, not the one that fits your previous unfortunate experience." She raised her hand to forestall another demonstration, and held Setha's gaze with her eyes. "Consider that your likelihood to jump to that conclusion might have been counted upon."

Setha grew still, and she saw the new thought take hold in his crafty eyes. Then his expression became almost bland, and he pursed his narrow lips reflectively. His tongue flickered.

"Hmmph," he said noncomittally.

"Consider also, Setha," she added, "that the

Takinaki trust Tanner. Do you think he could possibly deceive them? If them, what about the pseudobats? I've told you about T'wing and her gifts."

"T'wing?" Tanner asked.

"My pseudobat."

"You really have one?" the trader asked incredulously. "I thought that information had to be wrong." He looked around the room wildly, as if T'wing might pop into the air from any corner. That reaction also told with Setha. Had Tanner been more guarded in his character, pinched and sour like Lenart . . . but, then, the Takinaki had chosen well. She templed her fingers and looked at the two of them.

"Consider a hypothetical, gentlemen," she said. "Assume that it is an inviolate principle that a Guildsman never sabotage a legal trade. The locals know it to be so, and Terrans have heard it said. Am I right?" Both merchants nodded. "Assume further that, upon reviewing the fact-tapes for a proffered trade, the Guild orders team-first to use his skills to block agreement, oh so surreptitiously, and then to pursue one of the parties to prove him guilty of some fault. Assume finally the sabotage order is security-erased." Raome and human eyes fixed on her in intense interest.

"So?" Setha prompted.

"Upon his arrival, team-first finds one party storming out of the trade and the other mystified. And the circumstances may be such that all face ruin if that departure is not stopped. What to make of all this? What plots are afoot? And who is behind them? For there must be plots, with all involved as puppets on strings."

Setha leaned back and smoothed his robes, considering. "An interesting hypothetical, Guildswoman. A pickle for all concerned. Cause even for shouting and other hauling around. Cause even for breaking a

direct Guild order about sur-rep-titious?" Setha
drawled the word.

"Have I broken that order? I merely proposed a
fanciful problem."

"Hmph. Bend your principles as you must. But
sabotage? Proscribing a merchant?"

She bared her teeth as a reply.

Setha waved her away and looked at Tanner. "Ser
Tanner, I have my enemies, one or two who are
quite capable of such subtlety. Have you your own,
who would seek your ruin?"

"Any ruin would also affect my company," Tanner
replied uncomfortably. "I doubt any of my rivals
would pull down their own house of cards just to get
me."

"My anorphs say this Lenart looked sour. He
doesn't like you."

"He doesn't like anybody. Think of him as an
anorph whose plots are always outmaneuvered. It
affects the spleen." Setha snorted in amusement.
Then Tanner shrugged, reconsidering. "I admit Jay
has a grievance, from his point of view. I won't give
him special favors because his father's a big shot."

"And others at McCrory do? You are senior?"

"Oh, yes," Tanner said, with a grimace, "I'm supposed to be. But big shots are big shots."

"You humans have a surplusage of males," Setha
said condescendingly. "Raome don't have such
problems."

"Oh?" Jennan asked. Setha flicked dust off his
sleeve again, ignoring her.

"And you, Guildswoman, have you your enemies
in the Guild?"

"Three sets of enemies is a bit much, Setha. Coor-
dination would be a project in itself. Morgen and I
prefer other plotters named Li Fawn."

"Hmmph. Li Fawn get blamed for many puzzles."

"Yes, but in this case with some foundation. Tanner's company is successful in the sector. I tangled with the Li Fawn once and spoiled their plans on Hrauru. And so the Li Fawn have no reason to approve human influence in Sagittarius, and might bear a grudge against me."

"And why me?"

"You're a convenient tool."

"Setha is never a tool," the Raome said reprovingly. "Caught in a squeeze by unworthy rivals, betrayed by scurrilous offworlders, but never a tool. I won't permit it." He pursed his lips. "But an interesting idea. A Li Fawn ship was sighted near Ro three months ago and fled when challenged. Does it fit in? But why?"

"My pilot would love to catch a Li Fawn to ask."

"Yes, I heard about that. Bad, very bad." Setha shook himself slightly. "I suggest we go forward with the trade, Ser Tanner, to give us room to maneuver. The terms of the last trade were highly acceptable and I expected we would merely repeat that agreement." He looked inquiringly at the trader.

"The Takinaki were of the same mind, Ser Setha."

"While I dislike to rush a trade, even a trade with a proven party—" his eyes darted slyly at Tanner "—our speed may put our enemy off balance, whoever he is. We will watch the shipment from here to Taki's warehouse like gorphul spiders on the hunt, and hope the thief will appear. I doubt he'll dare to show his face on Ro."

"I should think not," Tanner said, his voice tinged with irritation. "That radio message accomplished all he wanted."

"That was a mistake. It forced our Jennan's hand. Perhaps he will make other mistakes, there on Taki. You and Jennan should be on hand to exploit it. I assume, Guildwoman, you would rather not return to Naberr to make explanations at this point?"

"I bow to your subtler and wiser mind, Ser Setha."

"Hmmph. As you said, there are no anorphs here. Let's not be irrelevant nor belated in our courtesy. How many Guild rules have you broken so far, anyway?"

"What do you mean?" she asked.

"Nothing. Everything. We Raome have watched the Guild as long as you've been watching us, with eyes trained by our subtleties. And I know quite well the Guild never proscribes a merchant for insults. And as for shouting at me in front of my anorphs? What would Nadashi say?"

"Nadashi isn't here." She scowled warningly at him, disliking the turn in the conversation.

"A good thing, too. He hasn't the constitution to stand it. A stickler for propriety, my good friend Nadashi. He'd have stopped you, team-second or not, and we'd be in the soup. What rules are you planning to trample next?"

"Oh, I don't know." Setha cut too close to the bone and she squirmed. She could see the confused look on Tanner's face, his eyes flicking from herself to Setha, and hated this disclosure, now and in this way. Setha knew better than to expose Guild vulnerabilities, especially in front of Terrans. She rasped her voice, warning him off. "I suppose you offer suggestions?" Setha promptly took the cue, but not in the way she intended.

"I do. Sneak Tanner aboard your ship."

"On *Ariel*?" Jennan looked at Tanner, aghast.

"What's one more rule?"

"Give me a break, Setha!"

"You two must coordinate. It is essential."

Jennan set her mouth, then looked at Tanner disgustedly. "All right. We'll sneak him aboard some-how. Good Lord."

"Are we then in agreement?" Setha asked, raising a wine glass. "Good. And, Ser Tanner, my most ines-timable friend, if I find there are shortages and you're their cause, I'll turn gorphul myself and feed you to my anorphs." He again saluted Tanner with his glass. "To your health."

"Thank you . . . I think."

"To you health also, Guildswoman."

"No thanks. I've got enough troubles already." Her emotions suddenly drained from her, leaving only the sour taste of disaster. She watched Setha and Tanner toast each other, and measured the prob-able cost to her career, all of it self-inflicted. Morgen had warned her, and in her black reaction she abruptly wanted no more of Setha and his smooth Terran traders. Without a word, she got up and left the room, not caring that they stared after her in surprise.

Setha's anorphs were clustered in the anteroom, and glared at her when she appeared. She gestured to Crai, indicating that Setha required him, and looked around for Morgen. He and Lenart were slumped against the far wall, the human in a sulky pout. Morgen twitched his ears, deliberately brush-ing them against Lenart's sleeve. She saw Lenart flinch at the touch, but he didn't try to move away. She was almost sorry she had missed the preliminar-ies; Morgen had obviously long since won the war.

Morgen saw her and raised an eyebrow. "The shouts were the best part," he said as she reached him, "though, of course, the *only* part from this van-tage. But am I complaining?"

"Not much. Let's go back to *Ariel* to talk."

"What about me?" Lenart whined.

"Do what you like. I'm not your employer." Lenart looked past her at the anorphs reentering the conference room. He hauled himself off the wall to follow them.

"A wonderful boy," Morgen said when he was out of earshot. "Such charm and grace. So human."

"That's a rotten comment, Morgen," she said angrily. "Does it apply to me, too?"

Morgen blinked in surprise. "Of course not. Forgive me, Jennan; I spoke stupidly." He blinked again, then looked concerned. "What went wrong? You did salvage the trade? Like you planned?"

"Yes, but . . ." She swallowed, and got herself under control. "I'm sorry, Morgen. We've both lost our manners." She made a conciliatory gesture. "Let's go home to *Ariel*. I need some better air."

They left immediately, without courtesies, and rode back to *Ariel* in silence, all too conscious of the anorph at the wheel.

The following morning Tanner dawdled over breakfast in the lounge of his small trade ship, the *McCrory Rose*. Through the narrow window band above his table he could see the Guild ship a half-kilometer away, glinting in Ro's pale morning. He watched the ship as he ate, considering the possibilities. Somehow, by some chance, his luck had blessed him again.

Lenart had left for McCrory's Portside compound to write another deathless report for his stockholder father. When Jay announced his ominous intention an hour ago, Tanner had merely grunted an assent. *Too bad an air lock can't slam*, he thought with a grin, and saluted the departed Lenart with his coffee cup. Eventually Jay would learn that McCrory still valued profits more than an owner's affection for stupid sons. And Tanner had the profits. Another year, maybe two, and he might deliver the whole of Ro/

Taki trade to McCrory, whisking it away from certain arrogant Daruma who thought they owned the sector for keeps. If he had the luck.

Luck: it all turned on luck. Tanner had chased his luck in Solar Trade while Lume and Tayna finished school. The kids had joined him later at Centauri Base, where Tayna promptly attracted the base commander's admiration. Luck, to have a pretty sister to catch Dobson's eye. By the time Tayna had shrugged Dobson off for good, Tanner had made himself indispensable to the old fart, enough to share in Dobson's promotion to the Gemini Worlds. More chances, more luck, and then, six months ago, Tanner had his long-awaited commission to Sagittarius, the current mecca for McCrory's ambitious underlings—a small commission, true, but one he promptly parlayed into the Ro/Taki contract. Luck there, in his unlikely friendship with a Takinaki chieftain. Now, luck again in this connection with one of the fabled human Guildsmen.

He stretched lazily. Let Lume and Tayna chase after their Shenda gewgaws, happy with a nowhere contract. He had higher ambitions—and would ride his luck as far as it carried him.

He dawdled over breakfast, content with his prospects, thinking about the Guildswoman and the luck she might offer to an ambitious man. As he dawdled, he idly pushed his eggs around his plate in an eggy *grand prix* before smashing the lot into a bacon wall. He had begun a third rendition of this satisfying catastrophe when the air lock chimed. With a grunt, he hauled himself out of his chair and keyed the lock release.

The door sighed open, revealing a Vang bent over uncomfortably in the inadequate space of Tanner's air lock.

"Good morning," Tanner said automatically.

The Vang brandished his spear in a courteous hello. "May I come in?" he asked in a deep voice.

"Surely."

Tanner backed up hastily as his guest emerged from the air lock. The Vang wore a helmet of fantastic design, a metal mask, and four arms. One of the arms held a small bundle of cloth and metal, another the spear. Tanner had often seen Vang around the port—they seemed to pilot everything—but he had never actually spoken to one. He looked up at the towering figure, delighted despite himself. A Vang, on his ship.

The Vang looked around casually. "Interesting configuration. Torch ship?"

"Yes, with modifications. Who are you?"

"I am Guildswoman Bartlett's pilot, named Chandra." He gestured slightly with the bundle. "We have decided on a double play. I'll dress you up in a light-mode, and Chandra will enter *Ariel* twice. You'll be the first of the twice, so to speak."

"So to speak. I understand." He looked Chandra up and down. "I've never been this close to one of your people. They really do look real, the light-modes, I mean."

"I interpret your expression as approving," Chandra replied in his deep voice, sounding pleased. "I find that refreshing."

Chandra unrolled his bundle on the flight-deck counter and extracted several pieces of apparatus. "I've adjusted this device to repeat my present appearance," he said, "and rigged the controls with a hold-pattern to minimize the need for actual operation. All you do is put it on and push the button." He sounded faintly disdainful. "It's not a real light-mode, of course—no solidity controls at all—but it'll look the part."

Tanner picked up the device and slipped the

straps over his shoulders. The assembly settled on
his chest and he buckled it into place. "Like that?"

"Yes. There's the button."

Tanner pushed the button and was abruptly surrounded by a shimmer of light. Startled, he raised
his hands and saw both encased in glowing steel
plate. He spread his fingers and saw flesh emerge
through the steel, like a weird ectoplasm. He hastily
flexed his fingers and they disappeared beneath the
coat of steel.

"I told you it had limited operation," the Vang
rumbled. "Practice a while to understand its limits;
then we'll set you in motion towards *Ariel*. You'll
have to walk—we can't trust that jury-rig around an
anorph driver."

Tanner walked around the flight cabin, watching
his legs and arms. If he moved too energetically, his
body slid out of the hologram, but after a while he
got the hang of it—sort of.

Chandra grumbled. "It'll have to do. Now, what
I propose is that you go out the lock and off to *Ariel*
a few minutes after I leave. I'll skulk around Portside, riding groundcars and berating bureaucrats and
such, then return to *Ariel* in an hour or two."

"I'll have to pack some clothes and leave a message for my aide."

"Yes. Do that."

Tanner fumbled at the hologram controls and the
shimmer of light disappeared. The Vang waited
patiently while Tanner threw some clothes in a bag
and then found a blank fax and his stylus. He hesitated over the plastic sheet.

"Perhaps a visit to Setha's mountain home," Chandra suggested. "We'll clear it with Setha after you
get to *Ariel*."

"You know my aide?" Tanner asked dryly as he
wrote.

"No. There is some problem?"

"No, never mind. It's not important." Tanner placed the fax on Lenart's desk and reactivated his light-mode. Chandra handed him the bundle of cloth he had used to carry it unassembled.

"Wrap your case in this. And remember to keep your arms down—you've got your left arms intersecting." Tanner looked down at himself and hastily extracted his lower arm from the other. As he gripped the case, his fingers emerged from steel again. He looked at Chandra through the haze of the light-mode, but the pilot waited patiently until Tanner adjusted himself back inside.

"Don't worry about it," he said. "You won't be close enough to anybody for it to matter. I hope. The Guildswoman wants this to be as secret as possible, in case anybody's watching."

"Are we being watched?" Tanner asked.

"I haven't the faintest idea, but we'll muddy the evidence as much as we can. Take it easy walking. The mode interface doesn't permit full atmosphere exchange. You might run a little short on oxygen by the time you reach *Ariel*, but not to worry."

Thanks, guy, Tanner thought. "Right."

Tanner gripped his case and followed the Vang to the air lock. The Vang cycled through as Tanner waited, sweating inside the alien light-shield. Then he passed through the lock and set off for *Ariel*. Every groundcar in the vicinity seemed to whiz by, the anorphs' eyes bright with suspicion. He ignored them and tried to concentrate on walking.

He was lightheaded enough by the time he reached *Ariel* and he fumbled a bit in and out of the light-mode as he circled the ship to its air lock. The lock door sighed open and he saw the Guildswoman in the doorway through the haze.

"Come in, Tanner," she said.

"How'd you know it was me?" he asked, trying to
be funny. The expression on her thin face did not
change, and he let it go. She wasn't happy about
this, although the reasons were obscure to him.

She waited for him to enter, then held up an oxygen canister. He pushed his chest button and the
light shimmered away. As she fitted the canister
mask over his nose, he closed his eyes to breathe in
the good clean air.

"Okay?" she asked. He nodded and she took away
the mask.

"Good morning," he said pedantically, and that
did earn a smile. Although attractive, she wasn't
beautiful, with a chin too strong for the thinness of
her face and dark hair too short. Nor did Tanner
care much for her quiet self-assurance. He preferred
his women more uncertain, more inclined to look to
a man for decisions—but at least he had the grace
to know his own bias. Tayna used to berate him
loudly about it—strange that she later picked Roycrai
from all the traders swanning around her. He wondered if Jennan might have the same female self-
contradictions. But she was tall and slender, and her
smile lighted her gray eyes. He felt another stir of
interest, intrigued. What was a human woman doing
in the Guild? Would she answer if he asked?

"Chandra said he'll skulk around Portside for an
hour or two," he said.

She nodded and turned away, moving gracefully
away from the lock. He looked around the room,
studying the counter-desks ringing the inner well—
a strange design, that—the long dining table by the
far wall, the twin couches on either side of the air
lock. Several doors at irregular intervals led to inner
rooms, and he guessed this level held the crew
suites.

One of the doors opposite from the lock sighed

open and a Daruma stepped out of an elevator, dressed in the same uniform as Jennan, a beige tunic with a high collar, loose trousers tucked into soft boots. Tanner thought he recognized him as the Daruma who had accompanied Jennan the night before, but wasn't certain. He hadn't paid that much attention to her aide. Did she have more than one Daruma aboard?

As the Daruma saw Tanner, he stopped.

"So you've arrived," he said in accented Terran. Jennan sat down in a chair near the well and swung back and forth, her head turned away from Tanner towards the Daruma.

"I speak Trade, Guildsman," Tanner reminded him shortly, and then belatedly realized the alien had intended friendliness, not a comment on human shortcomings. *Lenart has affected my mind*, he thought.

"As you do," the Daruma said smoothly, switching to Trade. "Welcome aboard. Stop scowling, team-first; it solves nothing and makes an unfortunate atmosphere."

"Yes, Morgen," she said, glancing at Tanner. The scowl stayed.

"You could invite him to sit down," Morgen said reprovingly. "Please excuse team-first, trader: she's in a snit. Everyone's in a snit—Setha, Portside, your aide, my esteemed team-first. Without emotion, where would we be? Would you like to see the report Lenart filed? Now *there's* a snit."

"Lenart was born a snit," Tanner said sourly. Then he sat down on the couch and stared at Morgen. "How did you ever get a copy?"

"The Raome gave it to us." He drew his face into a doleful expression, his ears waggling. "I'm afraid that the Raome like us better than they like Lenart.

A strange bias, truly strange." He glanced at Jennan again. "Raome are weird," he offered.

"Can it," she replied, and then grinned despite herself.

Morgen grinned back, his wrinkles deepening. His ears moved in a graceful pattern, and Tanner vaguely remembered some rumor about talking with ears. Did they? He suddenly realized how little he knew about the Daruma, with whom Terra had been trading for years. He could recite trade statistics, describe their ship classes, list the major trading houses on Naberr, but of the Daruma as people he knew very little. And he guessed Morgen knew all about humans, knew even before he had a human shipmate, learned as part of the Guild's impeccable training. The Guild seemed to know everything. He felt uncomfortable at their knowing—and at his own notknowing.

Jennan turned to Tanner then, and shook her dark hair. "Forgive me, Ser Tanner. I am in a snit, but a temporary one. Let me show you your suite; you can put your case there."

"Please call me Vaughn. And thank you."

"As you wish, Vaughn."

She got up from her chair and moved around the well with her feline grace, keyed open a suite door by the elevator. Morgen sat down and began working at a computer console. As Tanner followed the Guildswoman, he felt a new flush of anticipation: this could be a journey he'd never forget—with advantage he might find very useful. *Luck*, he thought as he returned Jennan's tentative smile. *Blessed luck.*

Chapter 6

In the slave pens aboard the Li Fawn ship, the daylight was perpetual, a nagging harsh light that struck at the eyes. Each day the Li Fawn interrogator, Ai-lan, took Lume to the crippled hulk of *Crystal*, demanding he explain the control boards wrecked by the electrical surge that had killed Roycrai, demanding he open access to the ship's computer. Lume refused, defying her.

"You obey!" she commanded, cuffing him roughly.

"No! Who are you? Where do you come from?"

Ai-lan ignored his questions, persisting in her demands about *Crystal*. He had learned a few names from her—Li Fawn, Pang-Ahit, Ngoh Ge, Kazuvi—but Ai-lan disdained any other answers. Lume looked curiously at the Li Fawn ship on the daily trips to *Crystal*, puzzling over the alien forms that scuttled at Li Fawn commands. On the fourth day, to his horror, he noticed a small disembodied brain in the door-lock panel of his cell, a living creature turned into a machine for the Li Fawn. He pointed at the panel and demanded the reason, but Ai-lan only shrugged coldly and named it "Kazuvi," then cuffed him into silence.

As each day succeeded the next, Lume watched Tayna's young face grow haggard and old, her eyes flicking anxiously, her hands waving without purpose. She had said little since Roycrai's death, and he worried about her sanity. On their eighth day in the pens, Tayna began rocking back and forth, chewing at her hands until he saw blood.

"Tayna," he called softly. She paid no attention and stared at the opposite wall, her teeth nibbling. "Tayna."

Lume crawled towards her across the metal floor. She shied away from him, eyes wide and staring, as if she didn't know him. He stopped short, bewildered; after a moment, Tayna resumed her slow rocking.

"I'll kill them for this," he told her. He crouched forward and pressed his forehead against the metal floor plate, hating the too bright light, the strange tasting food that made him dizzy and weak. "I'll kill them all."

The pen door swished and he jerked up his head, wary. A Pang-Ahit trundled into the room, searching for garbage. Its snout swayed back and forth as it examined Lume with each of its several eyes, tendrils flexing nervously along its elongated body. Then, with a snort, it circled around him, sniffing along the walls. Daring, Lume reached out his hand to touch it as it came closer. It avoided him.

"Pang-Ahit," he said softly.

The creature found the remains of yesterday's meal and gobbled it up, then rushed to the corner he and Tayna used as a toilet. Lume grimaced in disgust as he watched. Yesterday he had heard this Pang-Ahit—or perhaps another one—talk to the Li

Fawn outside the cell, clearly answering a question put to it. How could such a creature be intelligent?

Don't be so human, Lume, he thought. Maybe garbage, even *that* kind of garbage, could be a delicacy—if you're a Pang-Ahit.

"Pang-Ahit," he called again. "Friend. Me friend." He tapped his chest, trying to draw the alien's attention.

"Do not bother, human," a voice croaked harshly. Lume jumped in surprise, and jerked his head towards the pen door. Ai-lan lounged against the frame, watching him coldly with her crimson eyes. He had come to loathe that coldness with a passionate hatred he hadn't thought capable within himself. *I'll kill you first*, he promised her silently.

The Li Fawn smiled slightly, as if she guessed his thought, and flicked a graceful three-fingered hand through her feathered crest. "The Pang-Ahit know their role in the Great Plan," she informed him haughtily. "So will you—in time."

"Leave me alone," he snarled and turned his back on her.

"So—still defiant." She sounded amused. "You be careful, Lume. We Li Fawn not tolerate such slave defiance long."

"I'm not your slave!"

"Oh?" Ai-lan pointedly examined the narrow cell, floor, ceiling, walls, then fixed her attention on Tayna. "I speak to Tayna today."

"No!" Lume rose to his knees and a weapon instantly appeared in Ai-lan's hand, warning him back. "She's sick," Lume added lamely.

"Good. Perhaps answer better than you. Move back."

Ai-lan barked an order at the Pang-Ahit, who scurried past her into the corridor beyond, then approached Tayna. His sister looked up and cowered backwards, her mouth distorted with fear.

"Come, Tayna." Ai-lan grasped her arm and pulled her up. "You come."

With a cry, Tayna struck out and wrenched away, then leaped for the open door. As Ai-lan whirled and raised her weapon, Lume surged upward, batting the laser-gun from Ai-lan's hand.

"Run, Tayna! Run!" he shouted.

Lume aimed a punch at Ai-lan's jaw and swung with all his strength, connecting with a crack of his own knuckle bones. Ai-lan fell backwards heavily, then slumped against the wall, unconscious. For how long, Lume didn't know. He cradled his hand against his chest, wincing from the pain, then bent for the weapon and ran out of the cell.

The corridor was empty, a sterile succession of metal doors stretching for forty meters in either direction. He hesitated, looking one way, then the other, then heard a clatter and shout to the right. He raced for the far staircase and leaped up the treads three at a time. More shouting and a crash, then Tayna's cry of pain.

"Tayna!"

He emerged into a large room with instrument banks on every wall, a dozen control chairs on one side, a larger chair in room center. Tayna lay pinned beneath a crab-man Eschoni slave, struggling wildly, while a Li Fawn in golden robes angrily stabbed his fingers at several Li Fawn guards, croaking his commands. One of the guards spotted Lume and shouted a warning, then threw his body between Lume and the ruler. Cursing, Lume aimed and pressed the knob on his weapon. A ruby beam lanced out, burning the guard's chest to char. The Li Fawn slumped, his eyes wide with shock and pain, then fell forward on his face.

"Stop!" the ruler shouted at Lume.

Lume jumped for cover behind the central chair and peered over the chair back, then ducked back hastily as a dozen laser beams stabbed past him. The ruler shouted angrily at the guards.

"Let her go!" Lume called. Tayna answered incoherently, crying out words through her sobs.

He heard the Li Fawn croaking at each other, then a patter of feet behind him. He whirled in his crouch and fired at the pack of Eschoni boiling out of the staircase. They swarmed over him, chittering, their slack jaws snapping at his body, crushing him to the floor. He felt someone seize his hand and take the weapon from him. Then the crab-men jerked, squealing, and retreated, grabbing at their collars. A guard yanked Lume up to his feet.

Lume looked up into the furious red eyes of the Li Fawn ruler. "You be sorry, human," the Li Fawn promised him. "You be sorry for this."

He gestured at the guards holding Lume, then turned away contemptuously. Lume fought them all the way back to the pens, earning himself bruises from the cuffs and blows. They threw him back into the pen, and one watched Lume with weapon drawn as the others carried Ai-lan's limp body into the corridor.

"I'll kill you," Lume shouted at them.

The last guard spat contempuously and left, locking the door behind him. Lume sagged, his hands limp and useless.

"I'll kill you," he whispered.

He waited listlessly for hours, until his muscles cramped from inactivity. The Li Fawn had not returned Tayna to the cell and he worried, frustrated with his helplessness. What was happening? Would they punish her for Lume's atttack?

He got slowly to his feet, groaning, and stumbled

to the cell door. A narrow oblong of glass looked out into the corridor, but he could see nothing except blank metal walls. In the door lock near his hand, the Kazuvi shivered convulsively in its glass prison. Lume hastily snatched his hand away.

"Who *are* you?" he cried out, beating at the metal door. "What do you want of us?"

Later, in the night that had no darkness, they came for him, asking for the first time about the Light.

Chapter 7

Hyperspace travel was instantaneous, but a trans-sector jump from Ro to Taki would strain *Ariel's* modest engines and waste fuel in a fashion that would make a Guild accountant shudder. Jennan preferred to keep her explanation list as short as possible, and so they jumped to Prander first. Chandra exchanged some jocular insults with his relatives by radio while they orbited near jump-point, waiting for the engines to cool, then jumped *Ariel* to Taki. *Ariel* descended in a long curving trajectory into the ecliptic and assumed a low orbit around Taki, awaiting the arrival of McCrory's freighter.

Tanner had fit into the ship's company extraordinarily well. T'wing chirped at him sweetly, and even Morgen, who hadn't much use for Terran traders, had warmed to his winsome manners. And, by praising Chandra's light-mode on first meeting, Tanner had apparently won a friend for life. Jennan kept her distance, knowing she was rude in doing so. Human herself, she detected the faint traces of a purpose behind his suave manners and distrusted them for that reason—though, at times, she caught a strange expression on his face, almost a yearning, and it seemed a strange counterpoint to his smooth courtesy. He was a complicated man, not at all what she expected, and light years away from the prune-faced sourness of Naberr's Terran legation.

The second day after their arrival at Taki, Jennan sat in the ship lounge watching the verdant forests of the planet roll by the wide-view windows. The entire planet was forested, and, barring its small icecaps at the poles, had minimal oceans, infrequent lakes. But the sparkling strands of Taki's rivers wound through and through the forest, a meandering and random netting among the bursting life of Taki. It was a beautiful world: she had forgotten how beautiful.

She should go to bed. The others slept below as the ship adjusted to planet time, and she belonged in bed, too. But she continued to sit in her lounge chair, watching as Taki moved from daytime to night. Fairy chains of lights twinkled across the darkened landscape beneath her as the Takinaki lit their lamps against the night. Taki had no moons, no space installations, no star travel except the occasional offworlder ship spiraling down in controlled flame to land at Taki's single port. *Ariel* drifted through the upper air, a tiny solitary moonlet for Taki's skies.

She heard the elevator whine and shifted in her chair, unwilling for company. The door slid open, and Morgen padded out, dressed in rumpled bedclothes. The Daruma looked mildly irritated, the cant of his ears promising yet another lecture.

"Oh, it's you," she said.

"You should be in bed. How can you dazzle the whole of Portside while you yawn your head off?"

"I hear you, effrendi. The same to you, by the way."

Morgen settled into the chair beside her and

stretched out his short legs. He wiggled his bare toes comfortably. They watched Taki roll by.

"Taki is a nice place," Morgen said after a time. "I may retire here."

"It's a little early to talk about that," Jennan said. "You've only got another hundred years or so to make your arrangements." She cupped her chin in her hand. "What does it feel like to live two hundred years?"

"I don't know—I haven't done it yet." Morgen stifled a yawn with his fist. "The freighter should arrive tomorrow. What are your plans?"

"Oh, I suppose we'll follow the offloader down and sit around awaiting developments. If there are developments. I'm afraid, Morgen. I've afraid I've done everything wrong. Hauling Setha around like that, taking Tanner aboard *Ariel*. What if the crystals sit in the warehouse and nobody cares? We have to go back to Naberr eventually, and if I don't have answers, that's the end of my career in the Guild."

"Not all the end. We can always go into private trade together. Maybe we'll end up rich."

She looked at Morgen quizzically, and shook her head. "You're joking. You'd never leave the Guild."

"Maybe not," Morgen admitted. "But I can make waves, and I'm inclined to make huge ones if you suffer from this. You're depressed: it's probably just time-adjusting."

"Oh?" she asked, raising her eyebrow sardonically. "With the problems we've got?"

"Just a theory. Tanner likes you," he added irrelevantly.

"Another theory. And what does that have to do with anything?"

"Just commenting."

"Whatever are you batting around, Morgen?" she demanded. "He's a McCrory trader."

"So?" He grinned at her, unabashed. "One of the best things about team-second is that I can comment on all kinds of things. Oh, you're going? What a shame. We could have sat up all night watching the planet turn."

"I'm going to bed. Good night."

"Excellent." Morgen chuckled to himself as he followed her to the elevator.

The freighter arrived the following afternoon, and Chandra set down *Ariel* next to McCrory's offloader a few hours later. Men in McCrory uniforms bustled around the shuttle in preparation for unloading the crystals into storage. Tanner ambled over in the bright sunshine to talk to them, and then with a wave to Jennan set out across the field to catch a boat upstream. Jennan watched him stride off, then turned back to inspect the slight wrinkle in *Ariel*'s lower hull. One of the ship's landing pods had pierced the tarmac as they landed, tipping *Ariel* off her gyros. Only Chandra's prompt touch on her jets had saved the ship from a most ignominious arrival.

"Is it serious?" she asked. Chandra grunted noncommittally and continued his unhurried study. Jennan crossed her arms patiently and watched him.

Chandra shimmered in a tessellated pattern of simulated metal plate, a favorite light-mode resplendent with four gauntleted arms, each bulging with muscles inscribed in the living metal. On his head he wore a helmet festooned with jagged spires and metal loops, and his face was a carved metal mask, vaguely humanoid in Jennan's honor, with inset ovoid eyes gleaming with frosty menace. He had completed the costume with a ten-foot spear, and called it all the Steely Gaze. Morgen had called it a Steely Sight, as he always did when the Gaze appeared in their midst, which had led to breakfast comments.

"That depends," Chandra said finally. He toed the crumbling edge of the hole in the tarmac. "You ought to sue. That tarmac is only a meter thick. It's supposed to be three."

"I don't want to sue. I just want *Ariel* repaired."

Chandra looked around at the small port with its bedraggled warehouses and two dozen small ships. "I doubt if they have the facilities." He scanned the field again. "This is a spaceport?" he asked contemptuously.

"It's supposed to be. Save your scorn for Port Control—it'll help the cause. Come on."

Control had assigned *Ariel* a square on the far edge of the field. Control evidently feared dangerous overcrowding if it parked ships less than five squares apart, and so they hiked nearly the width of the port to reach the terminal. As they approached the tower, warning lights and a siren signaled the approach of another incoming ship, and scurrying grew intense.

"Amazing," Chandra muttered. "Oh, no, a ship, a ship! Oh, no!" Someone waved at them frantically from the observation tower two levels above, and Chandra promptly dropped into a slow swagger, twirling his spear in long swishing arcs, to and fro, up and down, artfully tossing from one hand to another to another. . . .

"Knock it off, Chandra," Jennan said. "You might distract the controller who's talking down that ship." She looked up at the daytime star of the approaching ship and picked up the pace slightly.

"So? What are nav-scans for?"

"You see any nav-scan housings on the tower?"

"Oh." Chandra stopped twirling and caught up with her in a few strides. They ambled on peaceably, heading for Control. "I wondered why Control got so chatty during descent. That could explain it, it could indeed." He idly tossed his spear to another hand.

"I like that outfit," she said.

"Thanks."

A half-dozen offworlder merchants lounged in front of Port Control, enjoying the late afternoon sunshine as they exchanged gossip. Jennan nodded to the Daruma traders in the group, and pushed through the terminal doors to the small waiting room within. A squat and very orange Hleri sat behind the counter, punching figures into an antiquated computer.

"Don't the Takinaki run their own port?" Chandra asked.

"Apparently not. The combines must trade off, like they do on Shann." She scowled with mock distaste. "Our luck to pull a Hleri."

She leaned on the counter and rapped her fingernails sharply on its plastic surface. The Hleri looked up and glared.

"What you want?" he barked.

"I had landing damage. I want it repaired."

The Hleri shrugged. "You can't land right, not my fault." Chandra stirred ominously, but she stilled him with a gesture. The counterman's yellow eyes shifted to Chandra, and he opened his wide mouth in a hiss, revealing a pallid sticky tongue covered with greenish mucous. A lovely sight.

"We did land right," Jennan said patiently. "The tarmac collapsed as we put down. How do I get my ship repaired?"

The Hleri snorted in acid disbelief. "Tarmac collapse? Ha-ha-ha. Human very funny."

"My pilot can drag you there, bump-bump-bump, along your shell-rotten tarmac to see for yourself. How about it?"

"Hokay, hokay," the Hleri grumped, and heaved his thick body to his feet. He waddled over to the counter and extracted some faxes from underneath. "Fill out form."

"Thanks," Jennan said ironically. The irony was wasted. The Hleri handed her a stylus, and she bent over the fax, printing neatly. Chandra wandered over to the window. The Hleri sucked his teeth absentmindedly as he watched her write. After a few minutes, Jennan shoved the completed fax back across the counter.

"Repairman start tomorrow morning," the counterman said. "Too late today. Repair charge eighty credits."

"Uh-uh," Jennan said, folding up her copy of the fax. "Port expense. You're the one with the rotten tarmac."

"You sue for refund."

"No sue for refund. No charge in first place."

The Hleri grunted in defeat. "Hokay. You come back and sign off form when repair done."

"Only if my pilot's satisfied with the repair."

"He be satisfied. We got good repairman. Byebye." The Hleri turned his back and waddled back to his chair. Jennan rejoined Chandra by the window, and then stayed to chat with the merchants outside the terminal as Chandra went off to inspect the port-repair depot. As she talked to the Daruma trade-captain, the incoming ship set down in a splash of flame behind the bulk of the Daruma freighter. They turned to watch, the trade-captain grunting admiration at the deft handling.

"Not bad," he said.

"I didn't recognize the prow markings. Did you see?"

"Sorry. And you're dodging my question, Guildswoman." The trade-captain smiled at her suavely.

"What brings you to Taki?" She heard the edge to his voice and repressed a grimace. Another conservative. The trade-captain smiled, watching her with suspicious dark eyes while he ear-twitched a command to his subordinate about ship listings and Guild inquiry. She wished, not for the first time, she had similar equipment to startle away a few Daruma assumptions about Terran inadequacy.

As she smiled suavely in turn, wondering if she could satisfy his suspicions with more inanities, one of the McCrory men came striding up and past, ship's manifest in hand, and walked briskly to the counter. Jennan excused herself and wandered back into the terminal. When the McCrory man got to the wild arm-waving stage, Jennan shifted into the Hleri's line-of-sight and exchanged a meaningful look. The counterman spat and began angrily stamping his stamp all over the McCrory papers. Then he hissed at the McCrory with heart and soul, making the poor man recoil three feet. The Hleri stomped back to his chair, leaving the shaken trader to gather up his faxes.

He stopped short when he saw Jennan, then glanced at the fuming Hleri with a sudden grin. He ambled over to Jennan, juggling the faxes straight in his hand.

"Thanks, Guildswoman!"

"My pleasure. Is that the manifest for the crystals?"

"Yes." He separated out one of the copies and handed it to her. "Give that to Vaughn, if you would. We're lifting in a few minutes."

"Would you show me where you stored the cartons?"

"Be glad to." Jennan followed the trader to the middle of the warehouse block. The man pointed out the cartons in the corner near the door, and she thanked him. He gave her a jaunty salute, and set out to rejoin the offloader.

Jennan stepped inside the warehouse to look at the cartons more closely. The building was more capacious than it appeared from outside. An elaborate frame of hardwood struts supported the corrugated roof, creating an air-space above the neat stacks of bales and boxes piled on both sides of a central walkway. The central walkway led twenty meters to a smaller door at the other end of the building, with narrower sidepaths between the towering stacks of goods. She recognized trade imprints of several offworlder firms, proof of a small but vigorous trade with the local clans. The muted sounds of Portside filtered in the open door.

She turned to the Ro cartons, and then, with a sigh, began a laborious check of the contents in each carton. When she was done, she restacked the cartons and dusted her hands on her trousers. Her back ached from the stooping, and she grimaced as she stretched out the kinks. As she turned to leave, she caught a furtive movement, tall and gawking, near the back door. A shadow darted behind a stack of bales, and she froze, her senses prickling with alarm.

"Who's there?" she called.

There was silence. Jennan was conscious of the light streaming through the doorway, the shimmer of dust suspended in golden sparks where the light touched. The rest of the building interior was shadowed, dim and musty from the inadequate ventilation. She listened, and heard a faint scrabble. She sidled quietly down the row of stacks, looking down each siderow to the side walls. Nothing. As she neared the last stack, she hesitated, then eased into the narrow walkway between the stores. She took a step, then two.

Something lurched into the bales from the other

side, and she cried out, raising her arm against the heavy bales tumbling down on her. They crushed her to the floor of the warehouse, and her head hit the concrete with a resounding crack. She struggled against the weight, panicked as she could not get enough air into her lungs to breathe. The warehouse door rattled shut, blotting out what little light reached her between the bales.

"Help, help!" she called, then cursed futilely against the weight that pinned her to the floor. As she heaved against the bale across her chest, agony lanced through her left arm. With her last shred of consciousness she felt the bales crush the remaining breath from her body.

Tanner whistled as he cycled through *Ariel's* lock, pleased with his meeting with the Takinaki. Although the Taki chief had seemed puzzled and probably hadn't understood Tanner's reasons, he had agreed to a delay in upstream transport of the crystals. Tanner spent some time amusing the chief's wives with his badly-accented Takinaki, and had laughed in turn as the lovely creatures tried a few phrases in Trade. The chief had looked on proudly, absently fluffing his silky fur, his great nocturnal eyes blinking in the muted sunshine of the leafy canopy. Finally Tanner stood up to go and began the long-winded courtesies of departure. A pseudobat, enough like T'wing to be a twin, clung to the intertwined branches overhead and chirruped approvingly as he left.

During the boat ride back, Tanner had gathered some brightly-colored blooms, leaning perilously over the side of the boat to snatch at the flowers as they drifted past, and had a satisfying handful by the time the boat reached the Portside dock. He laid the flowers on Jennan's desk in the common-room, and fingered one of the tiny sculptures she had brought

out from their tissued packing the night before. She
liked sculpture, especially the delicate Taki dream-
icons. The one he touched looked like T'wing,
vaguely, although few Taki icons had any obvious
referents to reality. He wondered if she'd accept a
present of another, assuming he could prise one
away from Chief Abegetto. He wondered what she
thought of him. Maybe that kind of gift was too personal. Maybe . . .

He hummed to himself absently. Maybe personal
was just the key. The Guildswoman's lover might
have a few stellar opportunities, might indeed.
Assuming, of course, he ever got that far. He
reached into his pocket and read the McCrory dispatch again. Whatever was *Crystal* up to? Stealing
Shenda artifacts? Not that Tanner didn't admire the
boldness, but Lume ought to know better. The
Guild had iron control over Shann, and had proved
it meant to keep it: they'd never get away with it.
Though it seemed they had. Amazing.

He scowled at the fax, reading the plea from a
furious McCrory Central for Tanner's help. Idiots.
What could he do? The Guild must be turning on
the screws; Central just might get desperate enough
to yank Tanner off to Shann. Anything to make a
gesture.

Not now, guys, not now, he thought irritably. He
stuffed the dispatch back into his pocket, considering
versions of a soothing reply to get Central off his
back. Now, waving money usually worked. . . . He
smiled happily, knowing McCrory too well.

The air lock cycle hummed behind him, and he
looked around as Chandra's massive form stepped
into the room.

"Where's Jennan?" Tanner asked.

Chandra halted abruptly. "Isn't she here?" The
Vang walked rapidly to the center rail and shouted

her name up the ship-well. At the sound of his voice, T'wing began screaming frantically, shrieking up and down an ultrasonic scale. As Tanner joined Chandra at the rail, Morgen looked down from the flight deck.

"Don't set her off again," he said sourly. "I've had enough of her caterwauling today."

"Has Jennan returned?" Chandra bellowed up at him.

"No. I assumed she was with you. Why?"

Chandra whirled and headed for the air lock. Tanner followed him hastily, and had to wait for the lock to cycle back to entry. As he emerged from the ship, he vaulted down the stairs and ran after the rapidly striding Vang.

"What's wrong?" he panted as he caught up. Chandra continued to stride along, forcing Tanner to half-run to keep pace with him.

"Jennan left me half an hour ago to look at the crystals," the Vang answered. "I saw her go into the warehouse, and I assumed she had come out while I was busy in the repair shed."

"Maybe she did and went somewhere else in Portside."

"Didn't you hear T'wing screaming? Morgen just doesn't *think* sometimes."

They reached one of the warehouses and Chandra yanked at the doorlatch. The door rattled back in its guide, and the two stepped into the dim interior. Tanner gasped as he saw Jennan's hand extended from beneath a tumble of bales, and ran towards her. He pulled a bale off the top. Chandra tossed his spear aside, and quickly grabbed another. Within a minute they had uncovered her, and Tanner dropped to his knees beside her still body.

"She's not breathing!" He maneuvered awkwardly in the cramped space, then leaned forward to blow

into her mouth. His other hand fumbled for her
wrist and he felt a pulse, thready and weak. Chandra
bent over them anxiously, and Tanner raised his
head.

"She's alive, but I have to breathe for her. Go get
a respirator." Chandra lurched to his feet and left
hurriedly.

Tanner steadied to the rhythm of breathing into
Jennan's mouth, his hand firmly on her wrist to monitor her pulse. By the time Chandra returned, Morgen running behind him, Jennan's heartbeat was
stronger and she had begun to breathe on her own.
Tanner slipped the elastic of the respirator over her
head, and then checked her arms and legs, searching
for broken bones.

"I think her left arm is broken. Don't move her
yet, Chandra. She might have a spinal injury, too.
Damn! How did this happen?"

"I brought a body scanner," Morgen said. "Move
out of the way, Vaughn." The Daruma slowly drew
the scanner down Jennan's body, then sighed
deeply. "Bruises, a broken arm, nothing major.
Thank the gods."

Morgen's shoulders sagged, the scanner sliding to
rest on his thigh. Tanner looked down at the Daruma's bowed head and felt awkward to see Morgen so
reduced. He had wondered about their relationship,
including some speculations he could never dare
voice to either of them. A girl raised by Daruma
might get odd ideas about most anything, even sex.
Have they? he wondered uneasily.

"Morgen, get up," Chandra rumbled. Morgen
started a little, then grimaced as he complied. He
looked shrunken, somehow, and Tanner felt even
more uncomfortable.

"I'll carry her," Tanner offered.

"Some things a Vang is designed to do," Chandra

said, and bent into the walkway to lift Jennan, cradling her in his upper arms. Morgen rocked from one foot to the other, then ran after the Vang. Tanner picked up the Vang's spear and followed, feeling like a fool with the thing. He swung the warehouse door shut, and then dealt with the questions of the several merchants who had rushed up, finally extricating himself to head back to *Ariel*.

Three of the merchants followed after him, pelting him with more questions. He ignored them and merely lengthened his stride. As he neared midfield, he noticed the McCrory freighter had left, and then hastily moved downfield as another small craft in the center squares began blinking warnoff lights. Tanner looked at the departing ship more sharply, realizing he recognized neither the design nor the symbols on its prow. It lifted in a rumble of flame and streaked aloft. Tanner watched it dwindle in the sky, then nearly fell on his face as he tripped on a crack in the tarmac. Wearily, he concentrated on putting one foot in front of the other as he followed the others back to *Ariel*.

Morgen was splinting Jennan's arm when he arrived, as T'wing flapped frantically overhead, screaming her distress. The Daruma ducked as T'wing swooped on him, and Tanner coaxed her to him. He talked nonsense syllables and scraps of Takinaki, trying to calm her, and the tiny creature finally clung to his shoulder, shivering. Through the door of Jennan's bedroom, he could hear Chandra's rumbling voice on the upper level, and a higher-pitched piping over the ship's radio.

"The radio was squawking when we came in," Morgen said as he wrapped gauze round and round Jennan's arm. "As you can well imagine. We must have made a fine progress across the field." Morgen spoke in his usual dry tone, but his voice caught and he fell silent. Tanner didn't know what to say. "I should have listened to T'wing," Morgen continued, bending over the injured arm. "She screamed and screamed at me, flying around like the ship was afire. But I didn't do anything."

"You couldn't have known, Morgen. How could you?"

Jennan's eyes fluttered open and wandered unfocusedly. She moved, and Morgen immediately stooped over her. "Don't move. Just breathe deeply." He readjusted the oxygen mask and gently stroked her hair. Jennan focused on the face bending over her, and her eyes filled with confusion at Morgen's distress. She raised her uninjured arm to tug off the mask, but Morgen firmly pushed the arm back to the mattress.

"Don't speak. don't move," he repeated. "You're back on *Ariel*, and everything is all right. Your arm is broken—that's why it's in a splint. And you have a nasty bump on your head." Jennan sighed and closed her eyes. "Jennan?"

T'wing squeaked a demand, and Tanner placed her on the blanket next to Jennan's pillow. The pseudobat fluttered her wings, cheeping in distress, and then curled up tightly into the curve of Jennan's neck. Morgen ushered Tanner out of the room.

"She needs quiet right now," he said. "I'll sit with her. I thank you for your comfort, Vaughn, though I'm not as gentle with myself as you are. I should have known better: there have been previous incidents. But who would have expected an attack so soon?"

"I'm not so sure it was an attack. Maybe the bales shifted on their own." He paused, thinking. "No, you're right. The crystals were near the door, and we found her several meters away. She must have surprised somebody inside the warehouse."

"Who left her there under the bales to suffocate."
Morgen's eyes glittered.

"Listen, do you have some sketching paper? I saw
something that might fit into all this." Morgen
fetched a pad of paper from a storage cabinet near
Jennan's desk, and watched as Tanner sketched the
ship he had seen. He drew the prow symbols
alongside the design, pausing several times to
remember their shape. He handed the pad to
Morgen.

"Do you recognize this? I've never seen a ship
like that, but maybe you know the symbols."

Morgen frowned at the sketch, then called up the
well to Chandra to come down. "I don't know," he
said to Tanner. He touched one of the symbols.
"This one looks vaguely familiar, but I can't
remember where I saw it. Chandra knows everything about ships," he added with total confidence
in the pilot's abilities. Chandra came hand-over-
hand down the ladder, and Morgen handed the
pad to him.

"Do you know this ship type?"

Chandra looked down at the pad, and an unreadable expression came over his metallic face. "Where
did you get this?" he asked hollowly.

Morgen turned to Tanner inquiringly. "I saw it lift
off just a while ago," Tanner answered. "Why?"

Chandra pointed to the middle symbol. "I don't
know the ship design, but I know that symbol. I
know that sign. It was inscribed all over the cartons
in the storeroom where the Li Fawn imprisoned me.
And you say the ship left?" Chandra's voice rose into
a half-scream, and he threw the pad violently against
the far wall. "It *left*?" Tanner and Morgen backed
away hastily as Chandra swung towards them.

"Chandra!" Morgen yelled. The Vang stepped one
way, then the other, flexing his mighty arms. Then

with a roar, he upended Morgen's desk, dumping its load of faxes on the floor in every direction. An arm swept across Jennan's desk, scattering the Taki flowers and sending the tiny sculptures ricocheting against the wall, smashing them into a dozen pieces. At the crash of the glass, Chandra abruptly stopped and looked down at the spray of shattered glass on the desk. Then he moaned, and fled past them into his room.

"Oh, gods, oh, gods!" Morgen said helplessly.

"Whatever possessed him?" Tanner asked, staring after the Vang.

"The Li Fawn kidnapped him and stripped him, Vaughn. You can't imagine what degradation that is to a Vang. When we broke into the storeroom, he was hiding behind some boxes, whimpering. I never want to hear a sound like that again." Morgen closed his eyes, his face pale. "And now he's broken Jennan's sculptures, after all she's been to him. He would have suicided except for her."

Tanner looked at Chandra's closed door with sudden alarm. He liked Chandra and could well guess the impact his death would have on Jennan. Impulsively, he circled the well with quick strides and pounded on the unyielding door.

"Vaughn, don't!"

Tanner reached down and flipped the emergency latch and barrelled into the room. Chandra's tall form whirled, and Tanner turned to gesture reassuringly at Morgan, then shut the door. He leaned back and crossed his arms.

"I'm here to make sure you don't do something stupid," he said in a measured voice. "If that means you tearing my arms out, go ahead and try."

"Get out!" Chandra hissed, taking a step towards him.

"You broke her things. She'll forgive you. You

dumped Morgen's research on the floor. She'll forgive that, too. You would no doubt have torn the Li Fawn limb from limb, but she would have forgiven even that, though it meant losing the proof that'll save her career. Morgen says you wanted to suicide after what the Li Fawn did to you, and if you're thinking any such thing now, I tell you she won't forgive that. She'll grieve and grieve, blaming herself for lying in there sick while you destroyed yourself. Is that what you want?"

"Who says I'm going to suicide?" Chandra growled.

"So I'm wrong," Tanner said, "but I'm not leaving until you get hold of yourself, and start thinking of Jennan instead of your pride." He glared at the Vang furiously.

Chandra stared back for a long moment, then sat down heavily on a chair. "All right," he said dully.

"Do I have your promise?"

"Yes."

"Then why don't you come out of this room? Morgen's your team-mate, too, and he's already had enough anguish over Jennan getting hurt. He thinks it's his fault because he ignored T'wing."

Chandra looked up. "That's ridiculous. T'wing wouldn't begin screaming until Jennan saw the danger. By then it had already started."

"Then go tell him that." Chandra stood up, and Tanner keyed open the door, still wary of the Vang's mood. Morgen was still standing where Tanner had left him, and, as Chandra followed Tanner out, he visibly relaxed. Chandra circled the well and stooped to pick up Morgen's papers.

"I seem to have rearranged your files," he rumbled.

Tanner righted the desk, and the three of them collected the scattered paper. Chandra refused any help with the glass, and sat far into the evening at

his desk, painstakingly gluing the sculptures back
together as Jennan slept nearby.

Luck, Tanner thought as he watched and felt his
neck hairs prickle at the risk he'd taken. *Just keep
riding the roll, Vaughn, old boy. It's your luck.*

Chapter 8

Two days later Jennan sat with the others in the common-room, propped in a chair with a pillow at her back, another under her feet, and a third under her injured arm. The pillows looked ridiculous, but Chandra had insisted. Her sculptures, neatly repaired, were arranged in her lap, and she fingered them one by one, her eyes straying worriedly to the Vang. Chandra was overly solicitous, insisting on this and insisting on that, but otherwise seemed his usual self. *Vaughn's doing*, Morgen had said, and she felt a wave of gratitude towards the trader.

She had drifted in and out of sleep for two nights and a day, and had awoken to find *Ariel* descending to Naberr. Tanner's mysterious stranger and the assault on Jennan had put Taki into an uproar, and the others had decided the Li Fawn would scarcely dare to return to Taki with every eye on the lookout. And so, with the hull repaired, Morgen had ordered *Ariel* to homeport. Jennan felt irritated at missing out on the decision but had to admit it was the reasonable choice. She only wished she had more answers for the Guildmaster than a headache and an escaped spy.

She tried to think, but her head wouldn't work. It was far easier to relax in her chair and watch the expressions of the others as they talked. She watched Tanner the most, noticing the aliveness of his eyes, the curl of hair at his temples, the mobility of his mouth. He noticed her watching, but she didn't care about that. She felt far too lethargic and Chandra's pillows were most comfortable. She yawned, promptly mimicked by T'wing clinging to her shoulder. Jennan scratched her pet's ears absently and yawned again.

The radio chimed on the flight deck and Chandra left to answer. He returned a few minutes later with a message fax in his hand. He silently gave it to Jennan, his expression unreadable. It was Guild official. She scanned the lines quickly, then crumpled it in her hands. The Guild ordered her to report immediately to the Hall to appear before a review board.

No preliminary reports, no discreet inquiry of a trusted Guildsman. *Why?* Well, she had the answer now. All this time she had thought the Guild's target was McCrory, perhaps Li Fawn, but the target—the bumbling, blind, trusting target—was Jennan Bartlett. She had her enemies, the Daruma traditionalists who hated the presence of humans in the Guild. She just hadn't counted the Guildmaster among them.

She stared down at the crumpled fax and felt herself turn deeply cold inside, beyond feeling and pain. She put the fax on the table, then lined her sculptures in front of it. Then she looked up, to see her friends staring at her in silence. Her expression must be deathly. She felt like death.

"A review board," she told them. "We haven't even filed our report and they've brought me up on charges." She struggled to her feet, cradling her injured arm. "I'll get dressed."

Morgen raised a hand in protest. "You aren't in any condition to go anywhere, Jennan."

She merely turned her back and walked into her room. She took her dress uniform from the closet and dressed awkwardly. As she was buttoning her sleeves, Tanner knocked at the half-open door.

"Do you need help?" he asked. "Morgen's making inquiries."

"I didn't authorize that," she snapped. "Tell him to stop."

"All right," he said quietly and left.

Jennan adjusted her injured arm in its sling and turned towards the door. On the shelf above her desk, in a clutter of fax memos and books, her Guild emblem winked at her in the soft light. She studied it a moment, then reached up and turned it to the wall. Then she caught up her burnoose and walked out of the room.

The groundcar ride to the Hall was made in total silence, Jennan retreated deep within herself, entering a dull lightless place where she felt nothing. Her head still pounded, settling into a steady ache that gripped her temples in a harsh vise. The Naberr sunlight hurt her eyes even through goggles, but she tried to ignore it. Physical pain was irrelevant.

As they entered the Hall, Jennan handed her goggles and burnoose to Tanner and motioned him to a bench near the door. As an outsider, he'd have no entry to the hearing unless summoned. He opened his mouth to protest but she stopped that with a furious glance. Tanner sat down.

She had sat on that bench the day the Guildmaster wrote the orders, she remembered. She forced down her despair at the memory. She and Morgen reported to the desk, the clerk's eyes widening at the sight of her sling. He called an aide to conduct them to the hearing room. She waited patiently, staring over the clerk's head.

The aide appeared, and they walked down a long corridor and then another. The aide keyed open a door, his eyes fixed on Jennan's face, and gestured her in. Jennan vaguely recognized him, thought to give some kind of greeting, but gave it up. She wanted nothing from him nor anyone else, not even pity.

Inside the hearing room sat three Daruma Masters at a long table—the Guildmaster himself, a senior councilman she knew all too well, and another senior she did not. Senior Tarthe cleared his throat as they entered and eyed her sling.

"Ah, Journeywoman Bartlett," he said. "Will you and your team-second walk forward to center?" He cleared his throat again. "Perhaps you would like a chair, Guildswoman." Jennan walked to the indicated spot and didn't bother to reply. Morgen stopped at her elbow, and she saw him think better about commenting.

She met the Guildmaster's eyes for an instant, and then determinedly looked elsewhere.

Tarthe rattled the papers before him, and she read his satisfaction in the cant of his ears. Tarthe had waited five years for this moment: he had furiously opposed the admission of humans to the Guild, protested their elevation to journeyman rank, still waged a constant warfare in the inner circles of the Council, for all that his own House had sponsored a human, too. Her misfortune to be Tarthe's first victim—if she was the first. Perhaps Rolf or Anitra had recently stood in this place, listening to trumped-up charges, the unwinding of Tarthe's neat plot, the end of hopes. She retreated even further within herself and watched Tarthe dispassionately.

Tarthe cleared his throat. "I will now read the charges," he said. "Breach of confidentiality. Disobedience of a direct order. Unprofessional conduct of a trade meeting. Admittance of a private merchant to a Guild ship. Unauthorized flight to Taki. Assault on a Li Fawn national."

Jennan blinked at that last but firmly clamped her lips. Tarthe continued reading, quoting Guild charter sections, reminding her of the terms of her oath, her probationary status, the penalties she faced if found culpable. He then asked for her plea to the charges.

Jennan said nothing.

Tarthe lowered his sheaf of paper and regarded her sternly. "Journeywoman, you will answer."

"After I receive three answers of my own," she said coldly. "Who informed you of the incident on Taki?"

"What do you plead?" Tarthe snapped.

"Answer or I will leave this hearing and this Hall. You have thirty seconds."

The third councilman jerked. "Impertinence! Who do you think you are?"

"Twenty seconds."

"I'll give you one more chance," Tarthe said furiously. "What do you plead?"

"Ten."

The Guildmaster interrupted smoothly. "Our report came from two Daruma traders present at the scene. They radioed headquarters and their House informed me. They said you assaulted a Li Fawn in a warehouse, though I must admit it looks like you got the worst of the fight."

She could not bear the kindness in his voice, and her anger kindled, a cold still flame. "They got their facts backward," she said harshly. "The Li Fawn, if it was him, pushed a stack of bales down on me. I broke my arm, got a concussion, and nearly suffocated. If Chandra and the human trader had arrived five minutes later, I'd be dead and you'd be spared this hearing."

The Guildmaster regarded her impassively. "I see," he said. "What is your second question?"

"Why is the Guild hostile to McCrory?"

"We received rumors of shortages in the Taki shipments and verified those shortages with the Takinaki. A McCrory agent recently tried to sell drugs to Hrauru. Tanner was apparently McCrory's agent for the same subversion, and may be involved in McCrory's theft of a Shenda artifact three weeks ago. The Guild will not tolerate illegality of that sort in Sagittarius."

"An impartial Guild is ill-advised to police trade in Sagittarius. Perhaps your apparent facts are not true."

"Your third question?"

"Who gave me the order to sabotage Setha's trade?" Tarthe's jaw dropped, and the other councilman rose to his feet, his face a mask of spluttering outrage.

"I did," the Guildmaster said. The councilman slowly sat down, staring at the Master in shocked disbelief.

"I see," Jennan said mockingly. "So much for your oath, gentlemen. So much for your honor and high-sounding words. This hearing is a farce. I resign." She turned on her heel and headed for the door. Morgen cried out, made as if to stop her.

"Jennan!" The Guildmaster's voice cracked across the room. She whirled to face him. "Come back here, you young firebrand," he said more quietly. "We haven't betrayed you, whatever you think."

"Oh?" Jennan asked savagely.

"My plan," the Guildmaster said equably, "was to find you guilty of all the charges, propose extenuating circumstances to excuse the lot, and put a commendation in your file. You performed admirably and we now need you to . . . Catch her, Morgen!"

Jennan sagged to her knees and pitched forward onto her face before Morgen could reach her. The room spun wildly and then went completely black. She floated unpleasantly in the darkness as voices jangled over her head.

". . . serious concussion . . . turned white as a sheet when she read the fax and . . . shut down all emotions . . ."

". . . I never intended . . ."

". . . she supposed to think! . . ."

"Tarthe . . . the physician . . ."

". . . Tanner . . ."

She floated past the voices down into the darkness, falling deeper and deeper into a black void until all awareness vanished.

She awoke in a hospital room. She studied the white walls, then watched the window curtains move in the breeze from an open window. She belatedly became aware of somebody sitting beside her bed. She turned her head on the pillow and saw Tanner.

"Good morning," he said, smiling.

"Morning?" she asked confusedly.

"You slept around the clock. We've been taking turns—though, for Morgen's sake, I was hoping you'd wake up when he was here. He left only an hour ago to get some sleep." Tanner raised his hand and showed her a bouquet of flowers. "These are for you. Chandra raided the hospital garden and got socked with a fine. But they let him keep the flowers." Tanner pressed the flowers into her hand and watched her anxiously.

"Pretty." She raised them to her face and breathed in their perfume.

"How do you feel?" Tanner asked.

"A little dizzy. Lazy as hell."

"That's the concussion. They x-rayed your skull and found a hairline fracture. Morgen hadn't suspected—and what he said to the Guildmaster when he found out!" He chuckled. "I never saw so many Daruma jaws drop at one time."

"What did the Master say?" Jennan asked, appalled for Morgen's sake. A human shouting at a Master was one thing, but the Daruma lived in other patterns. If he trashed his career, too . . .

Tanner winked at her reassuringly. "I gathered that the Guildmaster agreed with Morgen. So don't worry. Don't worry about anything." He patted her arm, and she abruptly dropped the flowers to seize his hand, pulling it to her lips for a brushing kiss.

"Thank you," she said. "Thank you for all you've done."

Tanner gave a shuddering sigh, then, with a determined expression, leaned forward to kiss her on the mouth. It made Jennan's head spin faster. As he released her lips, she laughed up at him.

"Dizzy."

Tanner grinned, then kissed her again and sat down. "Later we can experiment and see if it's me or your concussion," he said lightly. "I mournfully suspect it's your poor head."

"I like you very much."

"We can discuss that later, too," he said firmly. "And I'll tell you what you do to me. Right now you're supposed to rest."

"When can I go back to *Ariel*?"

"Not today. Probably not tomorrow. Sleep now."

Jennan obediently closed her eyes. She heard him quietly leave the room, and then she drifted away for a time.

That afternoon, Morgen dropped in, bearing a tape reader, two of her sculptures, and T'wing. The nurse let Jennan keep the reader and the sculptures, but drew the line on T'wing. While Morgen was arguing, Jennan fell asleep again.

She awoke late at night and found new flowers scattered across her bedspread—with a note from Chandra that magnanimously informed her he would forego a voucher for the fines but that he hoped she appreciated how much her hospital stay was costing him. She chuckled over the note, snapped off her bedlight, and lay awake in the darkness, drowsy and content.

The following day, her nurse opened the floodgates, and she had visitors all afternoon—her old nurse, Narena, bent and infirm but having the same loving eyes; her adoptive siblings from her House, most parading in merchant finery but a number in Guild uniform and determined to talk shop as long as she wanted to listen, fierce in their support. She gathered her House had filed a formal protest, putting the Guild in an uproar. She smiled and joked and renewed all her acquaintances, happy in their company.

Then, in the evening, Morgen brought his two young children, Laren and Vareshi, and somehow sneaked in T'wing, too. The nurse discovered T'wing almost immediately, infallibly attuned to such infractions of her rules, but Morgen was unrepentant. The two argued out in the hall while T'wing hid herself as an invisible lump—or so T'wing thought—under Jennan's covers. Five-year-old Laren showed her his reading with a letter from his mother, now on outsystem assignment, while baby Vareshi happily ate

several of Chandra's flowers from the vase. Then the
nurse swept in again. Morgen ear-twitched several
comments behind her back, and the nurse caught
the last one.

"Out!" she said, pointing to the door.

Tyrant.

"Out!" Sometimes even propriety had its pinches.

On the third day, Jennan was eating breakfast
under Morgen's supervising eye when the Guildmaster walked in. Morgen's ears curled in extreme non-
welcome, but the Master blandly ignored him. He
regarded Jennan with a warm smile.

"How are you feeling?" he asked.

"About me or you?"

"That sounds ominous," he said mildly, walking
around Morgen to the other side of the bed. He
perched one hip on the mattress and crossed his
arms across his chest, the picture of ease and
affability.

She narrowed her eyes, thoroughly irritated with
him. "It was the security erase and don't-tell-Morgen
that frosted it. How *could* you?"

"The security erase was just that, security. Guild
ships have been broken into before."

"Sure," she said deflatingly. She put another bite
of eggs in her mouth and chewed busily. She was
rewarded with the first faint glimmer of anxiety in
those too-subtle eyes.

"Don't you believe me?" the Master asked.

She put down her fork and glared at him. "Let's
just say that I have a new appreciation of revolving
options. Let's say that I think your choices were still
open, right up to my stalk-out on your little game,
Master. I know Tarthe, and that other councilman is
probably Tarthe's bosom friend. Tarthe surely isn't
one of mine. I've read the speeches he makes."

"Tarthe has been in clover the past few days, I will admit. One down, five to go." The Master smiled benignly, and she felt like braining him with her tray. "A hypothetical, my dear Jennan. You're good at hypotheticals," he added wryly. Jennan winced despite herself. "The Guild has a puzzle it can't solve, some apparent skullduggery by a Terran firm of impeccable reputation—at least so far—with incontrovertible facts we want to add up otherwise."

"Otherwise?"

"Yes, otherwise. The Guild favors Terra, at least if the other choice is the Li Fawn. Outsiders have come into the sector and we cannot turn them out now. So, to continue with my hypothetical, what must I do to solve the puzzle and find that other conclusion? Do I send in one of my finest Daruma mediators, one I can rely upon to keep every rule and formality—and by that, of course, behave exactly as expected? Or do I call on one of my human Guildsmen with the flexibility and nerve to take the risks I need for answers?" He spread his fingers rhetorically, then smiled at her skeptical expression.

"Plausibility is a Daruma gift," she said. "But if McCrory were crooked, who goes down the tube with them?"

"You do, my Jennan, for the sake of the Guild."

"You can stuff your . . ."

"Hush. Let's not be hasty. And you will uncurl your ears, team-second, before I snip them off."

Morgen looked startled. "Yes, sir."

"But I have a problem," the Guildmaster continued. "My human appointee has been thoroughly indoctrinated with Guild principles, as she must be to serve in ordinary situations. She would regard violation of the Code with the same horror as any of my Daruma, so I must push her into the flexibility with which she is graced. I decided if you had one code violation in the necessity of telling Morgen, you'd be less inhibited about racking up others when they became necessary. Is that not reasonable? Isn't that exactly what happened?"

His voice dropped. "A success, except on one point. I forgot you were a human Guildsman and that the pieces might fit an entirely different picture, a piece of self-immolation for the Guildmaster who betrayed you."

"You mean you didn't expect me to figure it out."

"Jennan, if you persist in this . . ."

"Master, I appreciate your subtlety. I know quite well that the Masters move their Guildsmen like pawns on a board. I just wasn't aware you pushed them so far afield. What do you want now?" She looked at him, her jaw set.

The Master's ears canted into an expression of regret. "Loss of innocence is always a blow," he offered.

"Trust isn't the same as innocence, and its loss is not inevitable. What do you want now?"

The Guildmaster shrugged and stood up. "We've spotted Tanner's mystery ship near Shann. A remote-post briefly picked up its transponder signal in the cometary plane before it dodged. I want you to find that Li Fawn and learn why he wants McCrory discredited. You're heard about the McCrory theft on Shann?"

Jenna blinked at the sudden change of topic. "You mean *Crystal*?"

"Yes. *Crystal* vanished four weeks ago, shortly before Taki complained about its shortages; curiously, the captain is Tanner's brother, Lume. You didn't know that? I'm surprised Tanner didn't tell you." He shrugged, dismissing the point. "It's too odd a coincidence. I can accept one in that Hrauru deal—that McCrory trader is a known maverick—

but not three. What is the pattern? Why McCrory? More curiously, *Crystal* never arrived at Centauri." The Guildmaster considered a moment. "I'll ask McCrory to lend Tanner to us for a while: they've been agitating to get him to Shann, anyway, for whatever use he might be in finding his brother. Would that suit you?"

"And if the plotter is McCrory after all, you have the convenience of my humanity when you go to treat with the Li Fawn."

The Master regarded her soberly, his lips drawn thin. "You will not be reconciled?" he asked.

"No. But I'll go to Shann, Guildmaster—for the sake of the Guild and the hell with McCrory. At least our motivations can be the same."

"Very well." He made a slight bow and left the room.

Morgen had grown very still. Now he fingered the edge of her bedspread, hesitating.

"You disagree?" she asked.

"No. It's just not a Daruma option, I guess. A Daruma would either join the game or walk out: I didn't know there was a middle ground." He looked at her a moment. "Maybe you're still feeling dizzy," he said judiciously.

"No, just human. We're good at holding grudges. In this case, my biggest grudge is against the Li Fawn. If they're the cause for this, they'll pay for it, believe me." She resumed eating, stabbing the food with her fork.

Chapter 9

As *Ariel* lifted away from Naberr Field a few days later, a small ship drifted into the receiving bay of *Ngoh Ge*, named "Pride of Nations" in the elder language and currently Lord-Son Chaat's base of operations in Sagittarius. The massive Li Fawn cruiser lay hidden in the cometary shadow of Shann, the future Seventh Colony of Chaat. In time, the worlds of the system, like all others in Sagittarius, would be rid of their animal infestations. Chaat would add new worlds and a wealth of new slaves to his father's holdings, far from the political nets of rival lords who held his family in cruel captivity at Antares.

In Sagittarius lay a power base to crush those rivals, an empire to match even the glittering suns of Home-Space, and a matching destiny for Chaat's line. Already his fourth lady-wife had borne him twin sons, two-fingered like Chaat himself, heirs to a proud line. The spy hoped for mercy in that happy news, for he brought failure with him, with no ready excuse.

Nineteen hastily unbuckled his flight belts and

loped past a pack of scrabbling Eschoni crab-men towards the transport well. His tall hulking figure instinctively moved to the sides of the shaft, concealing itself in shadow. As the well mechanism moved him upward, the bright contact lights of each level washed him in a blinding glare. He flinched at each illumination but endured it, holding to himself the robes of his caste for what small protection they offered.

At the top of the well, he stepped onto solid deck. A pack of Zaruti clinging to an overhead transom shrieked in warning, their body light flaring as alarm chemicals rippled through the nested bodies. The House Guard on duty stirred at the alarm, then recognized him and made slight greeting with her seven-fingered hand.

"He is waiting," she said.

The spy nodded and slipped along the corridor, then darted into a side door. He passed through a Kazuvi detector field, hurried past a multi-legged Pang-Ahit bent on its endless search for corridor garbage, then entered Command. The large room was a bustle of quiet activity, as Li Fawn Command caste calmly performed their duties at their boards. A dozen Guards in ceremonial dress stood at attention near the door, seniors in their caste and proud in their honor stations as Chaat's personal attendants.

To the left, a naked Eschoni crouched at a floor monitor before a complicated bank of machinery, watching a screen with its multiple eyes. As the screen pattern changed, the tech whimpered in alarm and scrabbled its claws at the floor control before its collar convulsed its wasted muscles for slowness. The screen steadied, and the tech blubbered with relief, its fear odor spreading through the room. The spy wrinkled his nose with distaste. He never could abide Eschoni gibbering and smells.

To the right, near another bank of controls, a Li Fawn supervised several Baroni as the small worm-like creatures ate their way into the flesh of a pregnant Mervit. The Mervit shuddered as she aborted her young onto the polished surface of the generator ledge, discharging her body currents into the wire face of a crystal generator. Nineteen looked away uncomfortably. He had spent part of his youth on the Mervit world, had even kept a Mervit pet until his body-mother found him out. It was the Mervit's misfortune that her body frequencies during pregnancy could regenerate the rare and precious *shoran* crystal. The animals had no other value, and the Li Fawn kept only a few in the pens. Still, the spy felt uncomfortable, and was ashamed of the feeling.

"Your name?" a Guard asked haughtily, her ceremonial lance raised to bar Nineteen's further entry.

"I am a worthless spy, Nineteen, come to report to our Lord Chaat."

"I will inform him." The guard walked stiffly forward and bowed to the Li Fawn lord seated in the center of the room. Dressed in the golden robes of Rule, Chaat's lean body lounged comfortably in the padded chair, jewels winking at his collar and ankles. Mottled ivory skin stretched tightly over the delicate inbred bones of his two-fingered hands. His blue-black feathered crest, dusted with gold, made a stark contrast to his pallid, ascetic face. As the guard murmured the introduction, Chaat raised his head and fixed Nineteen with a cold glare of his crimson eyes.

"Lord-Son Chaat," Nineteen murmured and prostrated himself on the metal floor.

"You failed." Chaat's voice was icy with displeasure. Nineteen flattened himself to the deck, twitching. Chaat allowed the silence to lengthen, then stirred himself in a soft whisper of his fine robes. "But I will excuse it this time. I allowed your predecessor one extra chance, and he wasted it on Hrauru. You can expect the same future, spy, if you fail me again."

"Yes, my lord." The spy began to twitch again, and Chaat grunted with satisfaction.

"Stand up and look at me. I have something to show you: remember it and then listen well."

Chaat rose to his feet and padded towards the far door. Cringing, the spy followed him out of the room. Chaat led him through a dim corridor, then down a winding metal stair to a confinement pen. Chaat keyed the small monitor screen on the door.

"Look."

Nineteen obediently leaned toward the screen to look into the room within. A human lay on the floor in ragged clothes, its face hidden in its arms. The spy recognized its rags as the remains of a McCrory uniform, and said so.

"Yes, McCrory. I caught his ship as he tried to sneak outward from Shann past the Daruma guard-beacons. His name is Lume, and he is stubborn. This one was trade-captain. He knows something he won't tell, something about Shann that another one, before she died, called 'Mad Roy's Light.' "

Chaat studied the unconscious human for a long moment, then switched off the monitor. "The name may be a corruption of some other name. The language banks offer nothing concrete, but I suspect it is Shenda. Fifteen millenia ago, the Shenda animals ruled Sagittarius. They had weapons, artifacts, machines now forgotten. I think this Light is such a Shenda machine. I want to know what this human found, and why he chooses to be stubborn."

"Yes, my lord."

"If you find it, spy, you may advance the Great Plan by decades. Your reward will be proportionate."

"Sire!" The spy lifted his face and met Chaat's eyes with fierce resolution. Chaat nodded approvingly.

"Guard will give you the transcripts of the interrogations," he said. "Study them and make your plans." He paused and fixed Nineteen with his crimson eyes. "And do not fail me again, spy."

"Yes, lord." Nineteen dropped to the floor, abasing himself, and Chaat impatiently dismissed him with a flick of his hand.

"Sire?" the spy ventured, greatly daring.

Chaat turned. "What is it?"

"Perhaps I should take my Siang?"

Chaat snorted irritably. "Of course not. This must be a quiet search by one spy, not a pack hunt by spy caste's slaves. And since when must I advise you about proper methods? You grow too attached to your tools, spy." Chaat's voice was heavy with displeasure.

"Yes, sire. I'm sorry, sire." Nineteen abased himself again.

"Even so, I name you Tsor del-Chaat and first of your caste. That name became yours by right when Sixteen died, but you must still earn it to keep it, spy. Find me this Light."

"Sire! I will!"

Chaat grunted noncommittally and left him. Tsor del-Chaat crept back up the stair, following at a discreet distance and keeping to shadows, exultant to be still alive.

Deftly, he slipped through long corridors toward spy-caste quarters near the outer hull. Zaruti warned of his approach twice, conditioned to sense all except Guards as intruders, but each time the Guard passed him safely. He moved from shadow to shadow, silently as only spy caste could move, and flinched from every revealing light, an inbred instinct of his caste. For this he had been born, this silent passage through streets and corridors, even those of home-ship. Now he had the name of Tsor del-Chaat, the name given to each primary in his caste. He relished the honor, long awaited, but would still think of himself by rank number, Nineteen, the name he had borne since childhood. To be named Tsor bore its own perils and was often a transitory honor: he did not yet, in his inner heart, call it his own.

He passed through other levels, slipping deftly from shadow to shadow, until he reached spy-caste quarters, his sanctuary within the enclosing bulk of *Ngoh Ge*. As he entered the outer room, a Siang challenged him in her rasped voice, then, recognizing him, leaped forward in welcome.

"Mass-ter!"

"Tiu," Nineteen murmured in answer and knelt to caress her smooth pelt. As he touched her, Tiu's four eyes gleamed and her tongue lolled from cruelly-weaponed jaws; she pranced in joy.

"Mass-ter," she repeated. "We have missed you." Behind her, other members of the pack peered from their den alcove, then bounded forward in their own welcome.

Nineteen looked around quickly but saw no other Li Fawn in sight. "And I have missed you, Tiu, all of you," he said, his voice a loving croon. He touched each one of them, giving greeting, and then stood up reluctantly.

Alone among his caste, Nineteen truly loved the Siang, the slave race ruled by the Li Fawn spies. Such attachments were disapproved—Li Fawn weakened themselves by caring too much for slaves—but the Siang, to everyone's surprise, obviously returned Nineteen's affection. Usually surly, sometimes uncontrollable in their instinctive rage, the Siang constantly simmered with rebellions that edged on madness. Only careful conditioning begun *in utero* kept the more passive Siang as useful servants; the more restive were inevitably destroyed. Nineteen had a gift with them—and valued it despite the criticism.

He touched Tiu's broad head, caressing her soft eyelids. She shivered with pleasure. "You stand guard well, Tiu."

"Thank you, Mass-ter."

"Where are the other masters?"

"At a meeting with the Lady Ai-Lan—except for Thirty-One. She waits for you, Mass-ter."

"I will see her."

Nineteen walked to the far doorway that led to inner suites and displayed his palm to the Kazuvi brain within the door monitor. As the Kazuvi recognized his pore pattern, the small light above its casing winked green. The inner door slid open, and he slipped into the darkened corridor beyond, the Siang padding behind him.

"Resume guard," he commanded sharply, and the pack reluctantly retreated to their usual post in the anteroom.

"Nineteen?" a voice called hesitantly.

"Yes. Where are you, Thirty-One?"

"Here." Thirty-One's graceful form appeared in a far doorway, wrapped in the dark robe of their caste, her crested head uncovered. Nineteen stopped short as her scent drifted to him.

"I am waiting for you," she said seductively.

He smiled. "Apparently my timing . . ."

". . . is flawless. My estrus began only this morning." She held out her arms. "Welcome, Tsor del-Chaat."

"Take care," he said warningly, raising his hand. "Our Lord Chaat is none too happy with me."

"I'll take the risk." Thirty-One smiled and rubbed her body languorously against the door sill. Her voice dropped to a deep croon. "I have confidence in you."

"Like you had in Sixteen?"

Thirty-One frowned prettily. "You didn't have to say that."

"Only noticing a fact. You never invited me to mate before; what has changed—besides the obvious?" He moved forward, approaching her.

Thirty-One stretched her thin lips in a warning grimace. "Only the obvious, Nineteen. Nothing more."

"That's what I thought." He slipped an arm around her slim waist and pulled her to him, thrusting his pelvis against hers to stimulate her further. She gasped and her responding scent swirled through his senses. "Not that I mind that much, of course," he said.

"Why should you mind?" She smiled up at him and drew him into her room. "I have noble blood, you know," she added, raising her four-fingered hand. "Perhaps Chance will favor our child, if we make a child, to rise above our caste. Perhaps even to Command itself."

"I'm content with our caste," he muttered and again breathed deeply of her drifting pheronomes. Smiling at him, she undid the clasp of her garment and let it slide slowly to her feet.

"A woman has other ambitions, Tsor: come, help me with mine, as Sixteen could not."

His vision blurred with her scent and touch; he circled behind her, preparing to mount. "I will," he growled.

She crouched before him, her buttocks raised enticingly apart, her swollen vulva gleaming pinkly between her thighs. He pushed aside his own robes, not bothering to remove them, and thrust into her. They mated quickly and roughly, both crying aloud with their passion, and then lay together far into the evening, apart from the others, as Thirty-One deftly cemented the sexual bond between them.

"I love you," she said later.

"I don't believe it," he answered.

"Ah, well." She caressed the stiff feathers of his crest, playfully disarranging them with her slender fingers, then pressed them smooth again. Her crimson eyes gleamed mockingly as she looked down at his face. "It doesn't really matter, does it?"

He smiled thinly. "I suppose not," he said and pulled her closer to him.

Chapter 10

Tanner examined his appearance in the silvered door of a common-room locker, turning back and forth to admire the lines of his new Guild uniform. Jennan watched from her vantage point at her desk, sipping at a glass of wine.

"Well, do you like it?" she asked.

He met her eyes in the mirror reflection and grinned. "You must think I'm ridiculous."

"Not at all," she replied. Her feelings were mixed, but from another cause. Tanner looked too good, and her inner voice protested the easy privilege, the oddness of a human in dress she had associated with Daruma since childhood. A tall human in Guild uniform somehow made the Daruma look dumpy and short. It provided a glimpse of how she appeared to the Daruma, and she found in that glimpse some forgiveness of Tarthe's small-mindedness. A minuscule forgiveness, a negligible blot . . . but still, the sight of Tanner bothered her.

She glanced at Morgen, who was immersed in his trade histories, and felt aggrieved for his sake, knowing he would only laugh at her feelings. Morgen had

113

zero insecurities—or at least he hid them well. She envied his calm, and wondered if the Daruma mind really was clearer of the frets she found usual in herself.

Tanner leaned forward to examine his collar emblem more closely, and looked a question at her in the mirror.

"Journeyman class," she said, answering the look. "You'll be masquerading as Dave Renner, one of my classmates. Besides, anyone familiar with Guild gossip—which probably includes the Li Fawn—knows that the human journeymen haven't made master grade yet."

"I see. Aren't I little old, though?"

"Actually, you're about Dave's age. He was a merchant captain for several years before he applied to the Guild under Hashami sponsorship. And you're forgetting that locals tend to think we age like the Daruma." She nodded at the preoccupied Morgen. "Morgen is fifty years older than I am, but looks much less—about your age, in fact."

Morgen's ears twitched slightly, and she knew he was listening. Matchmaker Morgen, all at ears for the developing romance. Jennan felt sourly half-inclined to skew the romance just to prove a point— whatever point that might prove. She put down her half-finished glass and rubbed her temples tiredly, and felt the dull throb of a returning headache. Bone regeneration had cured her broken arm-bones; she wished the Daruma had similar treatment for bruised brains.

"You'll pass, Vaughn," she said. "Don't worry about it." Tanner returned to his self-admiration in the mirror.

"I've never been to Shann," he said. "I visited Lume and Tayna at Out-Station last year, but unless you've got a Guild permit . . ." He shrugged.

Jennan smiled. "Prepare for a treat," she said. "The Shenda make a business out of artistic disorder. But everything they do makes sense, if you look at it from the right angle. It's looking at things from their angle that's fun."

"Oh? Most of what I've heard is, uh, unflattering."

She raised an eyebrow. "Just like the Raome are stuffed shirts and the Takinaki flutterbys? Think like a Guildsman, Vaughn. The Shenda are family, like a batty old aunt. We can regret the changes, all that they've lost, but they don't miss them. Or so they say. The Shenda live in the Now, as they call it, and are far more preoccupied with their language games than regrets for a lost empire. Right now they're cycling through a complete linguistic change every twelve years; it drives the Guild computers crazy."

"Doesn't sound like they'll be much help in finding that Li Fawn ship," Tanner said, and she knew he had missed her point.

"Oh, they might. We'll ask around Portside first."

She picked up her wine-glass and blinked at it. Although she had put it down half full, most of the wine had disappeared. She repressed a shiver and put the glass back down, wondering if she had blanked out. The Guild medicos had said her near suffocation had not caused brain damage, but she still felt strange, not quite in tune with reality.

She felt a stir behind her and looked down at the glass again. A slender tail whisked quickly out of sight, spattering tiny drops of wine on the desk top. Jennan leaned over her chair arm and glared at the pseudobat clinging to the back of her chair. T'wing looked back blandly, sucking on her tail tip, then smacked her mouth. A quick arpeggio of laugh-notes sounded in Jennan's mind.

"That's not funny, T'wing," Jennan informed her pet.

T'wing flicked her slender tongue around her muzzle and then crooned prettily for more. Jennan indulgently poured more wine into the glass from the decanter, then watched T'wing hitch herself onto the desk and drain it dry.

"Just what we need," Morgen said, "is a drunken pseudobat."

"I sometimes think," she drawled, "that T'wing has more sense drunk then some Daruma do sober."

"I won't argue that."

"Have you found anything more in those listings?"

Morgen leaned back and stretched. "I'm discovering fascinating things," he said. "According to Out-Station records, a Li Fawn ship has been whisking here and there around Shann for some time, though to no particular purpose I can see. For some reason, they seem to have special interest in the Shenda. The ship is hiding near Shann now, lurking around with the comets. Out-Station has challenged it four times as they crossed orbits, even sent out a Port embassy ship, but it refuses contact."

"That's nothing new." She rubbed her temples again, distracted by the throbbing behind her eyes. "What about *Crystal*?"

"No sign—no debris, no radiation, nothing. McCrory denies all knowledge and the Guild is inclined to believe it. Is your head hurting again?" Jennan shrugged. "Then why don't you rest? I faithfully promised the medico I'd watch over you."

"You always watch over me, which I much appreciate."

"Then rest. If T'wing is a bother, shove her out the door and I'll keep her occupied."

T'wing puffed her fur and hissed at him, bridling at the aspersion. As her pet began waggling her ears briskly, Jennan clamped her hand on T'wing's head.

"Sorry."

"Is nothing. Go lie down for a while."

"Okay." Jennan got to her feet and swayed slightly as a wave of dizziness swept over her. She took a step and got herself moving, made it to her room. T'wing flapped after her, then hung herself on Jennan's bookshelf for a nap, a happily contented process of busy wing-rustling and delicate yawns.

Jennan began to undress. As she teetered on one foot to pull off a boot, the dizziness struck again, harder this time, like an explosion of light within her skull. She swayed and lost her balance in the vertigo, falling backward against the mattress of her bed. Her boots skittered on the polished floor, and then her feet went out from under her.

She hit the floor heavily, striking hard enough to make her gasp. The room tipped and began to spin wildly, around and around in a frightening disorder. T'wing shrieked in surprise, and something crashed in the common-room. She dimly heard the sound of running steps.

Before her in room center a pillar of mist took shape, a swirling pattern of white streaked with gold and scarlet. A fever-red eye looked out at her from mid-cloud, its stare tinged with uneasy madness. A wide mouth, wickedly ringed with serrated teeth, opened beneath the eye, and the room rang with a mocking echo of T'wing's shriek.

T'wing screamed furiously and threw herself at the apparition. Then a hand slapped on the room's doorguard and the column of mist winked out, gone in an instant. Jennan had one glimpse of Morgen's face as he knelt beside her, then passed out cold.

She spent the next day in bed. Hazily she heard voices through her open door as the others debated on a return to Naberr or a Shann hospital (naively offered by Tanner and promptly vetoed by Morgen and Chandra) or a wait-and-see, her own preference which she pressed on Morgen whenever he visited her bedside. She lay inert in her darkened room, T'wing curled by her side, her breathing a slow counterpoint to the pounding in her temples. She felt deeply, deeply ill, a malaise she hadn't felt since her bout with Sarbian fever as a child. It racked her bones, settled into her gut, filled her body with an uneasy rippling sensation.

I'm sorry, Master Larovi, she thought weakly. *I'm sorry I'm so sick.*

On the second night, she awoke during sleep cycle and saw Chandra's faintly luminescent bulk sitting in her desk chair, a tight fit for the Elf and probably as uncomfortable as it looked. She smiled, amused. Only a Vang would use the Green Elf for pajamas. Despite the earlier quarrel, Chandra still liked the awful thing best—and so, they had compromised.

The Vang slept with open eyes—the Elf did not have eyelids, she remembered—and the fanged jaw hung slackly open, the rapier tongue undulating with the slow cycle of respiration. A faint rumbling snore with curious watery overtones buzzed from the open mouth. She shifted comfortably, smiling sleepily, and remembered her own vigil for an injured pilot.

Her headache pounced with a vengeance and she winced. *Oh, stop! Please stop!* The room blurred strangely, stretching tight with a harsh light that struck painfully at her eyes. She heard the roaring of a great wind and, in its midst, the faint cries of alien voices that rode the wind, were dashed to the ground, were crushed by its force. Her heart pounded in response to the terror, but she could not move, could not call out. Fire flickered along the ceiling in long streamers of a corpse-light fire, an eerie radioactive glow that danced and flickered in malevolent celebration.

The Steely Gaze marched from the storage room, his helmet rings twirling. The Vang smiled at her with frosty menace, and touched his spear to his helmet in salute. A second spear appeared in the opposite hand, then a third and a fourth, a forest of spears that all saluted her in a single pointy meeting.

This is madness, she thought and closed her eyes. When she opened them, the second Chandra had disappeared. She watched herself ooze from the far wall, then shorten and blur into Morgen, then shorten still further to T'wing, then wink out. A misty column formed in the shadows, watching her with insane gaze. It faded, reformed, and began drifting towards the bed.

She closed her eyes, unable to watch, and felt the strange malaise ripple again through her body. She sensed the wraith's approach, imagined its touch, and a shuddering wail echoed through her mind. Violently, she spun away from it into the darkness, buffeted by the wind as she fell. She cried out soundlessly, a cry of the terror and loss that surrounded her.

"The Light!" a thousand voices cried in agony.

"The Light!" she screamed in response, and fell helplessly into the void, torn to fragments by a ruby light. . . .

When she opened her eyes again, the room was lit for day-cycle and was empty of strange lights and mists. T'wing stretched full-length on the mattress beside her and yawned widely. Jennan heard a snatch of mind-song, then suffered T'wing's laborious thump-crawl across her stomach to the other side of the bed. T'wing curled up into a furry ball and sighed.

"Good morning," Jennan said to her.

T'wing raised her head and examined the room

from end to end, then settled back against Jennan's body. She chirped sleepily, as if to reassure Jennan, and yawned again.

"That's a relief," Jennan said wryly.

She sat up slowly and felt her forehead. Her temples throbbed badly, but she thought she could navigate a bit. She resolutely put aside the memory of her nightmare. *Nonsense*, she thought and threw back the bedcovers. After a quick shower, she felt even better. She dressed, and then stepped into the common-room. She heard a murmur of voices on the flight deck above her head and wobbled a little as she walked to the elevator.

Mind over body, she told herself, and made her legs work more efficiently.

She stepped onto the flight deck seconds later. Chandra sat in his usual chair, watching his screens, and Morgen looked around at her. "Back to bed," he ordered, pointing imperiously at the elevator.

"Nuts," she replied. She sat down at the computer console and quickly scanned the boards, then smiled as she heard Morgen's long-suffering sigh.

"I'm okay, Morgen," she reassured him.

"So you say. Nuts."

Jennan turned and grinned at him, amused, and then watched Chandra's screens. *Ariel* had steadied on a parabolic approach into Shann's system and was rapidly approaching the massive free-orbiting complex of Out-Station. By treaty-rights, all incoming ships had to check in at the Out-Station, even Guild vessels. The rule made the space around Out-Station look like a humble-jumble box of children's toys. Chandra radioed a few choice Vang words at the Daruma freighter drifting across *Ariel*'s course. The freighter hastily veered away.

"Vang are picky," Jennan commented. "Where's Tanner?"

Morgen pointed upward to the observation lounge. "Watching the view."

"Daruma can't fly their way out of a paper bag," Chandra rumbled. "Where's his Vang pilot?" Another ship veered close and Chandra promptly flashed *Ariel's* warn-off lights at the new offender.

"Probably asleep," Jennan suggested. "Or busy. Don't ruffle your feathers, Chandra. Not everybody's a Vang."

"Thank the gods," Morgen said feelingly, and ducked as Chandra pretended to swipe with his upper left arm.

"I don't have feathers," Chandra said and tapped his shoulder pointedly. "Steel plate."

"Right," Jennan said. "And Li Fawn wear white hats."

"White hats?"

"Obscure human reference. Skip it."

Ariel inched closer to dock and drifted. The comm chattered welcome and then began instructions for completing their dock connections. Chandra worked through the routine, and somehow got a few seconds ahead of the Daruma controller. Jennan grinned as she heard the controller increase speed as he tried to catch up with the signal lights on his console. The Vang easily stayed ahead, his hands moving smoothly across his own board. As Chandra completed the last sequence, the controller said a rude Vang word and snapped contact.

"You'll get reported for that," Jennan said.

"A charge I welcome to answer," the Vang said. "Daruma controllers think they own the universe. I can make comments about other Daruma, too. You belong in a hospital."

"I feel better." Jennan winked at a scowling Morgen. "Can I help it if Morgen is a pushover?"

"Hmph," they both said.

*   *   *

She took Morgen with her to check in at the station and to learn what news might be circulating through Port gossip. At the inner lock to their ship-bay, Jennan keyed in *Ariel's* ship code. The lock sighed open, and they stepped into the station concourse to join the flow of traffic passing outward and inward from the outer docks. They strolled onward, both enjoying the bustle of the station as they nodded to passing Guildsmen from other ships, then dodged an automatic baggage cart careening its way down the corridor. They caught a slide-walk leading to the inner station, and Jennan slouched comfortably as the slide whisked them forward at twice the pace of a normal walk. Her head had cleared, and she felt her spirits lift at the bustle of activity. It was her first trip to Shann, and she craned her neck like any tourist.

"I don't see any Shenda," she said after a while.

"They don't come out here near the docks," Morgen said. "After a few unfortunate incidents, the Guild made a rule and added it to the treaty. The Shenda generally observe it. Shenda do everything 'generally,' so the Guild station keeps an eye if one strays. Besides, there usually aren't many Shenda at Out-Station. They stay home and let us run things."

"Does that ever bother you?" she asked.

"Bother?"

"That the Shenda are that trusting. That the Guild has so much . . ."

"The word you want is domination. You know better than that."

"I'm just looking at things like they might look to Terra—or maybe Li Fawn. The Guild is everywhere, and you know it."

"True."

"Guild pulls the strings."

"What about the six centuries of getting where we are?" Morgen's ears twitched. "With all the races learning time and time again that the Guild can be trusted, that we Daruma are not interested in empire, that less sophisticated races benefit from our help?"

"Don't get huffy, Morgen. Like you said, I know better—but do they?" She gestured at a group of Terran traders wrestling with a baggage cart. "What do they see?"

"You're asking a Daruma to criticize the status quo. It's not in our character. We prefer enjoying our perfect reality and letting others change theirs."

"Right—like I discovered with Master Larovi." Morgen looked at her sharply but let it pass.

They pushed through the wide bay doors to the inner station and stepped off the slide onto the lower concourse. The station was constructed in the usual Daruma design of an inner well, although here the well measured several hundred meters across and a dozen stories high. Balconies and extended rooms ringed the well, complicated with ribbons of transport lifts dotted with people. Here and there, among the scurrying Daruma and a handful of offworlder merchants, a few hulking Shenda wandered in their distracted way. She and Morgen passed a Shenda male as he studied a station map. His large curved nose seemed a built-in guidance wand around the levels, but had brought no ease to his apparent frustration. Jennan looked back, and then stepped off the slide to walk back to him.

"Effrendi? Want help?"

Large gentle eyes, tufted by furry eyebrows, turned to look at her, and the Shenda's ears lifted inquiringly. Silky black fur covered him from head to foot, and, aside from squarish boots on his feet and a jewelled waist-belt, he contented himself with a costume of basic fur. An indenti-disk on a chain winked at his throat. Shenda towered over everybody, even tall and lanky humans, and so she craned her neck backward to look up at him. She repeated her question, and he waved his tufted paw at the map in despair, croaking some words she didn't understand.

"Where go?" she asked, and the Shenda burbled at her. She glanced at Morgen as he joined them.

"He's probably disassociating," Morgen suggested.

"You're a big help." She looked up at the Shenda. "No, he's a professor type. Whoever briefed him didn't include Daruma mapwork."

"A professor?" Morgen's ears waggled, and the Shenda obligingly tried to copy. Jennan grinned and patted the Shenda's furry arm.

"Sure. Come with us." She added a beckon-go gesture as she tugged slightly on the Shenda. "We go find what you want." The Shenda regarded her soberly, then took a tentative step. "That's it. We go find what you want."

"And what does he want?" Morgen asked.

"We don't know yet. We find out. I mean, we'll find out. Come," she repeated, and the Shenda obligingly fell into step with them.

"What your name?" she asked him.

"Name?"

"Jennan," she said, tapping her chest. "Morgen," she added, pointing to Morgen. She pointed at the Shenda. "You?"

"Marunda," he rumbled.

"Marunda," she repeated after him. "See, Morgen? It's not so hard."

"And maybe he said 'what-the-hell-you-crazy-human.'" Morgen scowled at her, half-amused, half-irritated. "Shenda males are not stray gorbats you

pick up on the street because they're cute. What are
you going to do with him?"

"Find out where he wants to go." The slide
whisked them along towards Control. "We just have
to figure out his dialect."

"Shenda have fifteen hundred dialects, all of them
changing daily." Morgen tried a series of syllables
on their tall companion, got an inquiring burble in
return. "See? He doesn't even understand Station
Dialect."

"Well, he has to understand some or he wouldn't
be here."

" 'Where ticket?' and 'strap down' don't get you
far once you arrive."

"Where ticket, strap down," Marunda said pen-
sively. "Where go. Jennan. Morgen. What-the-hell."

"Like I said," Jennan said, smiling up at Marunda,
"a professor-type." The Shenda's lips curled upward
into an answering smile, although smiling obviously
wasn't a natural Shenda accouterment. She appreciated the effort.

"You hungry?" she asked him, patting her stomach.

"Jennan," Morgen protested, "we're supposed to
check in at the Portmaster's office."

"We will. And stop nagging, team-second. This is
an inter-species experience. There's an eatery."

She grasped the Shenda's arm and tugged him off
the slide toward the inviting smells and busy gaggle
of the restaurant. Marunda staggered slightly as he
stepped off the moving slide, then plodded after her,
with Morgen trailing behind. She led them into the
covered shell nestled against the wall.

They found a booth near the front. The booth was
a tight fit for the Shenda, but he already looked less
upset. As Morgen scooted into the seat beside her,
she turned the ordering display towards Marunda so
he could see the pictured dishes.

"What want?" she asked him.

Marunda turned his attention from their surroundings, with its hum of voices and occasional laughter, and studied the display. She slowly dialed the selections, then stopped when his ears perked up at a dish of vegetables and tiny cooked beetles.

"Melasom," the Shenda said obscurely.

"Ymmmm, good," Jennan replied.

She dialed the order and added two bowls of joleki stew for herself and Morgen. The selector clicked to itself for a moment, then opened the wall panel to reveal their order. Jennan slid the big bowl of vegetables over to the Shenda and handed Morgen his stew. The three ate in companionable silence, as Marunda's large dark eyes flicked here and there, examining the occupants and furnishings of the eatery. When they neared the bottoms of their bowls, Morgen gestured at the Shenda with his spoon.

"Now that we've fed him, what do we do with him?"

"Is this a serious objection?"

"Not really. I just don't know how you do it. You attach a Taki pseudobat, who usually content themselves with rude comments about offworlders, and now you have a pet Shenda. I won't mention your effect on the Guild, stray Vang, and me. What do we do with him?"

"I told you. We find out where he wants to go." She tapped Marunda's knuckle to get his attention. "Where go?"

"Go with you," the Shenda answered, and contentedly crunched a beetle between his teeth. "Ymmm, good."

"Jennan, he's disassociating. Shenda don't follow people around like this. They think up contraries just to be contrary." Marunda waggled his ears.

"Not disassociating," he rumbled. "Just got to

where wanted to go, Out-Station. When got to Out-Station, what do now? Was deciding when you ask." The Shenda crunched another beetle. "Think maybe you disassociating, you Daruma, to make what you think is map."

Morgen leaned back in the booth and stared at the Shenda. "Why didn't you speak up earlier?"

"Way let Jennan be friends, you be idiot, Guildsman." Marunda sniffed, and turned his eyes to Jennan. "Not hear yet that Guild take humans in. You new?"

"Somewhat. Why did you come to Out-Station?"

"To see. Get away from females always a treat. Sometimes get away from males, too, particularly pesky brother." He studied her face and hair, flicked his eyes lower. "Think you female human."

"That's right. Does that bother you?"

Marunda considered. "Not decide yet. Morgen male Daruma?"

"Yes."

"You Guild-team?" Jennan nodded. "You friends?"

"Yes, friends."

Jennan saw the thought move slowly in Marunda's beautiful eyes. "I like concept," he said at last. "Not possible Shenda, but possible Guild. Not bother me you female, Jennan. Is female and female, two kinds—another concept, very intriguing." The wide lips curled up again in imitation of her earlier smile. "I like concepts."

"I told you, Morgen, a professor!"

Chapter 11

After they left the eatery, they toured a few of the
nearby Out-Station shops. Jennan pointed out things
to Marunda and he to her, and Morgen gave up
comments about prompt reporting-in. She finally
stopped in the middle of the aisle and looked back
at her team-second. Marunda picked up a perfume
bottle from a display shelf and fumbled with its
stopper.

"Yumm," he said, sniffing with intense pleasure.

"I am denting your propriety, effrendi," Jennan
said ruefully.

"A little," Morgen replied, but twitched his ears
in dismissal. "I like to see you having fun. How's
your headache?"

She grimaced. "Probably waiting in the Portmaster's office by now. First Chandra, now me. He's
probably fit to be tied." She turned back to the
Shenda. "Marunda, we have an errand upstairs. Do
you want to come?"

The Shenda waggled his ears affably. "Come with
you."

"Right."

Jennan led the way out of the shop and they caught the ribbon slide in the central well. As they stepped onto the slide, it responded automatically to their weight, making a small shelf in its smooth curve. It bore them upwards towards the roof in a wide looping spiral that touched a platform at each level, first one side of the well, then the other. At the top, the slide again neared a platform, and Jennan deliberately shifted her weight forwards. The slide paused to let them off. Jennan glanced down into the well at the foreshortened figures forty meters below, then looked around the balcony on which they now stood.

"That way," Morgen said, pointing at a sign in Daruma script. A second sign affixed below repeated the directions in Shenda and, to Jennan's interest, in Terran. But, then, Shann was the Sagittarian world closest to Sol, and she had heard the combines had a particular interest in Shann's antiquities—and, perhaps, a faint trace of a vulture instinct. An ancient race in decline might have attracted certain combines like a moth to a flame, despite the Guild's careful protectorate. She could easily guess at the stresses it added to Out-Station's responsibility.

They walked along the balcony, passing door after door that led to interior suites. "Do you know the portmaster here, Morgen?"

"Certainly. I spent my journeyman years here twenty years ago, and Beren has been Out-Station Portmaster for twice that. A good administrator, but he gets irritated easily. Running Out-Station is a hard job." They pushed past a group of Terran merchants standing in the middle of the balcony, and one turned his head to look at her curiously, then eyed Marunda.

"McCrory," she commented when they got out of earshot.

"And Ling-Choi. I hear both combines now have legations on Shann, though it took them a few years to get permission. The independents are still excluded, though that might be a matter of time, too."

"Speaking as a legation brat, I'm surprised Terra still puts up with it."

"Speaking as a Daruma, Out-Station has considerable teeth. It's the one place where the Guild is heavily armed. We borrowed a page from Terra here after First Contact, even shot up a few Terran ships as an example."

She looked at him with some shock. "I've never heard of that, Morgen. When?"

"A long time ago. It's not taught as history at the Hall, and everybody pretends it never happened, of course. But our ships are still armed." Morgen sounded strangely grim, and she wondered what had happened, exactly, during his "journeyman years." His ears did not invite further discussion, and she dropped it.

They reached the Portmaster's office and walked inside. Portmaster Beren sat in the front office, surrounded by machines and applicant chairs, with faxes piled high on shelves behind his desk. His years sat on him poorly, and he seemed a wizened gnome, with tattered ears, suspicious black eyes, and an air of harriment past endurance. A half-dozen aides worked busily at consoles in the suite beyond. As Jennan and Morgen walked in, with Marunda lumbering along behind them, Beren narrowed his eyes furiously, his ears canted in intense displeasure.

"What is *that* doing in my office?" he demanded, his finger jabbing at Marunda.

Jennan stopped short and stared, then collected herself. "*That*," she replied coldly, "is Marunda, a Shenda friend of mine. Have you other comment?"

Beren made a visible effort to control himself.

"Your pilot . . ." he began, spluttering, his face dark with rage.

"Yes?"

"And you delay reporting in! If this is the measure of your use to the Guild, journeywoman, I can well agree with . . ."

Jennan abruptly turned away and felt her face flush. "I don't need this, Morgen. You talk to him—he likes a monochrome universe and you fit the proper mold. I'll be on the ship." She took a step towards the door, but Morgen touched her sleeve.

"Wait a minute, Jennan. Master Beren," he said to the Portmaster, "may I inquire, in all propriety, if your insults come from conviction? Or are they merely symptoms of a disorganized mind?" Beren glared, but Morgen was undaunted. They stared at each other for a moment, and then Morgen pursed his lips shrewdly. He smiled with no friendliness.

"Or, perhaps, esteemed Portmaster, your attitude is freely transplanted from we-know-who on the Council? You *are* Sorema House, aren't you?"

Beren huffed. "I don't know what you mean."

"Nuts. A useful phrase, that, taught by my esteemed team-first to our pilot, and used by both with vivacity and elan. But then Sorema House has its own indignity; didn't you sponsor a human apprentice, too? Do you regret it so quickly?"

Beren clamped shut his lips and tightened his ears to his skull. Morgen skinned back his own ears and leaned forward, his eyes glittering. "I have lived among Terran savages," he said, "and I am about to send our pilot after you, you old reprobate. So send a message to Tarthe for me: if he continues this interference, I will ask my House and Jennan's House to arrange Sorema's ruin. Let Tarthe measure the odds. And while you do that, tell the Guildmas-

ter about this sweet reception. He'll squash you like
a treacle bug."

He turned back to Jennan and smiled benignly.
"Now we can go. A kind day to you, Portmaster."
They started to walk out.

"Wait!" Beren said.

They turned and looked at Beren inquiringly.

The Portmaster gave a gusty sigh and rubbed his
naked skull. "What **ever** happened to manners?" he
asked the open air.

"What the hell," said Marunda.

Jennan stifled a laugh, and then snagged a chair
with her foot. She sat down and crossed her legs,
one boot propped comfortably on her thigh. Beren
watched her suspiciously.

"I'll apologize if you will," she said. "How's that
for a trade? But you should tell me what I'm apolo-
gizing for. I think we both know what it is, but,
sadly, I can't change that." She shrugged. "I admit
that I've lived in a cushioned world. My pilot likes
me. My team-second likes me. My House likes me.
And the Guildmaster likes me. Unfortunately, the
universe is not unanimous. But I am here on the
Guildmaster's private mission, and I expect cooperation despite our differences—my lack of fluted ears
and your lack of tolerance, Portmaster."

Beren leaned back and steepled his fingers. "I'm
busy," he sniffed.

"As would be expected," she said firmly, "with
such an important charge as Out-Station."

Beren sniffed again, considering. "Shall we start
over?"

"An excellent idea."

"What is *that* doing in my office?!" he cried, pointing at Marunda.

Jennan dropped her foot to the floor and glared
back, furious at Beren's game-playing. "I've adopted

him." Marunda promptly burbled in pleased surprise, and Jennan glanced at him, alarmed. She wasn't that familiar with Shenda customs and had a sinking feeling she'd just acquired a very tall and furry son.

The Portmaster flipped his ears. "Then take him away, wherever you're going."

"This is cooperation?" Morgen asked coldly.

"The Li Fawn have disappeared, team-second. Haven't been seen for days, except heading out-system. I can verify that if you like." He looked at Jennan with a smugness Jennan wanted to wipe off his face. She tightened her hands on her knee, trying to hide her reaction, but Beren had clever eyes and only smiled more broadly.

"So your mission is over, journeywoman," he said venomously, "not even begun—and will get no further. The Li Fawn aren't here. *Crystal* is no doubt warp-lost. So go back to Naberr and tell the Guildmaster you've failed again. Tell him his coddling of human incompetence will be stopped, as will his pretenses about alleged Li Fawn plots and his continued attempts to destroy the Guild. Sorema is not deceived. Tell him that: it will comfort his remaining days on the Council."

Jennan stood up, shaken by the hatred in Beren's voice, then smiled thinly. "I think we'll hang around a while," she said. "You will authorize the in-system trip, please?"

Beren shrugged. "As you wish," he said.

"Thank you. A kind day to you, Portmaster." Jennan shepherded Marunda out the door, and they retraced their route along the upper tier. As they wound down the ribbon concourse, she glanced at Morgen.

"Thanks for the defense, Morgen, 'Terran savages

and whatall. I'm sorry it didn't work. I just didn't expect that kind of reception."

Morgen tightened his lips. "Apparently Tarthe doesn't take disappointment lightly, and, to be fair, the Terrans have pushed Beren lately. Not that it's any excuse. House loyalties aren't supposed to work that way."

"Even so, it looks like we're on our own here."

"Suits me." Morgen sounded quietly furious.

Jennan offered Marunda a ride home, and the Shenda accepted. Marunda seemed aggrieved about the disappointing marvels of Out-Station, and began mumbling to himself, a sing-song chant that rose and fell in formless pattern. After Jennan installed him in a chair in *Ariel*'s observation lounge, he began twisting his fingers in sinuous motions, his shaggy head turning back and forth as he examined every part of the room. Watching him, Jennan doubted the wisdom of bringing him along. The lucidity of his eatery conversation was already disintegrating as chemicals shifted in his brain, destroying his mind patterns. But he was a Shenda, and she was a Guildsman, and she had promised him a ride.

Out-Station's dismissal had been curt, and she knew she could expect little help from the Guildsmen on Shann itself. The Portmaster, here more than anywhere else, had too much influence: even if the duty-conscious Daruma were inclined to help, their knowledge of Beren's disapproval would probably constrain such generous feelings. A political stew was not to her taste, not when she was the body being fought over. Well, it would happen eventually as one of the human journeymen neared master rank, a time to "fish and cut bait," her father would have said.

Muffled clankings on the ship hull signaled *Ariel*'s

disconnection from Out-Station, and she felt the slight pull of acceleration backward as Chandra edged the ship away from the dock. Tanner sat quietly in another chair with T'wing in his lap, his eyes flicking from Marunda to herself. The Shenda began touching his eartips to his nose in a rhythmic chant, his fingers plucking time at the fur on his thighs.

Tanner scowled and gestured at Marunda. "What's wrong with him, Jennan?" he asked. "I've been wondering about what you said about 'what the Shenda lost.' I always thought the Shenda were, well, just Shenda."

"He's disassociating," she explained. "They all do now. At First Contact, the Daruma thought Shenda disassociation was only 'the working of an alien mind,' unquote, but later found clan records tracing their hereditary insanity back to the explosion of Shann's moon." She lifted her shoulders, then let them fall. "The Shenda always had a high rate of schizophrenia—it's built into the chemical evolution of their brains, and at twice the frequency found in humans and Daruma. But ancient Shenda valued their madmen for their inner worlds, and so sent them first to the safe places before Madringa exploded. They misjudged the disaster. Three-quarters of the planet's population died in the meteorite falls." She looked at Marunda sadly.

"And the schizophrenics survived."

"In enough proportion to shift the gene pool. The schizophrenia now runs at seventy percent, and even sane Shenda accept the cultural changes as normal. Those who aren't mad become so—*folie à deux* on a planetary scale. Every decade they lose more of themselves into their dreamworlds. Even the ancient disaster is now forgotten for what is was: they remember only their goddess Madringa, the Destroyer, the Bringer of the Light. They worship

their own destruction, Vaughn." She shuddered
slightly. Marunda fell silent and stared blankly at the
floor.

Jennan shivered again, then wrenched her thoughts
to other problems, some that might have a solution.
She had carried off a brave act with Master Beren,
but now had to think up some ideas about Shann.
Both *Crystal* and the Li Fawn ship had disappeared
out-system; *Ariel* was now headed in-system.

Smart, Bartlett. So what do you do now? She
scowled.

"Jennan?"

She looked at Tanner, and realized how much she
liked this McCrory trader. He had his smooth
points, his graspings for personal advantage, but perhaps his faults had their reasons. She felt more indul-
gent about those things as time passed. They hadn't
followed up on the kiss in the hospital, but she
thought she might, if he was willing. From the look
on his face caught at unexpected times, she thought
he might be. For now, she just wanted the chance
to talk to another human—this human—without the
barriers of her rank, the diversion of interests, the
cautions she too often endured.

"Just trying to organize my mind," she said, smiling at him.

He smiled and picked up his wineglass, took a sip,
and then let T'wing have the rest. "You know, I've
learned more about the local races in the past three
weeks than I had in twelve years inside McCrory. I
know the Takinaki fairly well, as much as anyone
can, but Setha surprised me. And once I came
aboard *Ariel* and saw your relationship with your
crew . . . There was a lot of talk about humans joining the Guild, not very favorable, either."

"Yes, I know." She looked away uncomfortably.

"We humans create divisions with our arrogance,

I think. Like Lenart, with his neo-imperialistic ideas. Even I'm affected by it—for a time, my only explanation for you and Morgen was sexual." He shrugged humorously at himself. "Don't feel offended, Jennan; it's a habit of the jealous male mind."

"I'm not offended."

"Anyway, all aliens look alike to us—or so I'm told." He smiled humorlessly. "It would have been better if Terra had come in this direction first instead of the Gemini Plane. Primitive savages in furs, blue-skinned or not, set the wrong precedents. Your Portmaster has some legitimate grievances—a lot of Terrans don't ask things like they should."

"*You'd* ask."

"So maybe I'm alien-happy," he said with another twist to his mouth. "Or so Lenart tells me." T'wing tugged too hard at Tanner's glass and pulled it out of his grasp. With a startled squeak, she rolled off Tanner's thigh and hit the floor with a thump. She sprang up, hissing, fur puffed in fury, then beat it over the edge of the well.

"Comedy act," Jennan said.

"Just soused." Tanner chuckled and leaned forward to pick up the glass. He set his glass on the side table, then stretched and ran his hands through his dark hair. "I admit it's good to be away from Lenart, but I do wonder what mischief he's up to now."

"Don't worry about it," she said. "The anorphs do their ritual combat in scorpion pits. Lenart may have a new experience he doesn't expect." She cupped her chin in her hand. "Has it been hard for you in McCrory?"

"Hard enough to envy you your rank, Guildswoman." Somehow that didn't sound quite convincing, but she let it pass.

"Right now that's not too enviable." She glanced away again and fidgeted.

"Are you going to tell me what's bothering you? You've been fidgeting for nearly half an hour."

"T'wing talks too much," she said, scowling.

"T'wing just burbles at me, you know that. Or are you so used to humans missing alien nuances?"

"Maybe by now I'm semi-human," she said gloomily. She held out her wineglass and he refilled it from the bottle on his table, then refilled his own and moved to the chair next to hers. With another smile, he lifted her hand to his lips.

"Gallant," she said.

"Always." He kept her hand tightly in his. "We lose the habits, I think, if our own kind cuts us off, or we retreat, as you have. Or so I think. It's not normal to cut yourself off from your own kind, Jennan."

"Normal? So what's normal?"

Tanner shrugged, conceding the point. "It's a kind of adjustment, I suppose. Others adjust in different ways; some Terrans never adjust at all. Lenart fights off his fears with denial; I play too many clever games. I get tired of playing games, Jennan. What have you tired of?"

She shrugged, then shifted her fingers for a tighter grasp on his hand. "It's related, I suppose. I guess we all grow up eventually. I always thought the Daruma were superior—more than equals, Tanner, but that's my upbringing. I don't know where I stand now. I'm being manipulated by the Guild, as if I'm being set up to take responsibility for closed minds, problems I have nothing to do with. I feel that I'm chasing after something that isn't there." She shrugged again. "Maybe there aren't any answers."

"And maybe there are," he said, his dark eyes flashing.

"Maybe," she said.

She felt another tug of acceleration, and the wine

in her glass tipped its level, sloshing against the rim
of the glass. She put down the glass on the side table
and stood up to stretch. The reflection of the lounge
lights blurred any view of the surrounding stars, and
she saw herself and Tanner in the glass like distant
actors on a massive stage. She walked over to
Marunda and stroked his broad head, wondering
who had the larger grief—not knowing the loss or
knowing it too well.

Halfway to Shann, the ship entered an early sleep-
cycle as the crew began adjusting to planet-time.
Jennan saw Marunda bedded down in a spare room,
and set a monitor on the wall-shelf to watch for
unusual movements. By now the ship computer had
established Marunda's behavioral parameters, and
could give alarm if the Shenda acted overly dis-
tressed. She looked down at the huddled form and
felt the despair move within her again. It was such
a waste. It was like watching someone die, someone
with a special light that, if extinguished, would make
the world a dimmer place.

She went to her own room through the darkened
common-room, and undressed for bed. T'wing was
asleep on the shelf above her desk, making little
buzzy snores. Jennan leaned on the desk, tipping
forward to look at T'wing more closely, and felt her
spirits lift just in the looking.

I have a habit, she thought, *of ignoring present
joys.* She thought about the day she had met T'wing,
of her pet's delicate antics ever since, of her uncon-
ditional love for one J. Bartlett. She remembered
forest shadows, the hushed shirr of the wind through
a million dancing leaves, water rushing over smooth
stones, and then wondered if her memories were
T'wing's current dreams. And then she thought a
while about Tanner—about what she had long

missed, about the risks of a painful mistake, and the promise of pleasure. It wasn't a hard decision to make.

She straightened and looked down at her simple sleep-suit of baggy trousers and sleeveless tunic, then looked hesitatingly at her bureau, mentally cataloging its contents. She had a nightgown of gorssilk, but the gown was practically transparent—quite suitable for the arrival in Tanner's suite, but inconvenient in transit if Morgen was still about. Or Chandra, though the Vang were very matter-of-fact about breeding rituals.

She walked into the bathroom and examined her face in the mirror, passed her brush through her hair, then grimaced to look at her teeth. The grimace made her laugh. Perfume? She rummaged through the cabinet drawer, then gave it up. She hadn't owned a bottle of perfume since her apprenticeship days—most Terran perfumes tormented sensitive Daruma noses, and she'd long since given up the fake aromas.

She hesitated, drifting around her suite from desk to bed to bureau, and then slipped out the door.

She padded along the carpeting past the several doors to Tanner's room, her heart pounding, then keyed open his door. It opened with a swish and she stepped inside, closing it behind her. The room was dark, illuminated only by a single baseboard panel on the far side of the room. She stood by the door as her eyes adjusted to the darkness. Tanner lay on his bed, his back turned towards her. She heard his slow breathing, saw the rise and fall of his ribs in a steady rhythm beneath the fabric of his tunic. She abruptly lost her nerve. This was very iffy. With a kind of panic, she fumbled at the door-latch, and her nails scraped on the metal. Tanner stirred and turned over in a start.

"Who's there?" he said loudly.

"Shhh. Not so loud."

"Jennan?" She heard the surprise in his voice. He lifted himself up to an elbow and leaned towards her, trying to see her in the dark room.

"I was . . . uh, just wondering how you were doing. If you were comfortable . . ."

Tanner chuckled. "Three weeks after I moved in. That's awfully lame."

"So I've lost my nerve," she said with some asperity. She fumbled again for the lock.

He hastily threw off the bedclothes and stumbled towards the door to cut off her retreat, barking his shin hard on the projecting bed-frame.

"Ouch! Oh, sweet Jesus!"

He bent double in pain, but continued limping sideways towards her and collided with her at the door. She caught at him to stop his fall, and they got tangled up against the doorframe. His arms went around her for support, and then tightened, pulling her full-length against his body. He bent his head to kiss her. Her arms slipped around his neck in response and held him tightly. Then he backed off slightly and bent to rub his shin.

"You'll have a royal bruise," she said. She touched his hair, caressed it. He responded by sliding his hand up her hip. He straightened and pressed close again, one arm slipping around her waist, the other cupping her breast through the thin fabric of her tunic. His lips moved against the side of her neck as he murmured something she didn't catch.

"What?"

He raised his head. The darkness made his face a shadow.

"I said, don't go." He moved his hand slowly down her tunic and then slid it underneath to caress her bare breast. As his thumb circled the nipple in an exquisite slowness, she felt an answering pang of desire between her thighs. She sighed.

"It's been a long time," she said.

"I'm flattered that I'm the cause for a renewal." His hand moved again. "Do you still want to leave?"

"While you're doing that? I'm not crazy." He laughed down at her, then drew her towards his bed.

Later, as they lay tangled together under the sheet, Jennan dozed contentedly. She idly caressed Tanner's bare chest, but he had fallen deeply asleep, and she pressed her palm against his skin, enjoying the touch of him. She ran her palm down his ribs to his hip and then up again, and he stirred in his sleep, tightening his arm around her in response.

As she slipped into sleep, a shadowy form emerged from the wall and watched the humans with a fever-bright gaze. They lay in a strange null-energy state, and seemed unaware of her. Madringa drifted towards the bed, expanding and compressing her energy volume, and studied both at close range. She sensed the completed pattern of the ritual she had witnessed, but wondered at the deliberate waste of energy. Even now, heat radiated off both bodies at a high-normal level. She added the energy to her own volume and tested the interstice. It was stronger now, even stronger than before.

Soon. Very soon.

She drifted back to the wall and entered it, distributing her force among the atoms of steel and beryllium. She stressed the wall's electron orbits, amusing herself with the patterns, then felt the irresistible recall of the End-Time. Not yet. She resisted briefly— but then, like a vanishing gleam, slipped forward and merged again with the Endless Light.

Chapter 12

Shenda Port was a massive enclave, dominated by Daruma ships. The ancient field stretched for miles into the distance, although only the quarter nearest the capital was now kept in repair. To one side rose the delicate architecture of the Shenda city, tall towers, wide halls, and ancient mausoleums dedicated to the Madringa's cult, interspersed with gardens and wide parks. Jennan looked over the port-field and counted a half-dozen Terran ships, an indication of Terra's interest in the system. At one corner of the field, to her surprised satisfaction, sat the mystery ship she had seen on Taki. Somehow Out-Station had slipped, probably because Beren was all too happy to think Li Fawn safely gone with their mother ship. But the Li Fawn were definitely here, probably that spy: now, how to find him?

She studied the small cruiser with *Ariel*'s long-range scanner, and then argued vigorously with Chandra about marching over right then and opening it up, with a drill-laser if necessary. In the end, Chandra gave in to a subtler approach by Morgen at the local Guild Hall. With her current bad odor in the local Guild, Jennan would get nowhere in inquiries, but her team-second had the requisite rank, aplomb, and flutey ears to poke around. Morgen took Chandra with him, partly as window-dressing about his interest in new ships, partly as a precaution against some independent Vang action against orders. Wearing a battery of lasers gave a Vang pilot too many ideas.

In the meantime, Tanner had his own possible inquiries and Jennan had an adopted Shenda to attend. She and Tanner took Marunda into the city to find the local Shenda clan hall. His identi-disk stated his home city as the capital, and they hoped for more specific directions at the hall. Marunda mumbled to himself as they walked along the stone-crumbled street; then the familiar surroundings seemed to lighten the fog in his mind.

"Shann," he said.

"Yes, Shann," Jennan replied, smiling up at him. "I brought you home, like I promised. Where go?"

"Home." Marunda pointed to the east, across the rounded domes of a nearby residential district. "Baige Forest Lane, near university. Small house."

Jennan looked inquiringly at Tanner.

"The McCrory substation's downtown," he said. "Do you want to take him home first?"

"We'd better while he's lucid again."

"Catch tram," Marunda said and stalked away towards the rail line. The humans followed him hastily.

Underneath a protective shell, an antiquated machine sat hissingly on a single pair of tracks. A half-dozen Shenda males sat on board, waiting, and a lone Shenda female swathed in yards of shimmering fabric sat isolated in a far corner. The Shenda males ignored her completely, despite her baleful looks. They took a long bench seat near the front.

Fifteen minutes later they were still waiting. Jennan stretched out her legs and slumped against the seat.

"Want to neck?" Tanner asked. He slipped his arm around her shoulders and played with a tendril of her hair. Then his finger began tracing the curves of her ear, as his joke turned half-serious. He leaned forward towards her.

"I can feel Shenda eyes boring into my back, especially that female's. Not a good idea."

She smiled to take away the sting, then chuckled as Tanner grimaced and withdrew his arm. Marunda sat lumpily on the other side and had resumed his ear and nose calisthenics. Jennan idly crossed and recrossed her booted feet, keeping syncopated time. Mere sitting was boring.

"It had better start up soon," she said irritably.

As if in answer to her words, the tram shrieked a warning, expelled a massive volume of steam, and jerked forward. It gathered speed and chugged along the winding track between the buildings, then emerged into a garden. Tall narrow trees, resplendent in multi-colored leaves, lined the side of the tracks. Then the tram plunged back into the city, its automatic controls whistling at every intersection.

At the third stop, Marunda hauled himself to his feet and climbed off the tram. Jennan and Tanner jumped off after him through the cloud of steam, and then followed the Shenda down a side street. They turned a corner and entered one of Shann's famous bazaars, a mile-long cavalcade of brightly-colored shop awnings, tables laden with wares, a bustle of foot-traffic as Shenda and offworlders hunted for bargains. They passed a Daruma Guildsman preoccupied at a stall of antiquities, then passed a small group of gesticulating Shenda beneath a display of bright silks crafted into flowers. The silks hung at the end of thin metal streamers, and nodded and bobbed in the slight breeze of the bright day.

Jennan looked around her, enjoying the bright colors and brilliant sunlight. A babble of muted voices floated through the air. Marunda plodded ahead, slowly turning his face from side to side. Halfway down the street, they passed a Vang pilot standing by a fruit stand, a tall rangy simulcrum topped by several glowing protuberances on his head. The Vang looked at them curiously from a visored face, and Jennan waved casually. The Vang nodded an acknowledgement, then turned back to the stand. Jennan thought of walking over to him, but gave it up as Marunda plodded onward. She hurried to catch up, drawing Tanner away from an enticing array of small jeweled statues.

"Madringals," he said, looking back at the display. "Lume says the Shenda make thousands of them."

"I told you—it's their religion."

Tanner snorted. "Absurd."

"And how would our religions look to them, Vaughn?" Jennan asked, a little irritated by his tone. "And not so loud: we're visitors here, remember?"

Marunda turned right into a narrow alleyway, then climbed a long rise of stone steps between towering stone walls into a covered bower. Lizard-birds twittered in the leaves overhead, as slender trees entwined their branches into a long cool canyon, a pleasant shelter against the hot sun. Tanner touched her sleeve and pointed to an ancient stone carving half-hidden in the shrubbery to the side, its tracings almost erased by time.

"Pretty," he said.

"Beautiful," she corrected, and earned herself a resentful glance. Marunda plodded on, oblivious.

After several hundred yards they plunged into the city again, entering a street-block of tall stone houses, their cornices and stoops rain-crumbled and fringed with mold. Jennan breathed in the scents, enjoying the walk more than she had expected.

She never noticed the Vang who followed them, for Nineteen kept a careful distance, alert to the dangers of discovery.

The spy had quickly learned the means of easy concealment in the Shenda city. First he learned to watch the Shenda animals for the signs of their frequent confusion, when he could be unnoticed. The reports stolen from local traders spoke of this "disassociation," and the oblivion of the local Shenda was an advantage the spy relished. Dressed in tall robes, his crest concealed beneath his hood, his multi-fingered hands kept carefully out of sight, Nineteen had wandered through the city, listening and watching.

The second afternoon he located the McCrory substation and watched from a shadowed corner of a building as humans went in and out of the building. He followed a group of the humans to the nearby bazaar, and had a heart-stopping moment when one human looked directly at him. He heard the drifted word "Vang" as the human turned back to his fellows, and, with the craftiness of his breed, knew the way to walk Shann's streets with impunity. But Li Fawn robes might be known by Daruma; he must find other resources.

At his ship he studied his supplies, and then looked up at the cluster of Zaruti on the ceiling light. Properly treated with chemicals, the Zaruti alarm reflex could be repressed, and their bright luminescence might be a useful decoration. He made a shell of metal, bound it with straps so he could wear it easily, and then gingerly detached the Zaruti from the light fixture. The creatures protested their separation, and he dropped them hastily into the chemical bath. The bath would begin a series of other chemical reactions fatal to the Zaruti, but their forced silence would last for several days.

He examined his costume in a mirrored door of his small living space, and felt pleased with the result. Then he went out again to catch rumors, watch and listen . . . and wait. He was an able spy, patient and longbearing, and a believer in the lucky chance. His caste worshipped Chance and the Shadows, and sought them both for honor and service to the Lord of their House. He watched and waited, waiting for Chance to know him again.

The fourth day he wandered through the bazaar near Portside and became impatient with Chance's inattention. The Shenda animals were incomprehensible, as likely as not to answer his careful questions, and even the answers made little sense. Even an Eschoni after its initial pain-conditioning had more ludicity. Nineteen was tired of Shenda foolishness, yet had come no closer to the Light. He dared not approach the humans directly, and a Daruma knew too much about Vang—and the spy too little—to guarantee his disguise. As he stood by a fruit stand, half-listening to the Shenda stallkeeper's babble, he saw the Guildswoman Bartlett walking towards him.

He recognized her instantly and froze in shock. She saw him looking at her and gestured some question. *How had she known him?* He automatically nodded the human affirmative-response gesture, then quickly turned away, his skin tingling with alarm. His body responded instinctively to his shock, raising his crest in display-threat within the confines of his helmet, quickening his heart-beat for the imminent attack. But she walked on, not looking back.

He surreptitiously watched her turn a corner into a side-street, and realized she was following the Shenda male who preceded her. For the first time, he noticed the other human near her in the crowd, also dressed in Guild clothing; his memory supplemented the notice—the same human had been on Taki, the McCrory trader who had eluded Lord Chaat's plan. He found the name: Tanner. The man, too, turned into the side street.

The spy narrowed his eyes, his disillusionment forgotten in this blessing of Chance. He pretended a momentary interest in the stallkeeper's chatter and turned over a fruit until he judged them a good distance ahead. Then he followed.

Marunda at last stopped at a door, examined the plate as if none too sure of the destination, and climbed the tall staircase leading to the door from the cobbled street.

"Problem with dialect change," Marunda rumbled as he put his palm to the doorplate, "is sign change. Even my sign." He turned to Jennan and waggled his ears. "You come in, be friend."

"Thank you."

He led them inside into a cool stone anteroom lined with curio display cases, then through a doorway into a wide room alight with the afternoon sun. One entire wall was windowed from floor to ceiling, the glass surface marred only by the faint tracing of the metal supports. An old-style communicator stood in one corner, decorated by a pot of flowers. Wide soft chairs were arranged in the center of the room around a sunken fire-grating where coals gleamed redly.

Another Shenda padded into the room from another door. Marunda said something to him in a melodic lilt, and the other retreated through the door, returning in a few moments with a salver and chilled glasses. Piqui. Jennan let her breath go in a deep sigh. Piqui had been Shann's most promising antipsychotic drug, but its promise had turned sour and had instead addicted a generation. Marunda's lucidity was measured in minutes now, the time of a single circulation of blood to his brain.

Marunda waved them to chairs and then arranged himself comfortably, toasting his feet at the grate. Jennan accepted a glass from the servant, nodding her thanks. Tanner crossed his legs comfortably and copied Marunda, though the tiny fire would do little but warm his boot-soles. He sipped at his glass, winced at the taste, and promptly put it down on the sidetable.

Marunda studied the fire, his glass cradled in his hands, then raised his massive head.

"Remember beetle salad and argument with Portmaster. Remember your face, Guildswoman, and kindness to this forlorn Shenda. Remember, too, blood adoption. . . ."

"I meant only companion-friend-bond, Marunda."

Marunda sighed. "Too bad. Would like you as senior brother. Only have junior brothers, am senior myself. Not easy." He took a deep swallow from his glass. "Where Morgen?"

"Back at the port. He had duties there." Jennan also sipped at the astringent liquid in her glass, and tried to repress her reaction to the taste. Marunda noticed immediately.

"You not like piqui?" he demanded.

"It's different," she said politely and determinedly took another swallow, knowing piqui to be harmless to her chemistry however it tasted—and however it affected Shenda. Marunda's eyes were already glazing, and he soon sank back into his strangely contorted disassociation. But at least he was safely home.

She put her glass on the sidetable and then stood

up, looked at the massive Shenda as he stared into the fire with unseeing eyes.

"Junior brother," she said softly to him, "dream well."

Tanner looked up at her from his chair, his expression bewildered. "What?"

"Nothing, Vaughn. Let's go."

As they emerged from Marunda's house, the afternoon sun cast long shadows across the block of weathered stone houses. Without speaking, Jennan and Tanner retraced their steps towards the park and the arbor tunnel to the bazaar. A few Shenda males strolled along the stone walks lining the street, their massive heads bobbing, and a hurried lone Vang disappeared around a corner of a building. Traffic clanged in the distance, and the long afternoon shadows filled the spaces beneath the trees, a tranquil, sleepy quiet.

They jolted down the steps into the park, and headed back downtown to visit the McCrory substation. Tanner pushed ahead into the arbor path, striding along quickly. Jennan tried to keep up with his longer legs, then finally dropped into a normal walking pace, panting slightly. Let him run if he must. She slipped her hands into her pockets and slowed even more, looking at the green shadows overhead.

Find a needle in a planet-wide haystack, she thought. *Read an alien mind of its intent while an old-minded Guildsman is destroying your career back home.* Tanner had disappeared around a bend, and Jennan stopped in mid-path, a little irked. Let him come back for her or go on, whatever he liked. She looked down at her boots and idly nudged a twig into a bump of soft dirt. The faint breeze shivered the leaves of the arbor, breathed on her cheek. *Something wrong here. Something I missed. What was it?*

She tried to reconstruct the conversation with Marunda, such as it was, then traced their journey backwards. *Something, something, ring-a-ring. Ding-a-ding, ming-a-ming, blong.* A mutable cloud with a single red eye. Tanner's caressing hand on her body, and the joy of sweet release in his arms. A pilot playing dominance games with a Daruma controller. The death of trust in a too-clever Master. *But you'll forgive him, you idiot, you know you will.* The crushing weight of tumbling offworlder bales. A crafty lizard playing one-uppance. . . .

Her head came up abruptly and she turned back towards the park. That Vang! It was the same one she had seen in the bazaar. What was he doing out here? Why was he hurrying away?

Vang?—or maybe Li Fawn? Her eyes narrowed, as her mind assembled the subconscious impressions from her brief glimpses of that Vang. He walked wrong, she decided. Vang always swaggered, challenging the universe to start something—but that Vang . . . skulked. Like the shadow in the Taki warehouse. She felt convinced of it. But where would he get the light-mode?

Then she clicked her tongue in exasperation. *He wouldn't need one, of course. All he needs is some kind of costume and everybody will assume it's a light-mode. And he followed me out here. Why?*

She walked quickly back up the path, then moved into a half-run, covering ground with long strides. As she reached the park, she looked around, but saw nothing out of the ordinary. Then, across the intervening velvet of park grass, through the screen of branches, she saw the gaping hole of Marunda's open door. She ran towards it, her body jolting with every stride.

She bounded up the stone steps and entered the cool passageway, then regained some of her native caution after the panic of her run across the park. She edged along the wall, placing her feet carefully for a silent progress across the stone flagging. In the inner room, she heard Marunda's murmuring rumble and a faint scuffling. It ceased. She stopped by a display case of stone artifacts, waiting, then edged around it to the doorway.

Marunda lay huddled on the floor, face-down, and the Li Fawn stood over him, a box-like device in his hand. She saw the spy take a quick look towards the other door, and then stoop to shake Marunda roughly.

"You will tell me why she was here," he hissed. "Tell me, or I will cause you more pain, Shenda." The box emitted a sparky hum.

Marunda's voice rose into a wail, and Jennan looked at the far door, hoping the servant would come. Then the spy moved his hands and Marunda shrieked in pain and writhed. Still the servant did not appear. Then Jennan cursed silently to herself: of course he wouldn't. Assuming he was lucid himself— which was problematical—he'd learned to ignore the wails and mumblings of another's manic fits, even those of his master's. There would be no help from the inner house.

Jennan looked around her for a weapon, and picked up one of the stone carvings from the display case. It was a cylindrical tube, a hand-span wide and half a meter long, finely etched with closely-set lines of carved figures. She wrapped her hand around it, shifted it until she found a firm hold, then stepped into the room.

"Why don't you ask me yourself?" she said furiously.

The Vang whirled and quickly raised its hand-device, clicking a control with its opposed claw. Jennan gasped and threw herself to the side as a ruby flash cracked past her, exploding against the far wall.

A shower of smoking, pulverized plaster pelted her and she coughed in the acrid fumes. She heard the Vang's running steps away from her to the back of the house. She followed cautiously, stooping briefly by the unconscious Marunda, then ran lightly across the floor to the far door. She listened, heard a crash deep in the back of the house, and slipped through the door into the walkway beyond, the cylinder still in her hand.

The interior door opened onto a garden ringed by a walkway enclosed in glass. Jennan ran along the stone flagging, circling the garden, until she reached another door on the opposite side of the square. She edged forward to look into the sunlit room, then slipped around the doorjamb. Across the room, yet another door stood open, admitting the bright sunlight of outside. She saw no sign of other Shenda in the small bare room—nor of the fake Vang—and hurried forward.

Behind the block of houses the Shenda males had created a series of gardens, walled with a bewildering variety of short fences. Some were carefully masoned stone, others a tangle of brambles, others a combination of slats and wire and metal junk that clattered in the soft breeze. To the left, several lawns away, a tall glowing form vaulted a bramble, moving fast.

Jennan looked down at the cylinder in her hand, repressed a curse, but kept the cylinder. Stone against laser was nearly futile, but tooth-and-claw of basic human was far worse. She leaped down the steps and vaulted the nearby stone fence. She concentrated on the efficiency of her run, pursuing the spy across several lawns. She began to gain on him as he leaped awkwardly over the barriers. Then he reached the street at the end of the block and vanished.

Jennan slowed as she reached the last wall and approached it cautiously, wary of an ambush. Then she palmed herself over in a low glide and dropped to the street. Nothing. She got to her feet, looking in both directions. Aside from a strolling Shenda who had stopped to stare, the street was empty. Jennan flexed her hand around her weapon. She had lost him.

"Damn!" Angry at her failure, she hiked around the block back to Marunda's house.

Marunda's servant—brother? son?—had put Marunda in a chair, and was bending over him when she reentered the entryway. As she replaced the cylinder on the curio shelf by the door, the glass resonated with a muted harmonic. The servant turned quickly, baring his teeth. Jennan began to raise her hand, opened her mouth to speak, when the Shenda charged.

"No!" she cried as he bore her backwards, smashing her into the damaged wall. The Shenda growled as it pressed his long arms around her, snapping at her head and neck as she squirmed. Jennan brought up her knee in a sharp jerk into the Shenda's soft underbelly. It abruptly released her and backed away, whimpering. Jennan stayed by the wall, her chest heaving.

"I didn't hurt him, you fool," she gasped.

"Saw you run," the Shenda growled. "Saw you run away. Kill you like you kill Marunda."

"I was chasing the . . . Kill? Marunda is dead?"

"Dead, dead." The servant's voice rose into a wailing shriek. "Dead, red, head, going dead, bled . . ." His cry sank to a low, sobbing mutter as he buried his face in his arms, hiding his face from her. Jennan stared at him in shock, then circled him to look for herself.

He hadn't a mark on him, but already his eyes

were glazing, fixed on the far ceiling in gentle, vacant thought. Jennan tested for a pulse, realized she didn't know where it would be, but the flaccidity in Marunda's arm was enough. She replaced the limp shaggy paw on the Shenda's chest and bowed her head.

"Junior brother . . ." she murmured. "Oh, damn, damn, damn."

Behind her, the servant sobbed brokenly in the shadowed sunlight of the open door.

Chapter 13

Jennan waited patiently in the entryway as the Guild investigation team poked and pried. The late afternoon neared warm dusk. Through the open front door, she could see the shadows gather among the trees across the street. A soft breath of warm air sighed through the hall, stirring the tendrils of her hair. She hugged her elbows to her sides as she stood against the wall, a slow pulse of grief aching in her chest. She watched Guildmaster Rotha, the team-chief, consult with an aide, then listened as he talked to Portside on the commset. Then she looked out again on the Shenda twilight.

She had liked Marunda, and now genuinely mourned him. It was such a waste, a stupid waste. Her anger against the Li Fawn spy prickled, but she tried to suppress it. Until she knew reasons, understood his motivations, she would not condemn even the spy. On Hrauru, when Chandra had been humiliated, she had felt a raging violence against the Outsiders who had attacked her friend. After her own assault on Taki, she had relished vivid thoughts of revenge. But outrage can cool with experience, and the Li Fawn was now more than an unseen shadow, had a purpose she needed to know. She had heard his voice, and now wondered about him. Who was he? Why was he here? What did he seek?

It was easier to hate a shadow, she thought. *Why can't I hate him now?* She felt uncertain, as if she had lost too many connections and fallen adrift between her Guild and her human heritage. She had expected to add this outrage to the Li Fawn's growing list, yet found herself wondering. Did he have reasons? And if she knew the reasons, would she forgive?

Where is the right? Have I lost my human passion, my capacity for outrage? Have I become too Daruma?

Yet some Daruma moved against her, although she had a shape and presence within their Guild, a voice, reasons. They saw only the form, the difference, and never sought the reasons. They saw only threat.

Where is the right? She studied the floor a moment, conscious of a gentle breeze from the open doorway, the scents of a warm alien world. *Do I try to understand? Or do I draw a moral line, say this cannot be forgiven?* Her thoughts chased each other dully in her grief.

As Tarthe refuses to forgive me my humanity? she wondered.

And yet . . . Do I lose myself?

She watched the Guild team remove Marunda's body and begin packing their equipment. Finally Chief Rotha dusted his hands on his crisp uniform and emerged from the inner room. Beneath his exterior calm and efficiency, Jennan could see his anger about Marunda's death in the controlled cant of his ears, the tension around his eyes. The Daruma had never resented their care of the Shenda, their older brothers fallen in dotage, for it drew from a genuine love, a love that transcended the alien.

What does he feel? Does he hate the Li Fawn? Must he?

The chief's eyes met hers in a flash of empathy. In this one respect, they shared a Guildsman's mutual anger about the waste of Marunda's death. At least they shared that. A Guildsman clattered past them in the hall, struggling with a portable analyzer. The chief reached out a hand to steady him as he overbalanced.

"Thanks, Chief."

"Be careful, Ton. Analyzers don't grow on trees."

"Yes, sir."

Rotha turned back to Jennan. "Piqui overdose," he said shortly. "I expect the autopsy will confirm it."

"But I saw the Li Fawn use a weapon!"

"I don't doubt that, Guildswoman. Stress often worsens the effects of piqui, especially in the initial stage of intoxication. You say Marunda drank only one glass?"

"Yes."

"Well, I'll tell the coroner. Maybe he can confirm the other cause as contributing."

Jennan frowned. "But maybe not. You're saying there's no proof that the Li Fawn killed him."

"None."

"But . . ."

The chief raised his hand to forestall her protest. "I believe your story, Jennan. Whatever your 'political' discussions with Portmaster Beren, I deal in facts, not politics. You're a Guildsman—a fact—with no reason to lie—another fact. Besides, I've had regular reports about that spy since Port allowed him to land." He looked grim. "I've left him alone, following directives, but no longer. I ordered a drill-rig to open up that ship if the Li Fawn won't. They've skulked around Shann too long and I want to find out what that spy is up to."

"To learn his reasons?"

"Exactly."

"Thank you, Chief." She smiled, bemused.

Rotha snorted, misunderstanding her. "I find it shameful that such an occasion is cause for thanks, as if the gift is unexpected. You've done well, Guildswoman." He flicked his ears wryly. "Like all good Daruma, I use my ears well. Your 'adoption' has already run around Portside rumors twice, and you did well to bring him home safely. We valued him." He glanced into the inner room. "Did you know he was a scholar?"

"I guessed."

"Even so, his nephew persists in charging that you murdered his uncle. That will be resolved once he's lucid again, but Beren will exploit the complaint while he can. Senior Tarthe and his supporters have great influence here, not only through his family connections with the Portmaster, but for other reasons. Shann Guildsmen see too many Terrans of the wrong sort."

"What do you mean?" Jennan stiffened despite herself.

"No offense intended, of course." The chief's ears flicked in irritation. "Whatever Terra complains, we Daruma don't claim to own Shann. We merely try to stop others from stealing it, as several have attempted and *Crystal* succeeded. Have you found any trace of her?"

"No. Is it certain that they intended looting?"

"Who knows?" Rotha shrugged tiredly. "To be fair, Daruma merchants can be as greedy."

"To be fair. Yes, of course."

Rotha studied her face a moment. "You seem troubled, Guildswoman. Can I help?"

"No; it's nothing important."

She smiled, appreciating his courtesy. Rotha obviously had an independent mind, which she also appreciated. Daruma tolerance, however dented by Sorema's plots, was the glue that bound the sector together into a greater whole, for the Daruma could encompass the others, bridge the gaps in culture and temperament, provide the common nexus. The Guild was merely the physical embodiment of that racial fact.

The bonds of diversity, she thought. *Yes, that is part of the answer*.

"I'm sorry that humans are plaguing you, Chief," she said.

Rotha shrugged, dismissing it. "They'll learn. As do we. Perhaps our peoples are too much alike. Perhaps the Guild has grown too accustomed to alien brothers content to sit at home, too comfortable with our role as leaders. Sadly, the universe rarely stops unwinding merely because we wish it. Another fact."

"I appreciate your liking for facts, Chief."

"I know." He smiled at her. "You have a gift, Jennan. Don't listen to Tarthe. A true Guildsman seeks the binding—Marunda told me that once. I think he found that quality in you; it fits what else I've heard about you and the other human Guildsmen. When this is over, if you're willing, ask Master Larovi to send you to Shann for a while." He scowled. "Beren may have his proprieties at Out-Station to shield him, but I have two hundred Terrans running loose in my city. I need a liaison, someone who understands both sides." He cocked his head at her, his eyes amused at her expression. "Interested?"

"Surprised." She chuckled, knowing he understood her exactly.

"Marunda had an attentive student. Keep me in mind."

"I'll do that."

Tanner walked quickly through the long arbor, his mind bent on the McCrory sub-station. As he reached the bazaar street, he realized that Jennan was not behind him. He turned and looked up the path, hesitated, then went on. Perhaps she'd catch up later. He preferred to contact McCrory without the Guild in tow, anyway; he belatedly realized he'd have enough to explain about his own Guild uniform. He well remembered the attitude of many McCrory traders about the human Guildsmen, a complex of envy and disapproval only accentuated in Lenart's spite. For all he had seen in Jennan's advantages, he wasn't that sure he still didn't share the opinion. The bias disturbed him vaguely, as if it were a small betrayal of Jennan, but he irritably shook off the feeling.

Three blocks uptown he reached the McCrory sub-station and stepped inside the shadowed coolness of the lobby. Several traders lounged in small groups on the polished floor. Three doors on the far wall led to the inner administrative offices of the company. Plaques and local art decorated the walls, and blue-green plants squatted in their planters in two corners. He glanced around at the decor with approval. McCrory always did manage to look well-heeled, even in the backwaters.

Tanner walked towards the inner doors, thinking to check in, then swerved abruptly as he recognized a face in a nearby group of traders.

"Vaughn!"

Silo's merry blue eyes sparkled with open pleasure, and the burly trader thumped him on the shoulder in welcome. Tanner and Silo had been shipmates on the old *Gemini Star* years ago, before their company fortunes had taken them in different directions. A good man. Vaughn grinned widely and thumped him back, then looked from face to face as Silo introduced him around the small group. McEnee, Joynson, Roberts. The other men eyed him curiously.

"But what's this?" Silo asked jocularly, gesturing at Tanner's uniform. "Gone native? Never thought it'd happen to you, Vaughn." Silo's teeth gleamed, ready for the joke.

"No. I'm on detached assignment. Had somebody try to sabotage a Taki trade, and so I got some camouflage to find out who." Tanner laughed self-consciously. The others had a strange expression in their eyes as they looked at him, one he did not like much. As they continued to stare at him, he felt even more uncomfortable.

"Well," Roberts said at last, "trade does take us in strange directions." He was an older man, well-grizzled, his tanned face creased with heavy lines. He lit a cigar and blew out a cloud of smoke over their heads. "Personally, I wouldn't be caught dead in a Guild uniform, special assignment or not."

"Shut up, Roberts," Silo said. "You'll have to excuse him, Vaughn. Guild bollixed one of his trades and he's peeved."

"Shut up yourself, Silo," Roberts retorted. "Much as I admire the pluck, Tanner, your brother has royally screwed up Shann trade for everybody. The Guild won't give approval for anything now—it's all 'under advisement.' " He spat at the floor. "I've even heard rumors that McCrory might be banned from Shann Trade."

Tanner's jaw dropped. "Banned? You're kidding!"

"Hell, no. You should hear the sub-station chief. He's going to skin Lume alive." Roberts smiled unpleasantly. "Hope your career will survive it, Vaughn."

"But I had nothing to do with . . ."

"Yeah—tell that to the Daruma. They think we're all in it together, and worse for you—you're Lume's brother. Daruma think that always means something—what, they don't know, but it's gotta mean something. McCrory Central might decide to hand your head to them on a platter, just to go along. It's happened before."

McEnee scowled, the expression unpleasant on his young face. "I don't see why we need Guild approval in the first place. Free trade is a fundamental principle, one that should have been written into the treaty. Roberts' trade was perfectly legitimate, and that Guildsman had no right . . ."

"Ancient history now, my boy," Roberts said sourly. "Station master said to drop it. We keep playing by the Guild's rules, like the Daruma owned the sector. As they do, of course, but nobody does nothing." He dropped his cigar butt on the floor and ground it out with his boot heel. "I hate these cigars. Why can't the station stock a decent brand?"

"Like I said, Vaughn, peevish." Silo chuckled again, his tone apologetic, then tried to change the subject. "So you're here on a Guild mission of some sort. I guess that's your luck," he added brightly.

"Yeah," Joynson muttered, his tone showing a different opinion of such luck. "How'd you arrange that?" He looked Tanner up and down, his thin face taut with disapproval. *What am I doing here?* Tanner thought in panic. He shrugged, trying to toss it off.

"Oh, I was factoring a Taki trade on Ro, and somebody tried to bomb the trade. Shorted the shipments. The Guildsman who handled the mediation is investigating and I went along for the ride. She thinks the Li Fawn might be involved."

"A convenient excuse," Roberts snorted. "Blame somebody who won't make contact. I'd say you should look closer to home."

Tanner plowed ahead. "The Guildsman wants to know if McCrory has seen any Li Fawn at Shann lately. Have you?"

"Li Fawn?" Roberts asked. "Are you crazy? Nobody sees Li Fawn. If you ask me, since you do, Guild probably made them up." He lit another cigar and coughed hoarsely at the bite of the smoke. Then his expression turned uglier. "Nice of you to trot over here on your errand, Tanner, but I still say you're chasing the wrong bilge. You ought to trot right back and tell the Guild that." He looked Tanner up and down, challenging him. "Nice uniform. Looks good on you."

Tanner felt himself flush, but said nothing. *Stupid, stupid mistake,* he thought. He should have known better to get too comfortable wearing a Guild uniform, should have remembered the way things looked to his own kind. *What am I doing here?* he thought again. *How did I let Jennan get me into this?*

"Hey, come on," Silo said, glaring at Roberts. "Vaughn's my friend. He's no turncoat."

"Yeah? So how come I get the impression I'm talking to a Guild spy? He looks like one."

"Thanks for your time," Tanner said coldly. "Good to see you, Silo. Wish you the best." Tanner turned away and stalked towards the street door.

"Hey, Vaughn!" Silo called after him. "Vaughn!"

Tanner emerged into the street and walked quickly away from the sub-station, almost trembling in his shame and embarrassment. He hadn't felt this way since he was a kid, when he let his liking for a home-town friend get himself identified with the wrong group at the Company academy. Tanner had learned from the mistake, quickly corrected it. And now, years later, he had forgotten that sharp lesson. Tanner set his jaw so fiercely that his teeth ground against each other. He was a McCrory man, a Terran, not some half-human who had forgotten his loyalties. As he almost had.

Well, you're not the first man to betray himself for a pretty woman. At least you've got the smarts to see it, Vaughn. At least you have that.

Tanner walked with long strides along the street. At the bazaar he hesitated, wondering if Jennan had returned to *Ariel* or still wandered elsewhere. *Not that I care,* he told himself angrily. *Why should I care?*

A Shenda male ambled by, muttering inanities; Tanner watched him pass with a new distaste. *Wrong group, Vaughn, my boy; keep to your own kind.*

Somehow, he had to find a way to extricate himself from this mess—without offending the Guild. A human in Sagittarius, whatever Roberts' complaints, had to deal with the Guild. They pulled the strings. Oh, she was so clever, leading him on!

"Luck," he snarled at himself. "Oh, sure."

The sun sat low in the sky, shedding reddish shadows into the street. He reached the park entrance and hesitated. Likely she had already gone back to *Ariel*. Well, he'd go there, too, and, first step, he'd change his clothes. He hurried onward, making for the port.

The spy crouched in the alleyway, concealed behind a stone wall. He listened and heard the Guildswoman's footsteps pass, then lifted his head over the cracked facing of the wall. The street beyond the alley was deserted, but he sank backward

to await dusk and its dark concealments. He
returned his weapon to an interior pocket of his disguise, then looked down and considered the disguise. Behind him, a low window led to an interior
basement in the tall house that loomed above. He
shattered the glass with a metal fist and slipped
inside.

He quickly stripped off the metal panels and
angrily kicked the cluster of Zaruti into a corner.
Naked, he padded forward through the maze of
machine parts and bundles, then broke open a box
and then another, until he found several lengths of
iridescent cloth. He fingered the material, remembering he had seen similar dress on Shenda females.
He lifted a bolt of the cloth from the box and
unwound it, then draped it experimentally around
his long body. He tried one arrangement and then
another, then, with a curse, threw the cloth away.
He paused to listen for sounds from the house above
his head, and then broke open another box.

Two hours later, the setting sun cast long shadows
into the alleyway. Dressed in a sober black he had
fashioned into his own Li Fawn robes, Nineteen levered himself onto the windowsill and listened for
sounds in the street. He reemerged into the alleyway, looked around quickly, and then headed for the
port. His need for caution delayed him. Although he
expected little hue and cry for a spy in Li Fawn
robes, he took no chances.

He slipped down alleyways and the shadowed
streets, watching carefully in all directions for any
observer, passing quickly through the shadows. His
pupils widened, gathering in the half-light of the
darkening streets, and his other senses sharpened as
his body instinctively responded to the sheltering
darkness. A hundred generations had bred such
senses into his caste, well beyond the capabilities of

other breeds, though other castes in turn bore their own enhancements. He felt the stir of the wind on his hands and hooded face, caught the alien scents it bore. As the twilight deepened, his vision expanded still more into the infra-red, and he stole through the faint reddish glow of the warm twilight, avoiding the red gleams emitted by house interiors and the blurred hot-blooded shapes of Shenda who scurried home in the gathering night.

Near the edge of the city, the lights of Portside sent a bright dome of light arcing over the port plain. Other lights winked from the prows of berthed ships, the metal bulk of the ships looming shadows beneath their lone beacons. Smaller lights scurried across the wide field as groundcars moved about busily. He heard voices abroad on the warm twilight air as crewmen returned to their ships, and caught alien scents, some pungent, some merely strange, as they moved with the evening breeze. He lifted his head and took in a large breath through his open mouth, classifying the smells.

He stopped in the shadow of a parked groundcar and crouched, examining the field ahead. As he expected, he saw shadowed figures gathered at the base of his own cruiser several squares ahead. The frame of a penetration device lifted above their heads, its drillhead already sawing at the ship's lock. He bared his teeth reflexively and felt his crest rise in response to his anger. He watched the Guild team resentfully for a moment, then dismissed the emotion and looked away to examine other ships.

Even Guild equipment could not pierce the hull in less than an hour. He had that long to arrange another escape. His ship's tamper-lock included a tiny crustacean exquisitely sensitive to barometric changes. The Treyin's convulsive reaction to pressure change would close a certain switch, and the resulting explosion would vaporize the ship, taking the drill-crew and a hundred-meter circle of tarmac with it. He would be elsewhere, exploiting the diversion. He moved downfield, away from his ship, keeping carefully in the shadows of other groundcars and the low outbuildings skirting the field.

The lights of Port-Tower shone brightly at the other end of the field, and the activity of groundcars and cargo-carriers was more intense. He hesitated, reluctant to move into such exposure, then slid into the shadow of a Terran cargo ship to reconsider. Four squares ahead he saw the *Ariel* and he grimaced, renewed anger throbbing in his temples. The Guildswoman. Twice she had appeared to interfere, twice too many. He studied her ship a moment and then bared his teeth again in a different emotion. Perhaps. He breathed a prayer to Chance, sketched a short plea with his hand, and ran quickly across the gap to the Guild ship.

Chapter 14

As Jennan completed her good-byes to Chief Rotha, she saw Tanner mount the house steps with long strides. He paused in surprise as he noticed the Guild van in the street, then moved aside as Chief Rotha left the house.

"What happened?" he asked, craning his head backward to watch the departing Guild team.

"The Li Fawn attacked Marunda. He's dead."

"Li Fawn?"

"The Vang we saw in the bazaar. I tried to catch him, but he got away."

"Apparently I missed some real action," Tanner said, then grinned.

Jennan stared at him. Didn't he care? Tanner's smile faded and he shifted uncomfortably, his face oddly defiant. Jennan blinked at him, wondering. What was this man? Perhaps all he saw was the odd body, odd mannerisms, that made a person nonhuman—and thus an unperson. She had thought he was different, thought he . . .

It didn't fit. Maybe something had happened at McCrory: would he tell her if she asked?

"Did you learn anything at the substation?"

"No," he said shortly and looked away.

"What's the matter, Vaughn?"

"Nothing."

"Vaughn . . ."

"Skip it, Jennan." He sounded angry and she stared at him again.

"What happened?" she demanded.

"I don't want to tell you, okay? Are you through here?"

"Yes," she said, controlling herself. Instinctively, she raised the old barriers and hid herself behind her Daruma calm, knowing it was a defeat. Vaughn looked away again, refusing to meet her eyes. A slow flush spread up his neck. They stood silently a moment.

"Let's go back to *Ariel*," she said tiredly. She turned and left the house, Tanner following after.

Nineteen found another hiding-place between *Ariel*'s pods and crouched down in its shadows. He listened, occasionally sparing a glance for the drill crew at his own ship far up the field, then removed his weapon from his inner robes and circled to the lock. He leaped onto the platform, glanced quickly around, and focused his weapon on the lock. Stolen ship plans of Daruma ships showed no self-destruct mechanism like his own, and he took the acceptable risk.

The ruby flame of his weapon bit at the metal of the lock, then penetrated the lock control. The damage broke the internal circuit, and the air lock sighed open. Nineteen slipped inside and quickly scavenged a length of metal from the interior light fixture to reconstruct the circuit. The outer lock cycled shut again, activating the inner door.

A shriek echoed from the interior of the ship, spiraling into ultrasonics that struck painfully at his dark-heightened senses. He turned quickly to meet the threat, fumbling in his robe for his weapon, then ducked as a small winged creature flung itself through the inner lock and attacked. Nineteen struck out at the furious animal, but it avoided him with a deft tipping of its wings. It attacked again, its shrieks echoing in the enclosed space of the lock.

Its wings battered at his head and he felt its teeth rake down his cheek. His fingers had grasped his weapon at last, but a chance blow of the creature's wings brushed it from his fingers. It clattered to the floor and skidded uselessly out of reach. Nineteen cursed. He struck out again at the creature and missed, then retreated to the air lock wall.

With one arm raised to shield his face, the spy reached out to the lock controls and snapped his repair with one hand. The outer door promptly reopened and his hand connected with the animal's body, sweeping it through the open door. The creature hit the guardrail on the airlock stair, then fell from sight to the ground. The spy hastily rebuilt the lock circuit and closed the door. Then he sagged against the lock wall and patted at his bleeding cheek with his sleeve, breathing heavily.

He listened for any sounds within the ship. Surely the animal's alarm would have brought investigation had anyone been aboard. As he heard nothing—no pounding steps, nor stealthy approach, no voices above—his heart thudded in exultation at his fortune. The guard slave defeated, an unoccupied ship for his taking—a fair trade. He still had few answers for Lord Chaat and would no doubt pay for that failure, but for now Chance seemed to bless him. Perhaps She would bring other opportunities. He was Tsor, and such spies often received Her special attention. He sketched another prayer with his multi-fingered hand.

He stepped into the interior of the ship, then made a thorough search of its four levels. Its sterile environment of metal and strange fabrics offended him, and his nose twitched at the unusual smells. He climbed back to the flight deck and looked around the banks of controls, then tipped back his head to peer upward into the half-well fronting the observation lounge. He looked around again, more curiously, and recognized several of the controls from the stolen data on his tapes.

He had studied the technological differences between Antares and Naberr, but had never had much opportunity to examine the Daruma's laborious substitutes for biocomponents. The other Guild ship had suffered extensive damage during its capture, some of it wrecked by its own Guildsmen— some of the tech analyses had been mere guesswork. Li Fawn had flexibility of understanding, drew upon their knowledge of other alien technologies they encountered during conquest, but *Ariel*'s expanse of machinery still seemed strange to him. He was used to the movements and strange forms of slaves working among machines.

He sat down at the computer and studied the controls, recognizing several inscriptions from his study of the captured Guild ship aboard *Ngoh Ge*. He sniffed at the laborious arrangement of dials and lights and doubted if the ship's computer even had a cyborg brain. Chaat had incorporated several of his worthier enemies into *Ngoh Ge*'s computers to supplement the slave brains, and Nineteen had overheard some pleased comments among the Li Fawn controllers about the result. He studied the controls further, then quickly entered a query, using the security code extracted from the captured Guild ship. It was old, nearly two years out of date, but . . .

"Query: name Lume," a thin metallic voice said. The spy looked around wildly, then found the speaker grille two feet above his head. He barely restrained an exultant cry at the response, and bit down hard on his inner lips to gain control. He tasted his own blood.

"Confirm query," the machine prompted.

He couldn't chance his voice, not with this unknown machine. He repeated his keyboard command and waited expectantly. The machine considered, then accepted.

"Source: Guild Confidential, Shann Port, authority Shann Portmaster," it said. "To all Guild ships: Subject Lume Tanner, Trader, Terran McCrory Line, Terran ship *Crystal*. Factor for shipment of Shenda madringals to Terran collectors. Currently negotiating with Shenda Clan Beraquit, but trade unexpectedly broken off upon *Crystal*'s departure from Shann four standard weeks ago. Report to Shann Portmaster if ship sighted. Additional data available. End message."

His heart thudding, the spy glanced towards the well, listening for any sound of the returning crew at the lock, then punched in the additional query.

"Acknowledged," said the machine. "Guild Confidential, Addendum. Subject: Lume Tanner, Trader, McCrory Ship *Crystal*. Inquiry to McCrory disclosed that Tanner had tested a Shenda artifact, ostensibly a madringal statuette. The test results, nature withheld by McCrory, prompted Tanner to abandon his trade and attempt unauthorized return to Centauri. Out-Station demanded *Crystal*'s return to Shann for Guild examination of artifact. *Crystal* ignored the demand and eluded pursuit. Protest filed with McCrory and the Terran Conclave. Whereabouts of

Crystal unknown, ship now overdue. Report if sighted. If *Crystal* boarded, retrieve Shenda artifact and return to Portmaster, Shann. Arrest of Tanner and crew authorized. End message."

The machine paused, then continued severely: "Security instruction. Vang light-modes are to be registered for security purposes of this ship, Guild Regulation 2.0334-j. Current light-mode not registered. Infraction logged. Light-modes without voice controls exceed security restrictions, Guild Regulation 1.0223-b. Infraction logged. Correction advised immediately." The speaker emitted a decided snap and fell silent.

The spy looked down at himself, then grinned highly amused. He ran his tongue around his lips, removing the blood that had trickled from his injured mouth. He considered, and felt himself riding Luck in all ways. Tsor he was now, with answers for Lord Chaat. His mind instinctively shied from the prospect of exposure, even of his own triumphant report to Chaat, but he relished the subtle conflict. *Tsor,* he thought exultantly.

"Register light-mode," he said aloud, his voice calm. "Including voice range demonstrated."

"Light-mode registered, voice-range logged into security control." The machine's lights blinked quickly.

The spy took a breath. "Begin lift-off sequence."

"Sequence begun. Assume position at flight controls."

Nineteen hesitated, remembering another datum from the stolen tapes. "Current light-mode not adapted to standard Vang senses. Can you adapt?"

The machine paused for a perceptible moment. Had he finally alerted it? Despite their limited design, he had no illusions about the intelligence of Daruma computers. "Explain further, please," it said.

"Confidential," Nineteen bluffed. "Consult Vang data."

It was enough. "I can adapt," the machine said in its flat voice. "Sequencing for non-Vang flight operations. Prepare for lift-off."

As the spy quickly changed his seat, *Ariel* began to tremble.

The journey back to Portside was silent. Tanner avoided her glances, keeping to himself, and finally she left him to it. Downtown, they left the tram and walked through the darkening streets back to Portside. Jennan felt her headache return as a tight vise around her forehead, and she squinted against the pain.

The bazaar shops were shuttered in the early twilight, their owners departed for their homes. A few traders, both human and Daruma, wandered through the streets, talking in quiet voices if they had a companion, ambling contentedly if alone. They passed a man in McCrory uniform, who nodded politely, then noticed their Guild uniforms with a start. But he was quickly past, strolling onward into the darkness behind them. The breeze sighed on Jennan's cheek, warming it with its soft touch, stirring her dark hair, tickling her nose with the scents of straw and dust and sun-warmed stone.

She took in a deep breath, tasting the Shenda night. She relished the taste as if she now tasted this world, this alien and beloved presence, for the last time. She felt the loss keenly, as if reality blurred into nightmare, as if a mocking light stretched tightly to obliterate all reason. Her emotion frightened her. One by one, she seemed to be losing her joys in life—her Guild, her trust, her rank and reputation, even her place to stand. She felt her life slipping away from her useless hands, unable to stop the erosion, unable to understand its cause.

For a moment, she felt an unexpected cry of despair rise in her throat. She wanted to turn to Tanner, but choked back the impulse. She struggled within herself, her head throbbing within its tightened vise, then finally found the coldness of her practical mind. The headache lessened, fading like a bad dream.

They passed through the remaining out-buildings at the edge of Portside. At the field apron, she stopped and scanned the array of ships in the darkness, her hands on her hips. To her right, the Li Fawn scout sat on its midfield square, a distant shadow against the illumination of the field and the starry sky. The drill-rig team scurried busily around its base, the ruby beam of the drill-bit biting at the ship door. It looked like Rotha would get his answers soon.

She felt a stirring in her mind as she caught a faint echo of T'wing's alarm. She looked around for her friend, confused by the impressions of flight through open darkness. Where was T'wing? How had she gotten outside the ship? Jennan tried awkwardly to reach out to the pseudobat, received a memory of a frantic struggle in an enclosed space. She raised her arms automatically, called T'wing to her.

"Jennan," Tanner said abruptly, "why is *Ariel* lifting off?" He pointed towards their ship. *Ariel's* warn-off beacons gleamed redly on the ship's prow, then began blinking in an accelerating pattern. The entry stairs slowly folded into their frame encircling the air lock. The ship was clearly taking off.

Jennan stared. "No!" Not *Ariel*!" she cried and ran wildly towards the ship.

"Jennan! Don't!" Tanner called and then, cursing, ran after her. They raced across the tarmac for *Ariel*, then fell flat as a massive explosion ripped through a ship downfield.

"Oh, gods!" The landing-square that had held the Li Fawn ship had become a smoking crater, the drill-team and its equipment blown to fragments.

"What in the hell?" Tanner asked, his voice hoarse.

"A tamper lock! Oh, gods!" Ahead of them, *Ariel's* lift-off lights blinked more urgently. "Come on, Vaughn!"

Jennan scrambled to her feet, dragging Tanner with her. As they pounded up to the air lock, Jennan leaped onto the narrow entry ledge and vainly slapped her palm on the air lock control, knowing that the lift-off sequence had already locked it beyond recall. The ship trembled in the first stages of ignition.

To her astonishment, the door responded. "Come on!" she said, and pulled Tanner after her into the lock. The engines sent a steady rumble through the metal floor of the air lock. Dimly through the hull, Jennan heard the warn-off siren begin its steady hooting. They had only seconds left.

"Brace yourself, Vaughn. *Ariel's* gravity controls don't cover the air lock."

"Right," he said shortly. "I know the drill."

The ship lifted, pressing them to the floor. Jennan tried to ease into the acceleration, shifting her muscles smoothly as she sank to the floor onto her back. From the corner of her eye, she saw Tanner do the same with practiced ease. As *Ariel* punched through the atmosphere, the acceleration made it hard to breathe as three gravities sat upon her chest. She felt a lance of pain in her arm as the acceleration pressed on healing bone. She tried to breathe slowly, felt her ribs creak under the growing strain.

Then the pressure began to ease and Jennan felt

her body become light as they entered freefall. She grabbed for a side-strut as she floated upward, then slowly brought up her knees, pushing against the strut to turn her body until she floated full-length, her head towards the inner-lock door. Tanner copied her maneuver deftly, bumping slightly against her as they floated in mid-chamber.

"Do we knock on the door or something?" he asked. The sound of his voice echoed around the small chamber.

"Sshh. That's not Chandra at the controls, Vaughn."

Vaughn looked startled. "Oh," he whispered. Then his expression turned skeptical. "How can you know that?"

"I just know."

"Right. So what do we do now?"

She shrugged. "We get inside, of course."

"Of course," he snorted. "Naturally. What else?"

"Vaughn . . . Oh, skip it."

She pulled herself to the inner lock control and studied it, wary of the alarms that could activate lights on the flight deck above. As the ship cleared the outer atmosphere, it should roll into a new vector for out-system, enough piloting activity to distract a Li Fawn perhaps unfamiliar with Guild warning lights. She waited, her hand poised by the lock control, until she felt the tug of lateral acceleration begin, then keyed open the lock. She quickly drew herself across the lock housing, bringing her feet beneath her into a controlled landing inside Ariel's gravity field. Tanner thumped down beside her. The lock-door swished shut behind them.

She looked upward towards the well, then tugged on Tanner's sleeve and quickly drew him towards the unoccupied suite nearest the air lock door. Inside the bare room, its bedframe stripped and the furniture rimmed with a thin film of dust, she led Tanner to

the door of the storage compartment. They squeezed
through the door into the narrow shelved room
beyond that ran the length of the suite. She slipped
to the far end of the darkened compartment, lit only
by a few tell-tales at the door, and sat down. Tanner
levered himself down in front of her, and they sat,
knees to knees in the narrow space.

"We don't have a weapon," Tanner murmured.
"This could be a bad trap."

He sounded irritated, an irritation she didn't
understand. He had been pleased enough when she
came to his cabin. She missed that pleasure in her
person, the admiration that had once flashed in his
eyes. He looked at her sourly enough now.

"*Ariel* doesn't have weapons," she answered sooth-
ingly, wishing she could be rid of the distraction of
soothing anybody, especially a balky human. "Chandra's lasers are more than enough protection."

"Chandra isn't here, if you're right about who's
flying this ship."

"True." She grimaced. "We do have a laser-pistol
on flight deck, but neither Morgen nor I ever had
any fascination for pistols. The Li Fawn had some
kind of laser device, so I know that he's armed. I just
hope he hasn't attacked anybody else." She stirred
restlessly, desperately worried about her team. How
had the Li Fawn got aboard the ship? Where was
Morgen?

"How did he get on board?" Tanner asked, echoing her thought.

She leaned up awkwardly, grabbed a shelf edge,
and pulled herself to her feet. Tanner ducked as she
climbed over him. "Stay here," she said. "I'm going
to prowl around."

He caught at her knees. "I'll do the prowling, Jennan. Sit down."

"We are *not* going to get into that silly argument.

I am team-first of this ship and you are team-third, Vaughn. Let go of my leg. That's an order." He did so. "I'll be back in a few minutes."

She crept out of the storage compartment, hoping Tanner would stay put, and then reentered the common room. She drifted around the circular wall, walking softly on the carpeting, with her eyes fixed on the open well above. When she had reached the point even with the well ladder, she moved cautiously forward and grasped the metal railing. She eased herself onto the ladder, listening for sounds. She heard the clicking of machinery, felt the vibration of the engines through the metal support—and a faint rustling of cloth on the flight deck above. She climbed towards the circle of open space three meters overhead, then hung on the ladder, her head just below the flight deck, listening intently.

She imaged the flight deck in her mind. The chief-pilot chair faced directly away from the well toward the navigation screens. The second-pilot station sat at quarter-angle before a bank of table controls jutting partway onto the deck. She tried to visualize the Li Fawn's costume that she'd only briefly glimpsed, and remembered the wide vision track across the top of the helmet. If the Li Fawn was at second pilot, he'd see her in his peripheral vision. She listened, trying to identify the place he had chosen.

Another rustling—to the right of the well, then a creak of a chair she recognized from all the times Chandra had shifted weight in it during flight. The Li Fawn sat at chief pilot. She eased herself upward, raising her eyes above the floor of the flight deck.

The false Vang sat in his chair, his back to her. His laser device sat on a nearby ledge, within quick reach. He had changed to loose dark robes that covered nearly all his lean body, and she saw no sign of his earlier disguise. The shape of his head beneath his wide cowl seemed strangely elongated, too tall for a normal skull. She remembered a blurred image from a Guild file that showed a feathered crest and other hints of an avian ancestry. The Li Fawn had been damn elusive to have only that vague indication in Guild memory. She wished she could see more of him, then checked her curiosity with a grim smile. *Later, Bartlett.*

The spy's pale multi-fingered hands moved over the controls, their skin strangely mottled, almost as if bruised. He clucked to himself with an odd high-pitched clacking, then flipped a toggle on another panel. She watched him, surprised at his easy handling of *Ariel's* controls. How had he learned to fly a Guild ship? He had already proved his craftiness to her—too many times—and now showed other gifts. She wouldn't underestimate him again.

She looked around the rest of the flight deck, then tried to crane backward for a view to the observation lounge, but saw no one else. She hoped all her crew had been off-ship when the Li Fawn entered it, for their own safety. It was not unlikely. Morgen's inquiries could have lasted well after dark, and he would have kept Chandra with him.

The Li Fawn clucked to itself, punched more controls. She saw the radar tracings on the large screen above his head shift slightly. He reached to the side to another control, turning his head as he did so, and she quickly ducked down out of sight, then inched upward again. She studied the screens, trying to read the figures at too far a distance, and guessed they were still headed out-system. To the Li Fawn's mother ship?

She looked upward again into the well, wishing she dared climb past to the lounge for a better view, but that would have to wait. She quietly eased down the ladder, careful to make no sound on the metal rungs with her boots, and retraced her path to their hiding-place. As she circled the well, she keyed the occupancy display on each of the crew suites, but found no one. The ship was empty except for two humans and one Li Fawn, and the Li Fawn had all the cards.

Tanner started as she stepped back into the storage compartment, then visibly relaxed.

"You were gone a long time."

"Subjective reality." He scowled in annoyance, but she was fast learning not to care. The loss of charm was turning mutual, and she looked at him resentfully.

"The Li Fawn's on the flight deck," she said. "We're heading out-system. I didn't see anybody else aboard."

"Did you get a weapon?"

"There are no weapons, Vaughn. Not with the Li Fawn sitting two feet from the pistol locker."

"Perhaps something else that could be a weapon?"

"I'll think about it. There isn't much." She smiled ruefully. "T'wing made too many problems poking around where she oughtn't. Once she nearly froze herself solid playing with a portable fire extinguisher. It was easier to modify the internal defenses into computer control."

"And the Li Fawn has the control."

"That he does."

"And we don't have the real Vang pilot with his laser suit, and we can't get at the one weapon you do have. So what do we do now?"

"We wait."

Chapter 15

In the slave pens aboard *Ngoh Ge*, Lume woke again, trembling from bad dreams, to the harsh light and narrow confines of his cell. The dreams came every night now, violent dreams of sky-borne destruction, a harrying wind, and a malevolent vapor who mocked him. *Madringa*, she called herself, and took a hundred shapes, each with a gleaming single red eye. *I AM THE LIGHT!* she cried and stabbed at him with her ruby light, slicing him to pieces. *I AM THE LIGHT!* he cried in his ecstasy, only to wake moments later sweat-drenched and shuddering in his cell.

He had slept face-down on the hard floor, his left arm curled beneath him. His arm throbbed dully from lack of circulation, and the pain slowly intensified. He cradled his arm, clenching his teeth against the shooting, tingling pain. The harsh ceiling lights glared, too bright for human eyes, but he stared up at them, half-wishing for blindness if he stared long enough, a stupid wish of defiance that had the gibber of near insanity. He could welcome even insanity, if it spared him the dreams. *Death is better*, he thought.

The pain in his arm sank to a tolerable level and he moved it cautiously, then slowly raised himself to a seated position and drew up his knees. How long had he been here? He had lost track of time in the endless day of the ceiling lights. His world was a room two by three by three meters, with metal walls, a pan for his daily ration of unidentifiable food, a jar of tepid water. He hoped they would kill him soon. He clung to the prospect of death like a drowning man clinging to a battered rock.

He looked down at his hands, studying the grimed wrinkles of his knuckles. Then he carefully examined his knees, pushing with one finger at a scab, then pulling at a string on the ragged collar of the blue fabric that surrounded it. McCrory uniform, what's left of it. *McCrory man, what's left of you.* He sank his chin on his knees, escaping into memories.

He remembered that last bright morning on Shann when he had found the Light. He and Tayna had met earlier with a local delegation of Shenda, supervised by a poker-faced Guildsman. The meeting went as it usually did with Shenda, but Lume hadn't minded. He liked the Shenda with their large bumbling bodies and elaborate manners. Tayna had less patience with them, Roycrai even less, but even Tayna thought they made progress that day.

A buyer could find at least a few madringals at every bazaar stall, and some clan stalls sold nothing else, with hundreds of goddesses carefully lined up in rows, each tiny deity regarding the world with a single mirrored eye. The statuette was only a few hand-spans tall, abstract in form and with a slender grace of line that caught the eye. It looked nothing like a Shenda, as did some lesser Shenda gods, but as the Beraquit stallkeeper carefully explained, the gods wore their true form when moved to destruction. A slender pillar, scored in swirling patterns downward from a jeweled eye, was apparently Madringa's catastrophic form.

They had detoured back through the bazaar as they returned to Portside, and Lume had paused by another madringal display. Among the array of wooden and pewter statuettes, he saw a madringal made of fire-blackened metal. A ruby gleamed with crimson fire above its eye. He picked it up to admire the shadow patterns in its damaged surface.

Tayna had walked ahead, then retraced her steps when she realized Lume had strayed behind. "What's up?" she asked. He handed the madringal to her. "Nice," she said, "but we already have several of this type." She put the statuette back on the table, and Lume promptly picked it up again.

"One more won't hurt. Four to one that's a genuine ruby."

"Fire-cracked rubies don't have much value."

"Don't be a philistine, sis."

"Who's a philistine?" she demanded irritably, then grinned. "Okay, one to you, twerp. Come on. Roycrai is waiting."

Lume grimaced sourly. "Mustn't keep Roycrai waiting," he said. "Never that." Tayna made an exasperated sound, but Lume ignored it. Their arguments about Roycrai never got anywhere, anyway. Roycrai was Tayna's only topic of blind stupidity.

He paid the Shenda stallkeeper, put the madringal in his pouch, then followed his sister along the bazaar street. She walked with long strides, her blonde hair swinging, and gathered some appreciative glances from several Terran traders along the street. Lume ambled along behind, liking the day, his pouch thumping his thigh with a comfortable weight as he walked.

That night they had sat in *Crystal's* ship lounge. Lume fingered the new madringal as he relaxed, admiring its lines. Roycrai had noticed his interest, and, typically, had begun another smart-mouthed lecture, this time opining that primitives often made common-day objects into something outsiders mistook as art.

"The Shenda aren't primitives," Lume said, glaring at him.

"No? Look at that statue. Take away the pretty design in the skirt, put a metal bracket in the eyehole, and you've got a warp hydrocoupler. Just imagine: the moon explodes, blam! and thousands of hydrocouplers rain to the ground from taxicabs, jaunt-hoppers, and cargo-freighters, all shivered to pieces by the atmospheric shock wave. A Shenda wanders by and picks up a hydrocoupler, shivers in religious ecstasy. Zap! A new religion founded on relics of ancient aircraft." He smirked.

"You're crazy," Lume said angrily. Then he had said some other things and they had quarrelled, and Roycrai set out to prove his theory just to show Lume. He sawed open one of the madringals from storage, installed a battery and bulb for a directional beam, then added several interlink circuits. He had tinkered at the thing all the next day, even though Tayna had asked him twice to stop. She had finally left the room, thoroughly upset. She always hated the way they fought.

"Why do you always start something, Roy?" Lume had asked. "It only hurts Tayna."

Roycrai made a final adjustment and switched on the battery. The madringal gleamed dimly along its seams, its wide eye blazing forth like an alien flashlight. Lume regarded it sourly.

"Who's fighting?" Roycrai asked. "I'm just demonstrating a scientific theory. You're the one with problems, little brother." He tightened a final gasket.

"There: your ancient hydrocoupler. Give me your new one and I'll fix it, too."

"You're crazy, Roycrai, really crazy. What have you got inside you, anyway? Don't you ever care about anybody?"

"Tsk. Let's not be nasty, Lume." Roycrai turned to him, smiling unpleasantly. "Crazy, is it, my little toy? Well, call it 'Mad Roy's Light,' then." He examined the glowing madringal with satisfaction. "Yes, I like that. A nice title—romantic, like you, Lume."

Lume balled his fists. "I'd like to deck you, Roy."

"Ah, but that would hurt Tayna's feelings. You care a lot about feelings, little brother. And if she had to choose between you and me, who do you think would win?" He turned back to his bench. "A woman gets one-minded about the man who beds her, especially when he's good at it as I am. Too bad you can't compete there. Tsk."

Lume had turned on his heel and stamped out, seething. The irony of that last argument haunted Lume, for Roycrai had been right, in a way. Roycrai had nagged him about the new madringal, just to annoy him, and finally had dragged him off to the McCrory substation lab for "tests."

"This isn't allowed," Lume protested, as Roycrai eased open the lab door, looking around.

"Quiet. Nobody's here at night, anyway. Give me your Light." Reluctantly, Lume handed him the new madringal.

Roycrai turned it over in his hands, then slipped it onto the scanner table. "Hmm. Not hollow like the others. Metal, too. Let's see what's inside."

Roycrai snapped on the scanner. As the machine warmed, the madringal responded with a high-pitched whine, then abruptly flooded the lab with a pulsing ruby light through its glowing eye.

"What the . . . ?" Lume stepped back in alarm.

They stared at the madringal in bewilderment, then looked wildly around the lab, now filled with the shuddering reddish light. It clung to every metal surface, creeping eerily along each seam, each cornered edge. Lume raised his hands and saw the same strange fire on his skin and clothing, writhing up his arms in an iridescent malevolent dance. The cycle intensified, shifting rapidly in new spectra, until the very walls echoed its violent hum and seemed to ripple uneasily. In the corridor beyond, Lume heard a great wind approach them, bearing Madringa upon her storm of destruction. . . .

"Turn it off!" he cried, and slapped at the scanner switch. The light slowly died, pulsing redly until it flickered out.

"So . . ." Roycrai said in an awed tone. "A moon is shattered by divine anger, and now ancient replicas of Madringa revere the memory. And, among the thousands of copies, a few of the originals, Madringa herself."

"What do you mean?"

"What I mean, little brother, is that fifteen millenia ago, when you and I and the Daruma were still living in caves, the ancient Shenda explored the entire Orion Arm using a star-drive beyond anything we've ever developed. We put our warp-units into canisters eight meters wide; the Shenda put theirs into that." He pointed at the madringal.

"This? A star-drive?"

"Or a component. Didn't you feel the tug of null-space? The walls *rippled*, Lume. And all in a device a few hands high." He touched the madringal warily, then picked it up. Deep in the substation building, Lume heard an alarm-siren begin to wail. "Let's get out of here."

"But . . ."

"Come on!" Roycrai stuffed the madringal in

Lume's pouch and grabbed his arm. Outside the substation, they ducked into a shadowed porchway as four men pounded past, then made for *Crystal*.

"Don't worry, little brother," Roycrai had said smugly after the argument Lume had lost. "We'll make our fortune with our pretty Light."

"Sure," Lume retorted and looked vainly at Tayna's set face.

Tayna . . .

Lume flinched away from her memory. Remembering her through waking dreams was enough; awake, he tried to forget how she had died. Instead, he wished all his energies focused on one thing, hating the Li Fawn for what they had done to Tayna. A shadow moved across the glass of the observation window, and he threw back his head, glaring defiantly at the shadowy watcher.

Lord Chaat turned away from the cell door, dissatisfied. This Lume had a secret and would not tell. The human's defiance had earned a grudging respect from Chaat, though it did the human little good. Occasionally slave animals showed a flash of the spirit and drive that characterized Li Fawn—surprising, unexpected, but undeniable. The Li Fawn had learned by unpleasant experience to weed such animals from their servants, and rarely made mistakes after their thousands of years of able mastery. This one would need to be destroyed once Chaat had his secret, and Chaat would consider the lesson in his plans for Terra.

Although his spies had brought him the intelligence, he had not at first realized the Terrans were also outsiders to Sagittarius, but dwelt in a half-dozen systems well beyond Shann. It promised an even more fertile field than he had expected. Two years before, Chaat had caught a lifeless hulk of a

Daruma merchant ship, turned inside out by a faulty hyper-jump, among the lifeless suns at the edge of Home-Space. He had followed its trajectory to Hrauru into this new garden. With gardens beyond: he had broken part of the ship code in the crippled hulk, and had learned of the names and places in Sagittarius. Later his capture of a Guild jump-ship had added still more to his store of information for the Great Plan.

Chaat climbed the narrow metal stairs from the slave pens, hesitated at the doorway to the control room, then decided to delay for another visit to Chaat-lama in her nursery. His fourth wife was not beautiful, but her three fingers bespoke her high breeding. She was unusual in Li Fawn noblewomen, for she had loved her first lord with an unhealthy fervency and now hated Chaat with an equal passion for his necessary destruction of that lord. The mating had been by force, and still she had not resigned herself. He had bound her afterwards while the sons grew in her belly, believing her wild threats to end her "slavery" by suicide. That a Li Fawn princess would believe herself an equal of slave animals . . . this Chaat did not understand. He did not understand her at all, and because of this, he was fascinated by her—enough that his senior wives had made pointed complaint.

At the doorway of her nursery, he took a Baruti from the cluster by the door and entered the darkened room. Chaat-lama lay on her pillows, her wrists bound to a padded ring by the bed. Blood ringed the bonds, naked skin showing where she had scraped the fur away, and her struggles had disarranged her clothing, revealing her lower body. A momentary thought of lust passed through his mind at the sight of her, but the sons were nursing and he had no hope of sexual response until they had been weaned. If she'd respond the next time. Why would she not be reasonable?

In a cradle at the side his tiny sons waved their limbs distractedly, kicking at each other with infant-weak legs. The Si-hah nurse retreated reluctantly on stalky legs as he approached, her several compound eyes still fixed on her charges in singleminded devotion. Chaat prudently waited until she had moved back beyond the reach of her sting, then leaned over the cradle, inspecting his sons with pride. Two-fingered sons, not three-fingered like Chaat-lama but sons after their father. He teased the crest of the darker-skinned one, and the infant batted at him, opening his mouth in a croak. Then he turned back to his wife. Chaat-lama glared at him.

"My greetings, wife."

"Damn you," she spat. "And your weakling sons, whom I despise."

"That aside," Chaat said affably, "how are you feeling today? The physician has told me you are quickly recovering your strength. This is good news."

"Damn you," she repeated, and turned away her face. The Baruti's yellowish illumination touched the hollows of her throat with shadows, gleamed upon the line of cheek and hands and thigh. Chaat knelt beside her and smoothed her crest into better order, but she flinched away from him violently, thrashing against her bonds. Chaat hastily withdrew his hand.

"Can't you be reasonable?" he said despite himself, and heard the plaintiveness in his voice. Chaat-lama stared at him, then laughed harshly, humorlessly, her voice soaked with her own pain. It was a revelation neither wanted, and Chaat stood up, breathing hard as he looked down at her.

"My regards to you," he said tightly, and abruptly quit the room. As he walked away, he heard a single sob and then adamant silence.

He forced himself back into his poise as he
returned to the control room, disciplined by years
of training and the skills bred into his genes. He felt
his mind grow cold again, and gratefully resumed
the accustomed ease of that clear thinking. He was
Command, and he relished the clarity of emotion
brought him by his caste.

He took his chair in the control room and arranged
his robes about him. The Eschoni chained to the
floor had been replaced by a younger female. A Controller proffered a written report on ship functions,
then another on supplies, fuel, and the count in the
slave pens. A guard from the lower decks was disciplined for inattention. Chaat relaxed in his chair,
attending to these minor tasks, and waited.

"Sire!" A controller seated at a control board swiveled in his chair, his expression surprised. Chaat
glared at him, and the youngling quickly schooled
his face.

"Sire," he repeated more respectfully, "a ship
approaches. A Guild ship that offers our own recognition signals!" He lost his poise again in his surprise, his crest rising in his agitation. Chaat glared
at him again, and the boy tried desperately to control
himself before he angered his lord even more. Chaat
relented a bit.

"What Li Fawn is aboard?" he asked. There was
only one who could be approaching from Shann, and
Chaat felt satisfaction—and a hope his spy had succeeded. The controller tapped out an answer to the
approaching ship.

"The spy Tsor, sire. He asks entry to *Ngoh Ge*."

"Permit it."

Another controller seated nearby nodded acknowledgement, and punched the sequence to open the
ship-bay doors. A screen above Ai-lan's head lighted,
giving a picture of the ship bay. Figures scurried

towards the inner lock as the siren hooted. As the dock cleared, the telltales on the ship doors blinked furiously as a jet of vapor stimulated the Ai-Baruti embedded in the metal. One bank of Ai-Baruti failed as the creatures succumbed to their latest exposure to the fall in air pressure, and Chaat watched Ai-lan quietly order replacement.

"The efficiency rate on the latest strain, Ai-lan?" he asked her.

"Eight exposures, my lord. The Rev-Baruti we took from Larat's ship has significantly improved the breed. He had a competent Baruti controller."

"You still reject partial shielding?"

"Yes, Lord. I hope to develop Ai-Baruti to live permanently on the outer hull. I ask your permission to continue breeding for vacuum-tolerant strains."

"Granted."

Chaat watched the ship-bay evolutions in Ai-lan's screen. The bay door irised open, and he heard a small snort of exasperation from Ai-Lan as another row of her Baruti failed. But the continued exposure would be short: already the tiny gleam of the ship on the blackness was visible in the opening to space. It grew larger as it drifted towards *Ngoh Ge,* first a tiny toy, its prow light winking redly, then growing larger and larger until its bulk filled the frame of the bay opening. A puff of flame at its belly checked its drift, and the ship landed neatly on the metal deck. The hold doors closed behind it. Ai-lan repressurized the ship bay and the spy emerged from its air lock. A dozen scrabbling shapes rushed onto the bay floor to their stations.

"Tell the spy Tsor to report to me immediately."

"Sire." Her nimble fingers worked her controls.

A dock slave on the bay floor lurched violently, its claws clutching at its control collar, then rushed away from its post towards the spy. It crouched before the spy, its head craned upward and its jaw worked briefly. The spy looked up at the monitor, then hurried forward towards the inner lock, passing quickly out of view. Chaat studied the Guild ship as he waited, admiring its sleek lines as a student of good ship architecture, and thought of the possibilities in his new capture.

He was still mulling over his ideas when the spy appeared in the doorway of Control. The spy abased himself, and Chaat signaled to approach. Spies were a different caste, allowed more independence and self-guidance than others, but Chaat had been well-trained in their management and had refined his training since. He well knew the value of spies.

"Your report?" he barked. The spy threw himself on the deck, covering his face, and visibly trembled. Chaat's feigned displeasure turned into a sharp pang of disappointment. Nineteen was an able spy, even gifted; Chaat would regret losing him.

"Sire," the spy began.

"Yes, yes," Chaat answered impatiently. Then the spy recovered himself and rose up without permission to his knees, then settled back on his heels. He looked at Chaat steadily, his face partly shadowed by his cowl.

"I do not have all your answers," the spy said formally, "but I have facts you may find applicable. This McCrory, Lume, was dealing with the Shenda for a consignment of Shenda artifacts, called madringals. The artifact is a small statuette of Shenda design, very numerous in the bazaars. 'Madringal' may be the Shenda word corrupted into the phrase 'Mad Roy's Light.' I suggest a linguistic study for probabilities."

"It shall be done. Continue, spy."

"Lume became very excited about one madringal

in particular, and tested it in the McCrory lab. His ship left Shann hurriedly thereafter."

"Why was he excited?"

"That I don't know, my lord, nor does the Guild. But the Shenda once had a high science. I have examined the madringals in the bazaar but found nothing but figurines of stone or glass."

Chaat considered a moment. "How large is this madringal?"

"Three finger-lengths high, my lord, a small object."

"Continue."

"The Guildswoman Bartlett is on Shann."

Chaat scowled. "This Guildswoman seems to be everywhere. Do you know why she was there?"

"No, except that she interested herself in a madringal at the bazaar, walked with a particular Shenda, and returned to surprise me as I questioned the Shenda. Her interference was such that I could not safely return in my own ship, so I appropriated hers. Her crew had left it unattended."

Chaat chuckled, not minding if the spy saw his approval—and probably better that he did. A spy's loyalty was intense and could not be guarded without some encouragement. The effect on the spy was obvious; his reddish eyes gleamed with pleasure, and he straightened his back with pride. And he well deserved it. Chaat rose to his feet.

"So! A small device, perhaps a madringal! I will act on this information, spy. Come with me. I'll need your assistance as Lume shows us which object on his ship is the Light."

"Sire!" Chaat left Control, the spy following.

Chapter 16

Jennan lifted her head, listening. The shadows of the compartment concealed Tanner's expression, but he, too, sat motionless, his head cocked towards the interior of the ship. Sounds were hard to judge through the muffling walls, but they had heard nothing for several minutes, and, before that, the faint cycling of the lock.

"Where are we? The Li Fawn ship?" Tanner whispered.

"Landed somewhere, obviously."

"But where?" Tanner demanded.

"Let's go see, Vaughn. Move your foot so I can stand up."

They maneuvered in the confined space, and then Jennan squeezed by the trader. He followed her quietly into the suite, then into the common-room. Jennan listened, but heard no sounds above, no sound at all except the familiar clicks and ventilator hush of *Ariel* at rest. She listened at the air lock door, and then they retraced her earlier path up the well ladder. The flight deck was empty.

Jennan clambered over the rail, Tanner closely

after her. "There's your weapon, Vaughn," she said, pointing, "in that storage compartment beneath the gravity controls. . . . No, not that one, over there." Tanner keyed open the compartment and removed the laser-pistol from its prongs, weighed it in his grasp.

"I say we may need it," he said.

"I'm not arguing." She activated the exterior monitors and gasped.

Ariel lay within a wide ship bay more than five hundred meters long and a third as high. It bustled with activity. To the left were two scout cruisers, lean and dark, attended by a scurrying pack of nimble-footed multi-legged aliens with naked reddish skin and a vestigial carapace on their shoulders and upper arms. Near them stood a taller alien, a bird-like humanoid in a lean gray uniform. He stood in an arrogant stance, a small device held in his spare-fingered hands, and his crested head turned languidly as he watched his charges.

Behind him were a bank of interior doors, winking with strange ovoid lights with a fluid gleam. Another bird-human emerged from the center door, made some adjustments at a nearby panel, then walked over to the other alien. The two clacked at each other briefly over the pulsing hum of machinery.

"Li Fawn?" Tanner asked.

"Those two fit the descriptions. Let's see what else is here." She turned the scan-dial on the monitor, giving them a slow panorama of the huge bay. Throughout they saw isolated Li Fawn among scurrying groups of other aliens, with the Li Fawn obviously in control. To the far right the camera picked up a small ship, its metal sides scarred by laser fire.

"That's *Crystal!*" Tanner exclaimed.

"Yes," Jennan said grimly. Beyond the McCrory scout she also saw the disassembled hull parts of a Guild ship, and she recognized the emblazon on the prow-tip. Maleto's ship had been thought lost in jump a year ago, one of the occasional casualties of star-drive. She pushed the record button and took pictures. The Guild would have a bit more than rumors and an ambushed Vang. She felt again her cold anger at the aliens who walked about, unconcerned, on the deck below.

She continued panning the camera and studied the hold doors behind *Ariel,* and clicked in a request for analysis from the ship computer. The printer chattered and she glanced at it, measuring the ship's meteorite laser-screens against alloyed steel. Or she could invert *Ariel* and blast them horizontally with her engine exhaust. She had no intention of staying around here long, now that she had control of *Ariel* again.

Tanner noticed her computer request. "What are you going to do?"

"Get out of here, and I don't care much about Li Fawn property in doing so." She queried in the two options and waited for the computer's recommendation.

"Option One," it said in its flat voice, "forty percent chance of failure due to variants in metal stress. Option Two, twenty percent chance of failure due to variants in attitude control and reflection of ship exhaust onto unshielded hull. Recommend Option Two, assuming Vang as pilot."

"And team-first as pilot?" she asked.

The machine considered. "Thirty percent chance of failure. Recommendation as before."

"Other possible options?" she asked.

"Possibility of voluntary opening of bay doors?"

"Probably nonexistent. Can you scan to locate the bay-door controls?"

"Assume non-detection of my scans preferred?"

"Definitely."

"No. Low-level scan indicates the bay is heavily shielded; the energy needed to pierce the walls to other levels would be detected. Second factor: ship technology is curiously incomplete. Presence of several life-forms suggest biocombinant technology. Control of biocomponents essential to operation of machines, perhaps including bay-doors. Can you acquire that control?"

Jennan sighed. "No. I wouldn't know where to begin, assuming the 'biocomponents,' as you call them, would respond to a human controller. Recommendation?"

"Option Two."

Tanner had grown increasingly impatient during their recital. "What about *Crystal*?" he protested. "The crew might still be alive."

"Or dead. You heard the computer. We haven't any workable scanners here. Tell me where to find them, Vaughn." She pointed at the screen. "Look at the size of that ship-bay and scale up to the rest of the ship. They could be anywhere within three square kilometers, all of it patrolled by Li Fawn and their slaves. Speaking of which, we may be running out of time." One of the Li Fawn controllers had gathered up a group of crab-men and was moving them towards *Ariel*.

"Maybe they won't come inside," Tanner muttered.

"Maybe they will, too." She swung towards him, exasperated. "What *is* your problem, Vaughn?" They glared at each other.

"I'm not leaving Lume and Tayna behind," he said.

She shrugged, knowing it would infuriate him. "*Crystal* stole an artifact and took its chances. I'm not going on a useless rescue mission when I've got information the Guild needs."

Impasse. Tanner smiled grimly and raised the laser-pistol.

"This says I win," he said.

"Don't be stupid. How will you get *Ariel* out of here?"

"Fly her out."

"Sure. The flight deck's security-locked. It responds to Vang and designated crewmen. I never added you, Vaughn. You touch the controls without my priority cue and *Ariel* does zero, even if you could fly the maneuver we need."

Tanner hesitated. "I've still got the pistol."

"That I can see. So?"

"I'm not leaving them behind!" he raged. "Look at that deck: those are slaves, Jennan. You're human, too. How can you just leave them to that?"

"I'm a Guildsman first."

The pistol dropped. "Obviously," Tanner said with contempt. He tossed the pistol on the control counter. "So do what you like, Guildswoman. And when Tarthe gets done, as he will, the Guild won't have much use for you, either. What goes around comes around." He turned away in dismissal.

Jennan blinked back sudden tears. She opened her mouth, then clamped it shut stubbornly as she turned back to the controls. Let him bluff if he must; she was still team-first, with her duty to the Guild. As her hand reached for the drive controls, she raised her eyes to the screen and froze.

Two more Li Fawn had emerged from the inner doors, and, in front of them, stumbled a brown-haired man, weak and emaciated, dressed in the tattered remnants of a McCrory uniform. One Li Fawn was dressed in golden robes and walked with an arrogant swagger that instinctively raised Jennan's hackles. He pushed at the man's back, forcing him roughly across the deck towards the McCrory ship. Behind them drifted a leaner Li Fawn in dark robes, its face concealed by a hood, its movements furtive. Her spy. It had to be. She glared at the image.

The spy saw the crab-man crew approaching *Ariel* and gestured abruptly at their Li Fawn supervisor. The other hesitated, as if to argue. A sharp bark from the golden noble brought instant response. The supervisor genuflected, almost cringingly, then hastily herded his charges away from the ship.

Thank you, spy, she thought grimly. *Want to loot my ship yourself, do you? We'll just see about that.* Again, she wondered about the spy. *What are his reasons?* She shook her head angrily to clear her thoughts. *Not now, Bartlett.*

The two Li Fawn and their captive disappeared into the McCrory scout. She looked at Tanner, who stood with back turned from her, arms crossed, staring haughtily at the other wall.

"Vaughn," she said softly.

"What?" His voice held the faintest trace of triumph, and she decided to not indulge him. This would be a one-girl operation, anyway. They only had one pistol.

She picked it up from the counter and tucked it in her waistband. "Wait here. If the Li Fawn want in, don't let them."

She went over the well railing, ignoring his spluttering, and ran lightly to the air lock door. As the outer door irised open, she jumped, catching herself on the ledge and letting herself fall lightly the two meters to the hold deck. She darted behind one of

Ariel's landing pods and transferred the pistol from her waistband to her hand. Then she considered ways and means.

The spy had landed *Ariel* near the hold doors, next to a line of equipment with useful bulks and shadows. In fact, as she noticed with some outrage, the bay doors had nearly clipped one of *Ariel*'s pods. Nice piloting, true, but she'd rather the spy play with somebody else's spaceship. She measured the distance overhead with her eyes, planning the take-off maneuver. Then she examined the route to the McCrory ship more carefully.

She peered around the pod, looking at each preoccupied Li Fawn in turn, waiting for her moment. Then she ran forward, keeping low, to the concealment of an offhandler. She edged forward, keeping behind the line of machinery, once dropping to her stomach to crawl forward on hands and toes behind a long cargo-arm. She reached the McCrory ship pod without an alarm.

The scout's air lock faced the main hold, without shadows. She circled the base of the ship, looking for another access. Near another pod she found a cargo port to the lower hold. She put her pistol back in her waistband to use both hands on the open-levers, then carefully lowered the panel. Grasping the sides of the port, she jumped up, reversing in midair to land on the ledge with her buttocks and thighs. She quickly drew up her legs and began climbing the short passage.

The open cargo-port admitted some light into the dark tunnel, allowing her to see the inner hold-door above her head. She climbed carefully, trying not to make a racket with her boots on the metal. When she reached the inner door, she raised the lever in the circle-lock and turned it slowly. The door opened easily and swung inward. She reached into the dark hold for a doorstop, found a small box, and propped the hatch open.

A murmur of voices filtered down from an upper deck through a ventilation shaft, and she silently crossed the hold towards the sound.

She paused a moment, trying to remember McCrory ship design. True, she hadn't been that interested in the study and the memories were sluggish. A Vang water-ship flashed into clear view and she tossed it aside, then her own jump-ship, a Daruma multi-cargo freighter, a Terran diplomatic courier (ah, Terran!), a Hrauru mud-skidder, a Vang . . .

She leaned her forehead against the ventilator grating, trying to concentrate. Nothing. Well, she'd go it blind. Since the voices came down the shaft, she'd climb up.

She pried at the grating with her fingers and pulled it free, then put her head and shoulders into the wide opening. She reached out with her hand, swinging her arm across the dark enclosed space. Her fingers brushed a metal bar on the opposite side of the shaft, then ran up a vertical crossbar to a horizontal rung. A ladder. She tugged on the bar, gauging its strength and condition as a precaution. She nervously rechecked her pistol and transferred it inside her tunic above her belt. Then she pulled herself into the musty darkness of the ventilation shaft.

She climbed silently towards the voices, passing hand over hand in careful rhythm with her moving feet. She passed an access grid at the next level, then reached another grating four meters above. The voices drifted through the grating, almost distinguishable. She carefully pushed open the grating and slipped to her feet on the polished corridor floor.

"I ask you again, human," said a harsh, croaking

voice, "and I won't ask much longer. Where is the Light?"

Jennan heard a thin murmur in response, which suddenly rose to a pained yelp. The sound impelled her forward. She pulled the pistol from her tunic and crept on, unconsciously drawing back her lips to bare her teeth. She placed each foot with care as she neared the door, her muscles taut, every sense focused on that rectangle of light and what lay within.

The McCrory man crouched on the deck in the middle of the room, huddled forward on knees and elbows. The golden-robed Li Fawn stood over him, his back to Jennan. She saw no sign of the spy, then heard a small crash in the farther room as someone searched through the stores there. She raised the laser-pistol, aiming at the base of the Li Fawn's skull. Then she hesitated, finding it hard to push herself to that killing blast. Reasons. What if he has reasons? *Am I nonhuman to even wonder?* The Li Fawn stooped again, twisting at the human's shoulder, and the McCrory man rolled violently away.

As he sprawled, he saw her in the doorway behind them. His eyes widened and then filled with an incredulous mad hope that made her catch her breath. Then the man suddenly caught himself, realizing what he had revealed, and looked up at the Li Fawn. The Li Fawn whirled in a fan of golden robes, squawked in surprise, and promptly threw his body towards the far doorway.

She reflexively squeezed the trigger on her pistol. A blinding flash hit the far wall. Missed. Jennan swung the laser snout hurriedly as the Li Fawn whisked around the edge of the far door, missing again.

"Stop blasting!" cried the man, and she promptly obeyed. The man pulled himself up on a counter

and smacked his hand on a control panel by the far
door. The door whisked shut, and he savagely
snapped the lock lever home. He panted, trembling,
then turned and grinned at her insanely.

"No way out," he said hoarsely. "No comm controls. Their slave pen!" He laughed, then coughed
and leaned weakly against the door, as if his emotion
had exhausted the rest of his strength. As it likely
had. She crossed to him quickly and caught him with
one arm as he nearly collapsed.

"Come on. We're getting out of here."

His arms went around her, clinging tightly, and
he abruptly kissed her. She struggled against him,
but he only held her tighter, his lips pressing painfully down on hers. Then she laughed deep in her
throat, and threw her other arm around his neck to
pull him closer into their embrace. Finally he broke
it off, though he loosened little of his hold on her.

"My name is Lume," he said. "And you are a won-
der-ful kisser."

"I have a feeling anyone would have suited," she
said dryly. As he bent his head towards her again,
she quickly interposed her palm. "Encores later,
Lume. Time is getting a little short."

"He can't get out of there soon," Lume said. "No
way." He looked at the door-lock with a proprietary
affection.

"But my Guild ship will, get out of here, I mean.
Are there any more of you?"

Lume sobered, his expression changing like a
cloth across a chalk-tablet. "No."

"No Daruma, either?"

"Daruma? No, I never saw any Daruma. I don't
really know. Is it important?"

She pulled away from him and did not answer. No
way to search, but Maleto would understand, even

approve, even if Tanner could not. Guild came first,
even if it made too many expendable.

Including yourself, Jennan. For the first time, she
fully understood Master Larovi's conduct—saw it for
what it was, the protection of the Guild, of fundamental order, of family and loyalty and the rightness
of things. Not human treachery, for all its common
guise—but the essence of Daruma honor.

But to a human it still seemed betrayal, to be
so used and thrown away. *Master, I see but cannot
see. . . .*

She shook herself abruptly, looked into Lume's
puzzled gray eyes inches from her own. "Come on,"
she said. She drew him after her, but he twisted
away.

"Just a sec." He threw himself down in front of a
panel cupboard, punched a code into the lock, then
rummaged inside. He pulled out a Shenda statue,
one she had seen in the hundreds in the bazaar. As
he turned back to her, he saw her expression. "No,
I'm not crazy." He got to his feet, staggering a little,
then joined her at the door. "What's your name,
anyway?"

"Jennan."

"You are a beautiful lady, Jennan. Let us get the
hell out of here."

They retraced her steps to outside. He helped her
lift the cargo door to toggle it shut, then stumbled
after her towards *Ariel*, the statuette held tightly to
his chest. He breathed heavily, weaving in his steps,
and she caught him around the waist, hurrying him
forward.

"Gonna make it," he said hoarsely. "Don't worry,
Jennan."

She helped him from shadow to shadow, keeping
one eye on the Li Fawn and another on the ship

ahead. As they reached the last off-loader, he sank
to the deck, his breath coming in painful rasps.

"One more run, Lume," she said, holding him.

"Right."

Together they shambled across the last space, and
Jennan flinched at the hoarse shout of alarm as they
were spotted. She hoisted Lume onto the lock edge
and jumped at the lock control. Her palm slapped
on the plate, and the lock opened, causing Lume to
fall through the door. She jumped onto the ledge
and dragged him inside. As the door sighed shut,
she felt *Ariel's* engines rumble and then choke into
silence.

"No, Vaughn!" she shouted, and dragged Lume
into the common-room. Then she leaped for the well
ladder.

"I told you they wouldn't work," she muttered as
Vaughn hastily vacated the flight chair.

"I only thought . . ." he began, then demanded:
"Where have you been?"

"Shut up. Computer, engage engines!"

Her hands moved deftly over the board, bringing
Ariel to roaring life. She spared a glance for the
screen and grinned as she saw the Li Fawn scurry
for cover. A laser bolt splashed on the hull, a puny
attempt of desperation.

"Not *my* ship!" she shouted at the screen.

Ariel lifted gracefully on her under-jets and swung
to a horizontal level, her prow pointed at the inner
hold, her engines aimed straight at the hold doors.
Jennan pushed the nose jets to full thrust as she
fed power to the engines, trying to hold the ship
stationary. *Ariel's* engines blasted at the metal of the
bay-doors, an unleashed fury that roared in the
enclosed space, melted the row of nearby machinery, and filled the bay with choking fumes.

Li Fawn guards burst from the inner bay-doors,

then hastily retreated into the safety of the interior levels. A group of crab-men panicked and ran wildly through the licking flames rebounding from the hull-doors, falling in agony as the heat burned the flesh from their bodies. Jennan bit her lip.

She fed more thrust to the engines, and *Ariel* began to inch forward as her engines overpowered the nose thrustors. Jennan hastily backed off the engines and allowed *Ariel* to drift backwards again. The ship trembled under the strain.

"Come on, come on," she muttered, watching the bay-doors in the rearward screen. She keyed her sidejets forward in their pivots and keyed them on, adding their thrust to the nose jets, and increased engine power again.

Ariel was swathed in flames of naked power from stern to bow. Telltales lit up across her boards as the heat ate away at the ship's hull, tripping alarms steadily as dangerous overheating crept up *Ariel's* body. And still the bay-doors held.

Thirty percent. Well, they were good odds for a try.

Then, with a whoosh, the bay-doors gave way, exploding into space. Atmosphere gushed out in a hurricane that lifted equipment and bodies and tossed them into the void, tore at the fittings on the walls, filled the bay with a choking cloud of ice crystals. Claxons sounded faintly through the roar of escaping atmosphere. Jennan swung *Ariel* on her gyros, flipping her end for end, wreaking more damage as the ship's exhaust swept over the inner hold. Then she cut the forward jets with a sweep of her hands and throttled full power to the engines. *Ariel* shot through the breached hull, escaping into the depths beyond.

"Whooee!" she cried exultantly. "Thirty percent!" Tanner yelled hoarsely beside her. With a triumphant flourish, Jennan slapped her palm on another control. "Computer, evasion course."

"Engaged," *Ariel* said coldly. "Beginning program."

"Strap down, Vaughn. The ride's about to get a little rough."

Chapter 17

Sitting at her board in Control, Ai-lan immediately ordered repair of the bay doors, her crew working in space suits on the debris-littered deck. One Eschoni failed to manage its pressure valve and drowned in its own blood; Ai-lan promptly ordered another from the slave pens and continued driving her crew. Mezoti coverings, crafted from the metallic casings exuded by the giant Mezot arthropods, were spread across the ruined doors, then welded to the inner bay walls with Mezoti silk. A dirigible crane driven by a low-caste Li Fawn maneuvered among the wreckage of the bay, then lifted new hold-plates into place. After fifteen minutes of frantic repair, the hold wall was secure enough to repressurize the bay. Ai-lan gave the order and left Control to inspect the damage personally.

She quickly dressed her lean body in a pressure suit and brushed by guard caste at the inner door. Her crest bristled as she swept her eyes over the wrecked bay. As severe as it was, the decompression damage at least lay within the bay's design limits; that design did not include unthrottled engine power deliberately aimed at the hold doors. The machinery along the bay wall had been melted into frozen slag, the liquid metal spread into broad pools across the hold floor. The interior hold walls and deck were scored and pitted, half-molten in places and the latter a treacherous footing. The nearer ships, the Li Fawn scouts, had extensive damage to their outer housings and hull. Ai-lan doubted they would ever be spaceworthy again, whatever the attempted repairs.

She flexed her fingers as she turned her head from side to side, and she felt a cold fury rise into her throat. Among her several functions as First Controller, the ship-bay had been a prime concern, not for the incoming and outgoing of ships, but for the promising strain of new dock-slaves, the Ai-Baruti, she had named after herself. That strain could make her reputation among the controllers of her House, win her rank beyond that of her birth-honor. All gone. She looked over the ruin of the dock-bay, seething.

She looked towards the human's ship, distant enough to suffer minimal damage from *Ariel*'s backwash. Lord Chaat had gone within; she had learned he had not come out before *Ariel* began its escape. She chilled her mind, preparing for the worst. If Chaat were dead, Controller caste would immediately begin their assassinations to replace him—here, far from home, with no Seniors to check the worst of the in-fighting. *Ngoh Ge* would be paralyzed, prey for enemies. With a flick of her three-fingered hand, she summoned three of the door guards and strode towards *Crystal*.

As they reached the air lock stair, one of the guards stepped in front of her and reached for the lock control.

"No, you fool!" she barked, slapping down his

hand. "Wait until the air pressure stabilizes. If that seal is secure, our lord may still live."

They waited, and Ai-lan looked around the littered bay again, her efficient mind cataloguing more damage. In a few minutes, the weight of her spacesuit began settling on her body, collapsing into folds and wrinkles under the exterior pressure. She glanced upward at the Kazuvi monitor inside her helmet, waiting another minute, then nodded at the guard.

"Open it."

The guard keyed open the door. They entered the craft and searched quickly, then found a closed compartment on an upper level. Ai-lan struggled with the lock, then released it. The door sighed open. As Lord Chaat stepped through the opening, Ai-lan expelled her breath in a hiss, then knelt at his feet.

"My lord," she said with fervent relief.

Chaat ignored her, looking angrily around the demolished room. Then he focused on something behind her. She turned on one knee, following his line of sight. A cabinet along the far wall stood open, its sliding panel shoved aside.

"Tchhah!" Chaat spat. He crossed quickly to the cabinet and stooped, rummaging with one long arm within. He straightened, his face quivering with an expression that made Ai-lan tremble. His crimson eyes blazed. Then, in a flash of his golden robes, he stamped out of the ship.

"Ai-lan!" She turned and saw the spy Tsor in the doorway. "What happened?"

"I pity you, Tsor," she hissed. "How could you let him be humiliated by slaves?"

The spy drew himself up and glared back. "I'm not guard-caste," he said with spirit.

"I doubt if the lord will think that an excuse." Ai-lan turned her back in contempt and left the room.

When she returned to Control, she found an

uproar. Chaat stood by his chair, gesticulating orders wildly, his voice raised to a furious shout. She had never seen him in such a rage and instinctively feared it. Command caste must command without passion, or all is lost. As Chaat's crimson eyes swung towards her, she sank prone to the floor, abasing herself in front of everyone. The shock of a high Controller in such dishonor silenced Chaat, as she intended. She waited for the rustle of his robes as he seated himself in his chair, then lifted her head. The room was deathly silent, with even the slaves struck dumb by her action.

"I am Ai-lan," she said proudly, her voice ringing through the room, "First of Controllers, sister to the Lord-Son Chaat. What does my lord Chaat command?"

Chaat's face had recovered its cold arrogance. Through kin-knowledge, she saw the flash of gratitude in his eyes, quickly erased. Chaat knew full well what she had done, and did not begrudge her the necessity. He had not been himself since acquiring Chaat-lama, and Ai-lan had twice considered private murder to heal that malady. Only Chaat's uncertain response had checked her.

Chaat fingered his chin, as if he considered her request. Then he looked out coldly over the Control room. "Pursue the ship that escaped us."

"Sire," Ai-lan responded and bowed her head. Half a dozen controllers turned to their controls, and the Honor guards visibly relaxed. High-caste Guard disliked a lord out of control even more than Ai-lan, for it struck at their loyalty and sense of purpose. Chaat eyed the guards, no doubt with the same thought, as Ai-lan rose to her feet. They exchanged a cold glance.

"Resume your station, Ai-lan," Chaat said.

"Sire."

Ngoh Ge stirred to lumbering life and moved after the fleeing Guild ship. Ai-lan took her customary chair in Command, and quickly read her scanners. One pulse on her board made her pause.

"Another ship, Lord," she reported. "Approaching fast in far orbit through the cometary plane."

"Identify."

Ai-lan made the necessary query on her board. "A Guild cruiser—one of their patrol boats. It is signaling the *Ariel*." Ai-lan again touched her controls, and a thin voice spoke from the speaker on her panel.

"Calling *Ariel*. Calling *Ariel*."

"*Ariel* responding," came the reply in a measured female voice. Ai-lan turned to Chaat in surprise.

"The Guildswoman?"

"Yes," Chaat said. He glowered, and Ai-lan wisely said nothing more.

The speaker crackled with deep-space interference, then steadied. ". . . ordered to surrender, Guildswoman."

"Gladly. Why am I surrendering?"

"Jennan, are you all right?" asked a second voice.

"What does he mean, Morgen?"

"Oh, nothing big. They just think you're an escaped murderer. Dimwits."

"That's enough, team-second. Bartlett, you are ordered . . . What? Well, send a recognition signal."

Ai-lan turned to Chaat. "They've seen us, sire. Recognition signal coming in."

"How long until we overtake the Guildswoman?"

"Ninety seconds. Do we fire?"

"Only a warning shot! I want that ship captured. Cripple her if you must, but I want it whole! If the other interferes, destroy it."

The cruiser spoke again. "Unknown ship, you are ordered to identify yourself."

"They're Li Fawn, you idiot," Jennan replied.

"And they're after me. Warn off! Warn off! Don't get in the line of fire!"

"We'll be there in six minutes."

"I don't have that kind of time."

Jennan looked at the approaching blip of the Li Fawn ship, and swept her hands across the controls. "Prepare for jump!" she warned. Lume staggered from the elevator, still carrying the madringal, and buckled himself into another chair. He threw her a grin of ragged exuberance. Bedraggled, dirty, bone-tired, and exalted out of his mind. She grinned back at him. What the hell, anyway, if they got vaporized.

"Lume?" Tanner sounded stunned. "She got you out?"

"Hi, big guy." Lume set the madringal on the side counter and patted it possessively. "What's up?"

"Them," Jennan answered, pointing at the screen. "Activating jump."

Ngoh Ge rushed down on them, and a laser bolt shot across their stern. Jennan jabbed her finger at the controls. *Ariel* leaped into the protecting cocoon of hyperspace, and Jennan felt the familiar ripple of Transition. In a twinkling, the Li Fawn ship vanished from her screens, replaced by the roiling grayness of hyperspace. Jennan sighed and began her system checks, then paused as she heard an odd humming behind her. *What . . . ?*

"Oh, my God! The Light!" At Lume's cry, Jennan swung her chair hastily to look behind her.

On the side-counter, Lume's madringal pulsed with a ruby light, its single eye ablaze. Its thrumming accelerated, until it filled the flight deck with a deep reddish glow, pulsing, compulsive, throbbing. Lume covered his ears in pain, and the throbbing rose to a whirlwind of sound and pulsing light, bearing voices crying out against destruction. The walls

and floor seemed to ripple in a massive wave, and
Jennan felt the wave pass through her own body,
sickening her.

A tall shape of glowing vapor coalesced before her
and raised its tendril arms in exultation, its single
ruby eye pulsing with a piercing light.

THE ENDLESS LIGHT! it cried soundlessly. *I
LIVE! I LIVE AGAIN!*

It stood transfixed in its ecstasy, and the light of
its eye slashed at the controls, the walls, the arched
ceiling of the well. *Ariel's* substance rippled again,
as the Light drew upon the very fabric of space to
create itself.

It struck at the three humans, drawing them into
itself. Jennan screamed as its ruby light ripped
through her body, slicing her to shreds. Dismembered, she fell into a black void, turning and
turning, as a fell wind whipped around her. *I AM
THE LIGHT!* shrieked a voice she recognized as
her own.

She cried out again, surrounded by other voices
and a great wind. Dimly she heard Lume scream in
the distance, a hoarse shout of fear and recognition,
then the chant of a dozen Shenda voices, deep and
rumbling. *I AM THE LIGHT!* she chanted with
them, caught in Madringa's ecstasy of rebirth. *I AM
THE LIGHT!*

Jennan reached upward, filling herself with Madringa's wild joy, slashing with her energies to draw still
more into herself. For an instant, the shreds of her
body rejoined, completing her transformation, then
fractured into Time.

The light wind sighed through the forest canopy,
stirring the leaf-filtered light into dappled patterns
that danced the Song of Life. The pseudobat chirped
upside down on her branch, her black eyes watching

merrily. A young human girl grinned back, one hand
on her hip, as she looked upward.

"You're a pretty one. What's your name?"

The Keeper of Songs, Heir of the High-Born and
Third of All the People, sang to her of firelight and
mind-song, of forest glades and water-coolness, and
of the binding together. The girl's grin softened to a
delighted half-smile as she listened, then fell into
her own waking dreams, strangely alien. And, for
those dreams, Twing chose, against all Tradition. . . .

The side-street bar was low-ceilinged and darkly
humid. A dozen orange forms sprawled in their
chairs near dank indoor pools, rumbling unpleasantly
to each other as they sipped their beers. The young
woman paused in the doorway, looking uncertainly
around the dark room. She walked forward, lanky
and still awkward in her youth, to approach a far
table. The Daruma Guildsman looked up crossly,
unwilling to be disturbed.

"I need your help, sir," she said. "I'm missing a
pilot."

"Shann Control, approach vector requested."

The Shenda ship-captain stood with practiced ease
on his command platform, his massive head turning
slowly from side to side as he watched his crew run
through the routine. He felt the old stirring of clan-
ties, the sense of familiar places. It was good to be
home after their long voyaging.

"Clan-Ship *Tavendor*, assume forty degrees, rad
twenty."

"Acknowledged," rumbled the comm-chief. The
captain watched Madringa Station grow larger in his
forward screens, with its crisscross patterns of habitats, fusion plants, and industrial parks. A dozen
interstellar clan-ships lay in their port cradles, their

bulk diminished by distance. *Tavendor* corrected its course downward to join them.

"Sir!" The captain turned his head towards the voice of his youngest son.

"What is it?" he asked calmly.

"More fluctuations in the ship-drive."

"Correct them."

"I'm trying! Sir!" The boy cried out, his collar-fur fully erect in terror. "Father!"

A deep vibration shook the ship from its bowels. The captain staggered as *Tavendor* lurched violently from an explosion below. He caught himself on the bridge rail, then fell heavily as another explosion ripped through the ship's bowels. *Tavendor* spun on its axis with dizzying speed, all gyro-controls lost, then began to fall helplessly towards the moon below. . . .

"Noooo!!"

Shavanda pointed upward, her iridescent veils slipping immodestly from her head as she looked upward. Meloka made to reprove her careless sister-daughter, even reached out a hand to replace the disarranged veils, when a glare of sudden light flashed into their night garden with the harsh brightness of noon-day. Meloka looked around her in bewilderment, as the garden turned blood-red, every leaf, every stone. Shavanda rose to her feet, crying out as she looked upward to the moon. And Meloka looked up with her, terror growing in her throat, as the moon dismembered itself before their eyes.

Jamandi bit on his fingers, murmuring magic words as he rocked back and forth on his haunches. His fur lay in uneven patches, untended and infrequently washed—the Caretender had long since tired of their battles about a daily bath, and left him

alone now to rock and make his chants. Jamandi
looked out on his sterile inner universe, an endless
plain peopled with strange plants and stones that
contained their hidden thoughts, thoughts only
Jamandi knew with certainty. They knew him and
honored him, his secret people, and named him
Caretender. And he guarded them with the Great
Magic, warding away the Dark that hovered vigi-
lantly above the silent plain.

Dimly Jamandi heard the Caretender leave the
long hall to answer a summons. Jamandi forgot him.
Only later, when hunger began to growl in his belly,
did he stir uneasily and look around the narrow hall.
A dozen collapsed figures lay near him, lost in their
dream worlds. The Caretender had never returned.

Then the lights flickered overhead in the ceiling
panels, once and once again. Jamandi cringed helplessly backward, shrieking out his magic, as the Dark
finally descended upon him.

Voices surrounded her, crying out against the
wind. Jennan fell through the void, fracturing,
rejoining, fracturing again. She saw herself as a
child, an apprentice at the Guild Hall, in a dark
warehouse of Hrauru: the Steel Gaze marched forth
from a bedroom wall, a Shenda lay motionless on
the stone floor, leaves whispered in a Taki canopy.
I am the Endless Light, created from darkness, she
cried with Lume, then merged to remember with
him. *WE ARE THE LIGHT!* they cried. In the distance, Vaughn shouted hoarsely in terror, lost in the
End-Time.

I endure, Jennan-Lume shouted in exaltation. *I
endure throughout time.* Madringa's willowy shape
throbbed and expanded upward, its torrential colors
scintillating with sparks of energy, bearing Jennan
and Lume with her. They divided and merged again,

then spun apart. Jennan lost herself briefly, became confusedly flesh, and then Madringa again took Jennan into her substance. In an instant, Jennan shattered horizontally into a dozen copies of itself, an array of goddesses reflected into Time.

I AM THE LIGHT! she shrieked, and fell into the void. . . .

. . . and entered her *Ariel* cabin as a glowing vapor

. . . uncomprehending, watched herself in Tanner's arms

. . . suspended herself over a Shenda street, as tiny figures walked below through the gathering darkness

. . . helpless, looked up into a bird-man's angry crimson eyes

. . . naked, she pounded her fists against her metal enclosure, screaming, "Bring him back!"

. . . and fell through the endless cloud of scarlet gas, accelerating relentlessly towards the star's massive core. . . .

I AM THE LIGHT!

A dozen glowing shapes repeated herself in series, taking sanctuary in Other-Time as the Light flickered . . . and died.

Chapter 18

Chaat saw *Ariel* vanish from the forward screen, then closed his eyes. He felt a coldness settle into his belly, a delicious keenness he relished. The Guildswoman would not escape that easily, for he knew his own ship's capacities. Her escape into hyperspace only delayed the inevitable.

"Follow," he ordered. The communicator chattered with renewed demands from the Guild patrol ship—stop, identify, relate: he ignored them. Let the animals clack and chitter: years of experience had shown they would do little else. As Ai-lan keyed in the course coordinates, he heard the Eschoni's faint scrabble as it obeyed its new commands. Some day, Chaat thought, he would place a Daruma at those controls, perhaps even this Captain Landoni who dared to bleat orders to the Li Fawn.

"Tracking," Ai-lan said. "Sire . . ."

Chaat opened his eyes. "What is it?"

"I have unusual readings for the warp trace—the power curve is unexpectedly high and not in the expected direction. I don't think she jumped for a Guild system at all."

"Can you track the warp?"

"Yes, sir. Activating our own warp."

The noise from the Guild patrol-ship was cut off in mid-word as *Ngoh Ge* leaped into hyperspace. Chaat watched the featureless screen for a moment, then looked at the guard nearest him.

"Bring the spy Tsor to me."

Within a few minutes, two guards returned with the spy between them, the spy strangely defiant.

"You failed," Chaat said coldly.

"I brought you the information you desired, Lord. I did not fail."

"The debris of your success litters our ship-bay. The Guild is now alerted, the Guildswoman temporarily escaped. And I still don't have the Shenda device."

"I did not fail," the spy said stubbornly, throwing back his head. He wrenched his arms from the guards' hold and gathered his robes about him.

Chaat felt his anger stir, but had to acknowledge some justice in the spy's defiance. Spy caste had its own degree of pride to fuel a necessary boldness, a useful gift for a spy and of benefit to his master. And Nineteen had brought useful information: what more could one ask of a spy? Chaat considered, his eyes fixed on Nineteen. He checked his first impulse and chose a wiser course, one that kept this spy's talents but would temper his arrogance.

"Put him in the pens," Chaat ordered. Nineteen's crimson eyes widened in surprise—he had no doubt prepared himself for death. Now he lay suspended between the prospects of mercy or humiliation, the restoration of his honors or the hopeless pains of an animal. It would temper him to wonder which for a time.

"Take him away."

Jennan awoke slowly, as if a great hand pressed down upon her. She struggled against the weight, knowing she was pursued by an unnameable thing, now in the next room, scanning, scanning, until its eye fixed on a single door, her door. She opened her eyes and shut them quickly against the vertigo, then tried to open them again, her head spinning with nausea.

She was sprawled in her flight chair. The instruments on the board before her clicked quietly to themselves, blinking their lights as the computer ran its constant checks on the ship. She lifted her head, though it sent an excruciating pain through her temples, and saw the blackness of interstellar space in the forward screen. In the distance were the brilliant discs of five suns, impossibly close to one another. Two suns were a matched pair of topaz jewels, linked by streamers of scintillating gas. Near them, close enough to interlock the cometary planes, lay a dwarf sun gleaming in deep yellow-orange, and, far beyond the others, another pair of suns flickered like reddish-orange embers of a dying fire. It could only be one system, the debris-poor wasteland of Xi Scorpii.

Most stars had companions, and most stars formed planets if the suns had enough separation. But the suns of Xi Scorpii with their overlapping gravity wells had torn apart the planetary material in their system. Those clumps of matter that did manage to coalesce fell, one by one, into solar fire. Aside from a few cold planetoids, Xi was a desert, without even enough remaining debris to interest the Raome. And *Ariel*, if she was not alert, was about to become another planetoid for Xi Scorpii to play with.

She straightened her body in the chair, groaning at the pain in her head, and tried to focus on the boards. The engine panel to her right read alarms across its face; she quickly locked down the warp-

drive to prevent any mistaken attempt to repeat their
jump. A raggedness in the intra-system engines, pal-
pable as vibration through the deck and into her
chair, showed the damage had not been confined to
the warp drive. *Ariel* might not have the capacity to
deal with the gravity wells it now entered.

Aside from the engine check, there was little she
could do at present. She turned in her chair to look
at Tanner. The trader slumped sideways in his flight
chair, his back to her, deeply unconscious. Beyond
him, Lume slumped forward, held in his chair only
by his waistbelt. Beside him on the deck lay the
Shenda madringal. She unbuckled her belts and
wavered across the floor towards it, watching it like
it was a dangerous snake. Her head spun suddenly
and she overbalanced, knees thudding to the floor.
She winced with the sharp pain, and wavered back
to her feet, more careful of her vertigo.

Tentatively, she reached out her hand to the statuette. Cool, but still with a subtle vibration she could
sense with her fingers. It was still alive, and she
snatched her fingers away. A Shenda statuette. Like
thousands of others. She choked back a hysterical
laugh and then reached out her hand again to lift it
gently to the ledge, setting it upright on its narrow
base. Its single eye gleamed redly in the deck-light.

She turned to Lume and crouched by him, check-
ing his pulse and craning to see his face. He looked
like Death warmed over, paler still beneath the grim
of his captivity, but his heart beat strongly. She levered herself upright on the back of his chair, and
wobbled over to Tanner, then leaned against the wall
with one hand, totally exhausted. But they were
alive, for a while.

She sank to the floor and leaned against the cabinet behind her, dully watching the screen. Gradually
the malaise ebbed from her body, bringing a renewal

of her strength and clear-headedness. She thought she might handle it now, for both men needed care, especially Lume.

She took the elevator to the common-room and rummaged in a storage compartment for a wheeled cart, then left it standing in the middle of the room. She brought sheets and bedding for one of the unoccupied suites, checked Tanner's own, then gathered supplies and wheeled them into the other suite. She filled a bucket of warm water from the tap, and set it by the bed with cloths and medicines. Then she wheeled her emptied cart to the elevator.

On the deck, she unbuckled Lume's belt and caught him as he slumped forward. She tried to lift him, and had to regather her strength more than once before she draped his limp body, face-down, across the top of the cart. She checked Tanner again, then she dragged at the cart, got Lume into the elevator, and finally into the bed below.

She removed his tattered shirt and trousers, taking care to ease them over the half-healed cuts on his arms and legs. She added antiseptic soap to the warm water, and dipped her cloth into the soapy water. Then she washed his face and arms, gave him a drink of water from the bedside jug, waiting patiently for him to swallow each sip, and then finished the bath. After she had bandaged his cuts, she examined the vials in her first-aid box, and gave him hypodermic shots of protein/vitamin concentrate, a neo-sulfa drug for infection, and an anti-nausea compound usually used for jump-shock. Then she covered him with the blanket and watched him sleep for a few minutes. He looked better already, and she felt a small tug of satisfaction.

He was a handsome young man, not much older than she, with laugh lines around his eyes and mouth. The shock and emaciation of his captivity gave him a deathly pallor and highlighted the strong bones in his face. She closed her eyes, remembering Tayna and the slave pen, and earlier, Lume's liking, a liking close to love, for the Shenda. *Marunda would have liked him*, she thought.

His dark hair, long unwashed, lay in greasy bangs across his forehead. She gently pushed them to the side out of his eyes, and smoothed the rest of his rough mane on the pillow. She would give him a shampoo later. She said his name softly, then bent forward and kissed him. Then she gathered up the bucket and medicines and loaded them on her cart.

When she emerged from the elevator, Tanner stirred, his head rolling back loosely. She crossed to him quickly and lifted his head, then slapped his cheek lightly with her palm.

"Vaughn!"

"Whaaa . . ."

"Wake up, Vaughn." Tanner opened his eyes and looked at her blearily, not tracking on her. His head fell back again, and she shook him slightly. He raised his head, blinking at her.

"Where are we?"

"Safe for now. Wake up."

He groaned. "I'm awake, but I'd rather be dead." He fumbled at his waistbelt, then bent forward to rest his forearms on his knees. "What happened?"

"Lume's little toy, that's what happened. Beyond that, I haven't a clue."

He raised his head sharply, and promptly winced. "Lume?"

"He's down below, in bed. Where you should be."

"I'm all right," Tanner said, and promptly passed out again.

Jennan checked his pulse and breathing, then decided to leave him where he sat. She hadn't the strength to repeat her mercies. She wobbled to her chair and sat down heavily. The madringal watched her with a reddish glare.

"Oh, shut up," she said to it. "Go endless-light somebody else."

Her voice echoed against the flight-deck walls, evoking in Jennan's mind an after-image of an infinitude of goddesses, each goddess staring at her with a crimson, malevolent eye. Jennan shuddered. She'd had a bout with warp-shock once and knew it often caused hallucinations. The subconscious mind sometimes rebelled against such unnatural bending of space and time, refused to accept the *not-when*. Yet this . . . this Light seemed something more. But what? Where is reality in the *not-this*?

Resolutely, she turned her back on the madringal to the flight controls. She sensed again the raggedness in the engines, and studied the stars in the screen. The F5 primary lay about eighty AU ahead, hours ahead at mere sublight speed. She didn't dare try the higher speeds of intra-system drive: they used pulsed micro-jumps. And the madringal obviously responded to warp-fields; recently activated, even the system-drive might set it off again. She looked over at the statuette and set her jaw.

Not on my ship, you don't.

"Computer."

"Acknowledged."

"Report on star-system ahead."

"Xi Scorpii, quintuple system. Source: Terran Combine survey ten years ago. Last Guild survey fifty years ago, now outdated. Suggest report in Terran astrometric equivalents based on most recent survey."

"Go ahead."

"Primary components A/B: F5 subgiants in highly eccentric orbit, period 45.69 years, average separation 18 AU. Component C: singleton G7 dwarf separated from primary by 650 AU, retrograde orbit, period 1256 years, currently approaching periastron. Components D/E: dwarf K0 and K3 stars, average separation 1026 AU, separated from primary by 7000 AU. Estimated system age from present cooling of dwarf components: seven billion years. No discrete planets, minimal cometary debris. Guild advisory against entering system."

"Explain."

"Possibility of unpredictable shifts in system gravity wells. Dwarf companions subject to flare-collapse of degenerate matter, with variable effect on stellar-matter exchange between A/B pair. A flare incident may render micro-jump calculation uncertain beyond safety margin."

"Great," she muttered. "Current distance from A/B pair?"

"Seventy-three point eight AU."

Jennan glanced at the madringal. The Guild had studied the relics of Shenda science for some time, but with little progress. Before the catastrophe the Shenda had delighted in inserting long philosophical tracts, even fiction and poetry, into their scientific discussions. To a Shenda, the interpolations added an artful mirror of Reality to the tedium of physical laws, and sometimes the artistry exceeded the facts. Later the Shenda had "refined" the records still further. By the time the Guild arrived at Shann three centuries ago, fact and fancy had become indistinguishable, a frustrating affirmation of the principle that alien science reflects the alien mind.

Some ancient records hinted at a technology exceeding modern Daruma theories in several areas, especially warp-drive. The ancient Shenda apparently journeyed farther in shorter periods of time than even the most powerful Guild ships—assuming the ship-logs could be trusted. Perhaps the Shenda madringal was such a drive, or a component in such a drive; Roycrai had thought so.

The Guild would want the Light. A working Shenda device might be the key to other parts of the technology, a way to resurrect a powerful ancient science. A ship-drive that can leap twice as far as the most powerful of ships in a twinkling of the eye. . . . Her choice. The Guild would want the Light, but the Li Fawn might arrive first, wanting it, too.

She felt an hysterial laugh rise in her throat. The Guildmaster had asked her to find Li Fawn and *Crystal*'s treasure; now that she had both, she didn't want either. She took a deep breath and rubbed her fists into her aching eyes.

A choice, but really not a choice. She couldn't risk the Light falling into Li Fawn hands, not with the Guild unaware it even existed. And the Li Fawn cruiser would arrive first at Xi Scorpii. Her crippled *Ariel* wouldn't last long in a determined chase. She took a breath and scowled.

"Elapsed time for sublight capsule to reach nearest star?" she asked aloud.

"Nine point three hours."

"Prepare sublight capsule for ejection."

"Acknowledged."

She went below to the engine room and stood for a moment, listening to the ragged whisper of *Ariel*'s engines. On one wall of the heavily-shielded room were the ship's messenger capsules, a fail-safe system if the ship's other communication systems became inoperative. She cracked the seal on one of the capsule compartments and tugged at the capsule. It slid out easily on its tray and automatically opened. Then she hesitated: perhaps she had another option.

"Computer."

"Acknowledged." The ship's voice echoed boomingly in the metal chamber. Jennan winced slightly as the sound aggravated her ragged nerves.

"Given Xi's unstable gravity well, how long could a rocket sustain a parabolic orbit?"

"Unknown."

"Well, speculate a little," she suggested, annoyed at the machine's caution. "At least give some parameters."

The computer paused a moment. "Four hours to four standard years, plus or minus eighty percent uncertainty."

Jennan stared at the ship's speaker. "Eighty percent? Maybe we should stick to 'unknown.' "

"A good idea," the ship said tonelessly.

Jennan snorted. The Guild computermen insisted that jump-ship computers were only machines, not like the larger semi-aware computers used elsewhere. *Ariel* sometimes tended to show more personality than the experts decreed.

"Compute a parabolic orbit towards the outer dwarf pair."

"Computed."

Jennan retrieved the madringal from the flight deck and carried it gingerly back to the engine room. She laid it within the capsule, padding the interior with soft material. Its metal surface gleamed in the muted engine-room light, its red stare unwinking.

"Madringa," she said to it. "I want you off my ship, but I can't throw you away completely. Stay quiet and whirl around the system for a while. You'll like it."

I am losing my mind, she thought. *Why are you talking to a statue?* In the distance, a flowing shape shrieked its exaltation, its ruby light striking at all space. Jennan felt herself slipping towards it, her body fraying. She shook her head violently.

"No!" The engine room steadied around her again.

She took a deep breath, fighting the grayness of
Madringa's presence. Too close: the ghost came too
close here. "Program parabolic orbit."

"Acknowledged." The capsule closed and its control lights blinked briefly.

"Launch."

The capsule disappeared into its compartment.
The door closed and then reopened a minute later,
the compartment empty. She was committed now,
but at least *Ariel* might survive. Maybe. She looked
dully at the empty compartment, her head throbbing
with fatigue, convinced she had made the wrong
choice. The capsule was detectable at short dis-
tances, its call beacon wedded into its machinery.
No time to modify, even if she had the shop tools.
If the Li Fawn found the Light . . .

What would they do with such a device? What
would the Guild do? Races might tear each other
apart for such power, destroying all in a frenzy of
greed.

And *Ariel*? Her fragile ship would be the first
casualty of that struggle. The ship's engines whispered around her, the comforting sibilant sound she
knew well. She listened for a moment to the ship
she loved, and the despair struck so unexpectedly
that she sank downward to her knees.

"No, no!" she cried, and heard her voice echo
from the metal walls. Eerily she heard yet another
echo in Shavanda's anguished cry. "Noooo!" It
silenced her. Jennan bowed forward on the deck,
her arms wrapped around herself, and rocked slowly
back and forth. *Ariel* whispered onward, oblivious.

Chapter 19

As *Ariel* disappeared from the view-screen, Morgen slowly expelled the breath he hadn't realized he'd been holding. He rubbed his naked scalp, and felt as if even his ears had cramped themselves into knots with the tension of the past several hours. He flicked his fingers in a swift caress to his ear tips, then dropped his arms to his sides.

"Thank the gods," he said to no one in particular.

Captain Landoni leaned forward in his chair and peered at the screen, his voice querulous. "Where did she go?" he demanded. "I want a plotting trace of that warp."

"Yes, sir." A Daruma navigator murmured to the Vang pilot near him, then moved his hands smoothly over his controls. The wide control room was muted as its several Guildsmen quietly carried out their duties, their calmness of movement a Daruma characteristic but one which Morgen, although Daruma himself, had appreciated only after Jennan pointed it out to him.

We see best through another's eyes, Morgen thought. He watched his fellow Guildsmen, and felt another stab of worry for Jennan as the light-marker of the Li Fawn ship flared briefly and vanished from the screen. Any reprieve given to *Ariel* by its escape could be short-lived.

"Second ship has entered warp," another Guildsman reported. "No response to our query."

"Just track *Ariel.*"

"I'd be more interested in where the Li Fawn went," Morgen said. "Aren't you even concerned? Their cruiser menaced a Guild ship and now chases it."

"Maybe," Landoni said irritably. "My authority only extends . . ."

"You once had some flexibility. . . ."

They both stopped short and glared at each other mildly. Then Landoni gestured peace and shrugged. "I'm tired, Morgen. Matters were simpler when we were journeymen—no decisions, no policy involvements, no Guild troubles. You create for me a problem I'd rather avoid."

"We aren't journeymen any longer, Landoni."

Landoni shrugged again. "A faint regret at most. With the troubles come the blessings, though I don't feel particularly blessed right now. Portmaster Beren is frothing at the mouth about your Guildswoman murdering a Shenda, and you stand there and adamantly deny any such possibility."

"As I do."

"With no evidence whatsoever for your position."

"Except my knowledge of her—and of Beren's alliance with Tarthe's faction on Naberr. Tarthe fancies himself the next Guildmaster."

"So I've heard. The Shann Guildsmen aren't that isolated, particularly with one of Tarthe's chief adherents as Portmaster. But I've heard other tales, too—that you've lost honor in this foolishness over your human Guildswoman. Sorema rumors, I admit.

But why should a Guildsman place an outsider above the Guild?"

Landoni's expression was genuinely troubled. Morgen remembered him as honest, if somewhat slow-witted in his dogged attention to the precise parameters of Guild duty. On this captain rested any feasible rescue, if Jennan needed it. Morgen considered his options, and first chose an appeal to old friendships. *Persuasion is a Guildsman's art*, he thought.

"Jennan is Guild," he began tentatively.

"To Tarthe, never."

"Landoni, we were journeymen together here on Shann. I brought you home a few times after a rough night and you returned the favor in your time. You knew me well: I haven't changed in the past twenty years."

Landoni still looked dubious. "People change in subtle ways."

"True, but the essence remains—and change can come despite limited choice. I'm caught in such a choice imposed by Sorema, and I choose according to my ship-honor, my Guild honor. For me, both are the same—the choice is governed, without true choice. I have only propriety, the duty of my honor." He gestured at the viewscreen. "Jennan has my loyalty as team-first, quite aside from other gratitudes. But mostly she is Guild—the best of Guild. Guild is a mentality, not a racial characteristic." He sketched a gesture of House honor with his hand. "My duty, Guild-brother. I ask your help."

Landoni flicked his ears in acknowledgement of the gesture and request, then looked back at the screen. "Hmmm. Taren, did you get the plotting trace of *Ariel*'s warp?"

"Yes, sir. Warp trace shows a destination of Xi Scorpii."

"Xi? *Ariel* can't jump that far."

"See for yourself, sir." Taren displayed the looping sine curve on an auxiliary screen. "Xi Scorpii, with no intermediate warp-points, only one long curve to its destination. And the warp trace is strangely distorted: I doubt if *Ariel* arrived."

"Lost?"

"Probably, sir. As you said, jump-ship class doesn't have sufficient power for that length of jump."

"The Li Fawn followed her there," Morgen said.

Landoni shrugged. "Maybe. Li Fawn aren't officially my problem, Morgen. You know that. I was given an assignment . . ."

". . . to investigate the *Ariel*'s unpermitted departure. You now have a clue." He waved a hand at the ship screen. "Li Fawn. I suggest you continue to investigate by following both ships wherever they went."

"Don't push me, Morgen." Landoni's irritation flashed again, but Morgen ignored it, unwisely or not.

"But Jennan is in danger!"

"If she arrived. You saw the warp curve."

"If she arrived, as you say, the Li Fawn ship outclasses *Ariel* by thirty to one. Why did it attack her? Why does it chase her? Your first duty is to the Guild, and to a Guildsman under threat!"

"If she arrived."

Morgen crossed his arms again and looked at his old friend challengingly. "So go see. That's my request of you."

Landoni grimaced. "I heard you the first time when you weren't that bald in asking. It's not that easy."

"Why not?"

Landoni rolled up his ears and scowled at him, then ear-twitched a comment about stubborn impracticality.

Morgen ignored that, too. "Why not?" he repeated.

Landoni hemmed, and Morgen tried to keep a tight rein on his patience. Landoni could not be pushed while in his honest doubt, and Landoni's cruiser was Jennan's only prompt chance of rescue. Even if Morgen sought help at Out-Station, Beren's opposition would cause more delay, then prompt a crisis between Beren and the Guild Hall that Morgen would rather avoid until Jennan was safe. Morgen waited, forcing aside his anxieties.

"I suppose I could ask permission from Out-Station," Landoni said at last.

Morgen tried to speak quietly, but could not contain his asperity. "Which will be refused, of course. I thought you were more venturesome than that, Landoni. Have the years ossified your brain?"

"Careful, my friend. Don't push away those who might be sympathetic." Landoni flicked his ears, then looked at Morgen squarely. "I only mentioned the possibility. I can guess as well as you that any request would be denied. Instead of options, we'd have a flat prohibition against what you ask. Yet not asking is a breach of procedure." Landoni returned to turning over his choices, his eyes abstracted.

Morgen sighed and shifted his weight impatiently. "Landoni . . ."

"I need to confer with my officers. Go below for now; we'll talk later."

"Later!" Morgen choked back his protest, bending to his sudden understanding of his old friend. As well as he knew Landoni, he could see that the younger Guildsman—a Landoni almost reckless in his vast enthusiasms—had been erased by the years of responsibility and careful tutelage by Beren. As Morgen had grown in one direction through his friendships and frequent change of assignments, Landoni had grown inward, just as Shann and its Guildsmen looked inward to their own affairs. Morgen had a new understanding of the frustration he sensed in the Terrans who traded here. The Guildmaster was right: overcautious propriety paralyzed the thinking mind. And, while minds deliberated their overlapping rules . . . He looked at the empty view-screen in despair.

Then he shook himself and schooled his expression, erasing all traces of his prior emotion from his face and voice. "I'll be in the lounge with my pilot. Please make your decision as soon as possible."

"I shall do so," Landoni responded, nodding his head. "As soon as possible."

Morgen turned and walked out of the control-room, aware of several glances towards him from other Guildsmen in the room. Rumors, indeed, although much of it could come from the overhearing of his request. He felt aware, as he had on rare occasions, of living within constant observation, a scrutiny that judged the merits of his behavior and cared nothing for the person within. A kind of paranoia, accentuated by his easy relationship with Jennan, an unavoidable part of a ritualistic society. Strengths, weaknesses—he hoped only that Jennan did not pay the price of his own culture's caution.

In the anteroom, he stepped on the upper landing and descended a spiral stair to the midship lounge. As he walked through the metal coping of the entryway, Chandra looked up from his easy sprawl in a wide chair. T'wing hung upside down from a nearby shelf, and chirped as Morgen approached.

"Well?" the Vang rumbled.

Morgen sat down beside him and grunted slightly as T'wing pounced on his unwilling shoulder. The pseudobat had calmed somewhat from the near-hysteria of previous hours, though Morgen thought it a natural product of time rather than any reaction to Jennan's distant mind. T'wing and Jennan had been rarely parted by any distance during Morgen's association with them; he had no measure of T'wing's empathic range. Perhaps she touched Jennan now; perhaps not. He reached up his hand and stroked her fur comfortingly.

"Morgen?" Chandra asked, more demandingly.

He looked up at the Vang, measuring his words. He felt more tired than ever, but rallied yet again to soothe his pilot. *When does somebody soothe me?* he wondered briefly. "Jennan jumped to Xi Scorpii and the Li Fawn went after her. Landoni is thinking about possibly following."

"Possibly following?"

"Take it easy. Landoni has his own problems right now. I think he'll come through." Morgen tried to sound more confident than he felt, and suddenly wearied of the effort to hide emotions today. He rubbed his naked skull. Sometimes he could almost envy Jennan her humanity—just barrelling around the universe, emoting however the spirit struck. No rules, no careful manners, only the rejuvenating flush of an honest rage, a quiet love, the exhilaration of being alive. . . .

Jennan. His fear for her suddenly flared, and he measured her worth to him. Jennan . . .

T'wing fluttered her wings in distress, and Morgen calmed her, trying to keep his own internal equilibrium.

Chandra crossed his upper arms and slumped deeper into his chair. "Landoni may find a few more pinches if he doesn't. And don't sound so carefully patient, Morgen. I have my own version of brains, not all of them controlled by my passions. However we Vang display, we know that threats go only so far."

"Oh, really," Morgen murmured.

Chandra disdained his sarcasm. "Besides, I'm outnumbered here: this patrol-ship has two Vang pilots. You will note I count the forty Daruma as inconsequential."

Morgen smiled. "Naturally."

Chandra shrugged, his metallic shoulders gleaming in the muted light of the lounge. The frosty humanoid eyes seemed to warm slightly in that cold mask. *Does Chandra really like me*, Morgen wondered suddenly, *or does he accept me merely out of loyalty, part of his Vang's loyalty to the ship? I wonder if I'll ever know.*

"I expected some move against Jennan," Chandra said reflectively. "It started on Taki and has been building ever since. Perhaps Tarthe merely took advantage; perhaps Tarthe was part of its inception. But something or someone is now on the move. I would like to know who." He stretched his neck muscles, then flexed the biceps of each mighty arm. "Yes, indeed. Tell me, my friend, why does the Guild turn on one of its own?"

"Not the Guild. Sorema House. Politics, fear, domination. Who knows?"

"Sorema is Guild. You do have your Daruma responses, including a death-challenge against Beren. Have you considered that?"

"That's hardly justified yet." Morgen looked away. He had considered it briefly when Beren issued his proscription, that incredible charge that Jennan had murdered Marunda and fled Shann because of it. Incredible.

"I only mention it to advise against it. Beren is too important to Out-Station, too entrenched in the Guild's hierarchy. The Guild will reduce the House-to-House combat to personal combat, perhaps even insist it be nonlethal. And so you can pummel him, crisp him a bit, and take that sorry satisfaction for your loss. I can't guess at the consequences to your career, but I hardly believe the Guild would approve, however your customs pronounce its honors. It's not worth it, Morgen: it wouldn't solve anything."

"This from a Vang?"

"That's a rather bigoted comment. I admit I've given cause from time to time, but, on the whole, my behavior has been rather mild."

"I'm sorry." Morgen bowed his head dully. "She may be dead, even now," he said.

"T'wing doesn't say so. She would know."

"Maybe."

Chandra shrugged again. "We'll find out, one way or another. I've been sitting here considering my own options as a Vang. My people have their own 'houses,' their own rankings, some of which not even the Guild has ever suspected. We are a secretive people, and our bluffs are a fine misleading. You're more perceptive than most, Morgen, but even you usually react as expected. But I have been considering."

Morgen smiled up at him, bemused. This contemplative, dispassionate Vang was not what he expected; Chandra had the right of that. His smile deepened when he remembered his stray thought about soothing. And he thought he knew this Vang: it wasn't the first time he had wondered if he was starting over again on the understanding.

"What could you do?" he asked.

Chandra paused as a Daruma crewman passed through the lounge on an errand. Then they were alone again in the narrow room. Chandra turned his metallic face towards Morgen, and its expression sent an unexpected chill down Morgen's spine.

"Chandra, what are you planning?" he asked in alarm.

The metal lips turned upward in a menacing smile. "So? Even your loyalty has its limits?"

"Nuts to that. You know how I feel about Jennan. But the Guild . . ."

". . . is the Guild, greater than House, even ship-oath. I won't ask you to place Jennan in that spectrum. I doubt if you even know. But I despise a philosophy that consistently weighs the whole greater than the single part. I have my own personal reasons, but we Vang think in different terms."

"There is more than one option, Chandra," Morgen said desperately. "Don't . . ."

Chandra smiled more gently. "Guild-brother, why do you think I've even brought this up? We must consider means, and I need your clever mind. When Jennan escapes her current peril, she will still face the Guild opposition that has taken shape against her. We must prepare. I need your deeper knowledge of the inner Guild and the power there, something I've never interested myself in. And you need the knowledge of what I could do on Prander for Jennan's sake."

"What could you do?" Morgen demanded.

Chandra stretched lazily. "Oh, I have a few possibilities. Like maybe withdrawing all Vang from Guild ships."

Morgen stared, aghast. "I don't believe it."

"Or maybe starting a war between Naberr and Prander. That ought to mix things up a bit."

"Chandra!"

Chandra smiled coolly. "It's a possibility—although not a serious one. A war wouldn't solve the problem, only allow Terra and maybe the Li Fawn opportunities they don't deserve. Do you know what Jennan is called on Prander? "Life-Bringer to the Prince." I'm the prince—one of many princes, true, but still a prince. And all of Prander knows Jennan's name. Oh, yes, I could do it."

Morgen looked him over skeptically.

"T'wing believes me," Chandra said.

"I didn't know Vang had princes."

"Rough equivalent. 'Pod-master' is another, or 'revered house-son,' or . . ."

"All right, all right. Save it."

"One should respect a Vang's lasers," Chandra said mildly. "Sorema should have considered Jennan's bonds to me—and mine to her. It is the unseen satellite circling its system, laden with menace. Does Sorema really wish Jennan's death?"

"I don't know. I think its circumstances are merely an acceptable solution, much regretted."

"I will consider that, too," Chandra rumbled. They sat together on the bench, waiting, each wrapped in his own variety of patience.

Chapter 20

After a time, Jennan lifted her head, then slowly got to her feet. She pushed back her hair from her forehead, staring unfocusedly, then dropped her hand as her mind began to work again. Options, what options? Her gaze fell on the remaining capsule compartments. Without warp capacity, *Ariel*'s communicators lacked the power to reach Shann, much less Naberr, at this distance, but . . .

"Computer."

"Acknowledged."

"Prepare a second capsule, interstellar flight, to carry a message to Naberr. Program message: "Guild Jump-Ship *Ariel* to Guild Central, seeking help. Stranded at Xi Scorpii after warp incident, possible hostile action by Li Fawn imminent."

She paused, trying to organize her tired mind. "Advise small capsule orbiting dwarf pair. Contains *Crystal*'s artifact, a Shenda warp device. Advise extreme caution in transporting through hyperspace. Repeat: extreme caution."

What else? By the time any ship arrived from Naberr, whatever game *Ariel* played with the Li

Fawn would be long ended. She cleared her throat. "Personal to the Guildmaster from team-first: my honor to you, Master. End message."

"Programmed."

"Launch capsule." The lights flickered on the control panel, then another capsule door slid open, revealing a second empty compartment. Options, now closed. Well, she would try to spin the others as long as they lasted.

She took the elevator to the flight deck, checked Tanner briefly, and then sat down at controls. She watched the arcing traces of both capsules fade as they fell out of range, then keyed her controls for a schematic of the system. She studied the configuration of the gravity well, then began plotting a course between the primary suns. Riding Xi's gravity well had its own risks, but she wanted some orbital momentum to help *Ariel's* ragged engines. And perhaps, just perhaps, the Li Fawn might be careless in rushing into the system—if they followed *Ariel* to Xi. That they might not was another chance, but she didn't hope for it.

"Computer, display the normal warp entry-point for this system, approaching from Shann."

A tiny point appeared on her plot of the system, forty degrees tangent to Xi's primary gravity-lines and nearly 100 AU away. She studied the well schematic in relation to that point. If she was approaching the nearest dwarf when the Li Fawn ship emerged, she might induce them to blunder across the deepest part of the well. However powerful its engines, the Li Fawn cruiser must lay within standard design limits. Guild observations had not shown any marked superiority in the ship's capacities, and, in any event, a culture that could handle the forces in Xi's gravity well, however encountered, would not have choosen the option of skulking around Sagittarius. That cautious approach suggested an equivalent technology, however configured.

"Elapsed jump-time from Shann to Xi Scorpii, Type A cruiser class."

"Ten point three hours, assuming nominal time distortion during warp." She glanced upward at the ship-clock, juggling the times in her head. She plotted a course between the primary suns, extrapolated the orbital momentum as *Ariel* swung around the farther F5 star towards the dwarf, then continued plotting down-system. Possible, even with *Ariel*'s crippled engines—enough to lead the Li Fawn on a merry chase for six hours and yet be conveniently close as the Light swung far around the system.

But eighty percent uncertainty, she remembered. *Ariel* might be inconveniently close to the dwarf pair if the Light went astray. "Expected effect of Shenda device impacting on F5 star?"

"Unknown."

"Right," Jennan muttered. "Let's just hope it melts."

"Query?" the computer asked didactically.

"Nothing."

She entered the ship-course into the navigational controls, then tentatively keyed in power to *Ariel*'s engines. The ship leaped forward, accelerating inward.

Jennan leaned back and rubbed her eyes, blinking wearily. She still felt bone-tired and odd, stretched out and pressed flat in the wrong ways. Her heart seemed to beat with the wrong rhythms, and something gibbered at the edges of her mind, barely felt but enough to send her body thrumming from the threat. She slowly stretched her muscles, trying to shake off the malaise, then slumped in her chair, eyes closed.

Tanner moaned softly, and she stirred herself to attend to him. She got up and walked the few steps

to his chair. She ran her hand over his hair, then
shook him slightly.

"Vaughn?"

Slowly the trader came around until he blinked
wearily at her, some understanding in his eyes.

"Where are we? What happened?"

"Xi Scorpii. How do you feel?"

"Embalmed." He groaned and straightened in his
chair, then shook his head dazedly. She laid her
hand on his forearm, and he reached with his other
to grasp her fingers tightly. He looked up at her, his
eyes shadowed by shock and fatigue.

"I said some things I shouldn't . . ." he said.

"Yes, you did." She looked down at their inter-
locked fingers, and moved her fingers slightly within
his grasp.

"Thank you for saving Lume," he added awkwardly.

"Of course. I saw the Li Fawn march him out as
we were talking."

"Please look at me, Jennan." She raised her eyes
to his.

"I'm a stupid man," he said. "I apologize for my
stupid behavior. Sometimes I have my good
points. . . ."

She smiled slightly. "You can be very suave."

". . . which isn't something you always admire.
And I'd like you to admire me, very much. I'd like
you . . . I don't really know what I want, not in
words. I . . . I guess I want you to feel about me
the way you feel about Morgen."

Jennan looked away uncomfortably. "That kind of
loyalty is earned."

"Yes, I know." He grimaced. "There was a time,
after my daring deeds on Taki, when I had a chance
with you. I could see it in your eyes, but somehow
I lost it, just by assuming. I'm great on fatuous

assuming, especially after I take a woman to bed. I turn into typical Terran, you would say. . . ."

"Terrans aren't that bad. I'm one myself."

"Oh, no. You're a Guildswoman, to the core. Loyal and smart, knowledgeable about things we Terrans should have learned about Sagittarius—and bound to your Guild rules. I need to remember that. I'll try harder, if you'll give me another chance."

It was a pretty apology. Jennan smiled again. "I haven't crossed you off, Vaughn."

He sighed. "Good." He leaned forward and kissed her lightly, then sagged back in his chair. "Like I said, embalmed." He looked around at the flight-deck. "Where is that gizmo, anyway?"

"Falling into the nearest star. I didn't dare keep it aboard." She straightened and gently removed her hand from his grasp. "Team-first decision."

"I'm not criticizing," he said hastily. "What are your plans now?"

She explained the plotted course on the screen, and saw him gradually recover his confident ways, as if a pretty apology and a kiss smoothed every-thing. She felt the distance between them remain, lost the impulse to tell him about her fears and the despair she felt in the engine room. He bent forward towards the controls to tinker with her course, still talking. His voice faded from her attention as the room stretched tightly again—for a moment, she felt a vaporous ghost watching from the walls. She turned nervously, looking in all directions, as the sensation ebbed.

Tanner was oblivious, and she shook her head irri-tably at herself. The line between reality and fantasy had become blurred, and she needed a clear head.

"What's the matter?" Tanner asked, looking up at her.

"Nothing. I'm going to go below and check on Lume. Call me if there's any problem."

"Okay."

She mistrusted her equilibrium on the well ladder and so took the elevator. Lume still slept, as if drugged, and she watched him for a few minutes. Then she straightened the bedcovers he had disarranged in his restless sleep, and sat down in the desk chair. She closed her eyes and sighed, her nerves thrumming unpleasantly.

Jennan Bartlett.

She heard the voice deep in her mind and opened her eyes abruptly. Lume still slept, his chest slowly rising and falling beneath his coverings. She turned her head, examining all parts of the room, every sense alert.

"Where are you?" she said aloud.

A wispy shape formed itself near the far wall in pastel gray and scarlet vapors, surmounted by a single ruby eye. It drifted towards her and she tensed. The shape abruptly stopped its approach.

I am Madringa. Do not be alarmed.

"Alarmed? You damn destroyed my ship." Her voice echoed eerily in the darkened room, then seemed to rush away into an emptied distance. Jennan's spine prickled with the cold touch of the void.

Not I, said the apparition. *The Endless Light destroys. It destroys as it creates me. Only as it fades do I escape into the other times, as this self now appears before you. You will meet my sisters, Jennan Bartlett. You are a part of us. You understand the Endless Light.*

"No, I don't. I don't understand it at all."

To experience is to understand. That is enough.

"Who are you? What are you?"

I am a creature of the Light, of its substance and power, I have my beginnings in another place, but

I do not remember them. I have my endings in the future, but they are my other selves. The voice became sad. *I live through death, and I myself die. As you have known, Jennan Bartlett, and will know again.* The vapor thinned until it seemed only a faint blur. *Be warned. Your enemies approach you.*

"When?" she asked, but the room was empty.

She sat on the chair, confused, trying to assimilate her impressions. A fevered dream, with a mocking ghost. A dispassionate watcher from the walls as she lay in Tanner's arms. Her strange despair in a Shenda street, and now this sorrowing voice in a darkened room. Hallucination? Madness? She pressed her hands hard upon her knees. Or perhaps an alien, of a type postulated but never discovered? Can a warp device create life? With what intentions? How does one find the bonds with a creature of pure energy?

She smiled at herself then: Tanner was right—she was a Guildsman to the core. She sought the connections, even with ghosts that oozed from walls, shrieked destruction, and tried to dismember her ship with light beams. When in doubt, be spectacular? Madringa certainly was that. She smiled again as she felt a stir of awed admiration, and recognized it as a cousin to her affection for Chandra's Vangish posturing. *Odd.* But she also felt strangely touched by this new ghost's sadness, as if it truly found a chord within herself.

The bonds of diversity. She smiled, and felt a knot loosen within her.

Tanner had claimed she lost her humanity by isolation from her own kind. Perhaps, just perhaps, it was a trade for something better.

She rose to her feet, then quietly checked Lume again. He slept undisturbed, frowning in his dreams.

She watched him a moment, then left the room for the flight deck.

Two hours later *Ariel* slipped through the embracing arms of the primary pair and rounded the farther sun on a tight orbit, heading for the singleton dwarf. The momentum of the ship's fall into the gravity-well accelerated *Ariel*'s speed to near-normal, and Jennan eased back engine-power, relieved to spare the ship's crippled engines. *Ariel* slid forward on the upper lip of the primary well, still accelerating, then fell down the intersecting slope towards the dwarf.

"It's going to work," Tanner said with some surprise.

"Apparently. Keep a watch on it, Vaughn. I'm going to check on Lume again."

"Okay."

Jennan got up from her chair. As she turned towards the elevator, the doors whisked open. Lume stood in the doorway and leaned weakly on the jamb for a moment. When he failed to walk forward, the elevator clacked irritably.

"Good morning," Lume said. "Or is it? Morning, I mean."

"Free choice," Jennan said with a smile. "Sit down. How do you feel?"

Lume wobbled on unsteady legs to the nearest chair and sat down heavily. He looked around the flight deck, as if trying to orient himself, then looked blearily at Tanner.

"Hi, big guy."

"Hi, yourself. You look awful."

"Thanks. Tayna's dead, Vaughn," he added dully. "So's Roycrai. The Li Fawn killed them."

Vaughn stared. "But why?"

"Do they need a reason?" Lume looked around the flight deck. "I remember this place. I remember other things, too." His eyes met Jennan's for a moment.

"So do I," Jennan said. "Courtesy of your madringal. I had to get rid of it—I ejected it in a capsule. I hope you don't mind."

"Oh, I don't mind," Lume said. He ran his fingers through his disheveled hair, then dropped his hands in his lap. He looked around the deck yet a third time, examining the instrument boards, then craning back his head to look into the half-well overhead. Jennan reseated herself in her chair, watching him.

"Where are we?" Lume asked.

"Xi Scorpii," Tanner said, pointing at the viewscreen. He punched a button to alter the schematic, a totally pointless change made mostly for show. Jennan again caught the arrogant nuance in his voice, as if Tanner had the leadership on this ship, and felt a prickle of irritation at his implication. For all his apologies and professions, the trader had reengaged his competition with her. What *was* his problem? And hers, for that matter, to think it even an issue?

Her eyes met Lume's, and she saw the glint of ironic understanding in his eyes. He winked at her and then yawned. "I remember many things, Guildswoman. An interesting guide, our Madringa." Jennan wondered what Lume had seen through the Light—parts of his own history? Or hers? "Have we really escaped?" he asked.

"No. The Li Fawn will probably track us here."

"I didn't think so. Lord-Son Chaat gets determined about things, and nothing gets easy when he does." He looked grim for a moment, a weight that lay strangely on his young face.

"Chaat?" Vaughn asked.

"The commander of the Li Fawn ship. He's a lord of some kind, the kind who makes others 'tremble when he walks.' Complete autocracy—and the wierdest technology I've ever seen. They use animals to run their machines—sometimes the animals are part of the machines." He grimaced. "And I think some of the animals are people."

"People?"

"As in slavery, Vaughn. Most of the 'biocomponents' are apparently non-intelligent and merely trained to do things like we train dogs and chimpanzees. A kind of crystal butterfly—I forget the name—monitors radiation levels. Zaruti colonies provide light and alarm bells. And so forth. Every animal has its function, with the Li Fawn in control. But one race is clearly sapient, judging from what I saw of them. They were chained to control monitors and working on the docks."

"The crab-men?" Jennan asked. "I saw them, too."

Lume nodded. "Their name is Eschoni. They seem to be the special pets of a female Li Fawn named Ai-lan." Lume shuddered slightly. "She wanted to make a special pet, too, I guess. If she'd had more time, she might have arranged it."

Tanner turned towards him and raised an eyebrow. "I can't imagine why you'd permit it."

"It's not a matter of permitting, Vaughn," Lume said irritably.

"Oh? Then what else is it?"

Lume shook his head, obviously angry. "This isn't the time for another big-brother act, especially when you don't know what you're talking about. The Li Fawn subvert entire species. The Pang-Ahit collect garbage—it's all they do, and apparently all they want to do. Yet they're at least partly intelligent: I heard one talk to Ai-lan. The Li Fawn control the crab-men with torture, but the Pang-ahit follow willingly. How do you redirect a race's purpose like that?"

Lume shook his head again, his expression perplexed and horrified. "And it goes beyond that. Some species are cut up and put into the machinery—as radiation monitors, alarm-lights, computer components. The lock to my room had an amputated brain in it. I could see it through the plastic cover. What kind of race does that to other life? I think the Li Fawn are far more dangerous than anybody realizes."

"Maybe," Tanner said, unconvinced. Jennan saw another wash of anger flush Lume's face. He turned his eyes back to Jennan.

"Did you really throw the Light off the ship?" he asked.

"Yes."

"Then I strongly suggest we stay out of Chaat's reach. He wants it—and now that we've demonstrated it, he'll want it more. Lord Son-Chaat is one honcho I never want to meet again."

"You sound unnerved," Tanner said, his tone maliciously light, his voice laced with the indulgence of a seasoned oldster for a tinhorn. Jennan scowled at him. Lume, too? What *was* Tanner's problem? The tension between the two men tightened into a vise.

"Chaat killed our sister," Lume said coldly, "so take off the nasty smirk, Vaughn. I know damn well who runs this ship, whatever your little games with that board." He pointed at Jennan. "She came for me, got us off *Ngoh Ge*, not you. She is Guild and this is a Guild ship. I don't know why you're here— Madringa didn't show me enough in the dreams— but if anybody gets us out of this, it'll be the Guild."

Tanner flushed angrily. "Now wait a minute. . . ."

Lume raised his voice, overriding his protest. "You and Roycrai are just the same. You don't care about the locals—to you, they're just grist for the mill, like the Li Fawn use their slaves. I heard the engines ignite: you would have left us there, just to save yourself."

"That's not true. I only . . ." But Lume had looked away, his face heavy with contempt. Tanner clamped his jaw shut and turned back to his board, seething.

Jennan watched them both, slightly shocked by the raw emotions unleashed between them. She lacked pieces of the foundation, if the interchange had a foundation besides family stresses. What had Lume seen in the Light? Why did Tanner feel he had to compete? And why did Lume feel such disdain for Tanner's pretensions?

Maybe I have to relearn my humanity in several ways, she thought. *Maybe it's not me at all*. She remembered her father's bewildering rages and ambitions, her own inability to cope with him in any positive way. *Maybe I should swear off men*, she thought. She crossed her arms and slouched in her chair, amused by her own conclusion. *When in doubt, be sexist*.

"What's so funny?" Tanner asked her irritably as her smile caught his eye.

"Nothing, Vaughn." She leaned forward and studied the view-screen intently. Then she stood up and bent past Tanner, her sleeve brushing his, her hand keying through the system display to warp-point, touched another button for magnification. The distortion of impending ship-entry was obvious. The small patch then flared into a light-marker.

"Computer," she said, "identify incoming ship."

"No Guild beacon discernible," the machine intoned. "Identity unknown. Solar distortion and distance make ship type ambiguous, but parameters resemble the Li Fawn cruiser."

"Well, if it's not a Guild ship, it couldn't be much of anybody else. Here they come, gentlemen. Let's hope we give Lord-Son Chaat a very long chase."

Chapter 21

Ngoh Ge reentered normal space at optimum distance from the primary pair of stars. Chaat sat impatiently in his command chair, watching the screens over the heads of the controllers. They set their scans promptly, studying the system ahead for any sign of the Guild ship. To his right, the Eschoni tech scrambled to complete its sequences, gibbering quietly to itself as its claws worked the floor controls. Chaat watched it a moment, frowning at its thinness of body, its palsied limbs—even its shell seemed shrunken. Chaat needed full efficiency, and sick slaves threatened that efficiency.

"Tracking," said a controller, distracting his attention. Chaat saw the scans display on the screens, one after another, as the computers analyzed the incoming data. The information was a welter of overlapping fields: gravity curves, magnetic bands, electron storms—all in constant flux as the components of the system subtly influenced each other in their orbits. The primary pair were ribboned by a bright exchange of gas; the three dwarf stars stirred and

trembled under the forces of their own collapsing
gravity.

"Report," he ordered.

Ai-lan turned her head towards him. "Tentative
fix on a craft approaching the singleton dwarf. Speed
exceeds light-maximum, with discernible pulses of
warp-drive. Definitely a ship under power, although
the readings now diverge from the last readings
taken of the Guild ship."

"Overtake it."

"Sire."

The monitor controller transferred his data to the
navigation board in front of Ai-lan. *Ngoh Ge* leaped
forward to intersect the distant ship. Chaat rose from
his chair and stood behind her, studying the readings. The Guild ship's earlier arrival and the strange
readings in its warp-trace indicated that the Guildswoman had the use of the Light. Yet now her ship
moved at a crawl, almost struggling to reach the next
star.

He scowled, considering possibilities. Perhaps the
device had damaged her ship, or perhaps she
tempted him into some folly, like a *quaseti* female
luring predators into its mate's ground-trap. Why
was she moving so slowly? Surely she could see
Ngoh Ge rushing down upon her.

I'll ask her later, he thought coldly, *when her ship
has fallen into* my *trap.* Then he scowled again.

He felt a grudging respect for this Guildswoman,
and it annoyed him. But this human had proven an
able adversary, dealing him setbacks he'd not sus-
tained since Antares. Twice his spy had dealt her a
crippling blow, only to find her at his heels again.
Strange. Was it her Guild training? He had heard of
the instruction, but found that it provided no particular grace to the Daruma. Indeed, it made them
soft-minded and careless, too focused on their har-

monies to recognize true threat. He had outsmarted
the Guild for years, stealing knowledge of the sector
while they continued to discount him.

Perhaps because she was human? He fastened on
that thought, seeking its implications. He had studied the humans at long distance, seen their frustra-
tions with the local Daruma, but had dismissed them
as casual interlopers into Sagittarius. Perhaps his
assessment should be revised; perhaps these humans
were the true quarry.

He had heard they controlled four star-systems
beyond their own, exploiting the worlds through
control of the native races. He wondered at their
means of control, then wondered further—incredible
thought!—if they might be another race of Masters.
Chaat stared at the control panels, trying to adjust
his mind to the concept. The philosophers had spec-
ulated about such a possibility, although Command
caste had always ridiculed the theory—had not the
Li Fawn dominated every slave-race they encountered? Yet . . .

Possibilities are always part of Chance, and thus
worshipped as such by spy caste. And Chaat knew
that Chance affected even his own Law of Rule. Possibility—a House could fall, sending a father into
captivity and a son into exile. Possibility—a capital
ship could prove too careless, and fall to a deft
attack, gifting slaves and a wife to the victor. Possibilities could become events, and a ruler who trusted
the Right too much eventually met Chance's substituted choices.

Who were these humans?

He would ask the Guildswoman . . . and make her
answer to his satisfaction.

Ngoh Ge slipped down-system, hurtling towards
its small prey. The ship whispered through the arcing gas-streams of the primary stars, then emerged

on the far side at a greater speed, aided by the forces
which shaped the system's immense gravity well.
Plot-trace calculations indicated the Guild ship had
chosen the same option, another odd similarity that
annoyed Chaat further. Ahead lay the larger of the
three dwarf companions, winking sullenly orange
against the limitless black of space.

"Reading on the degenerate star ahead?" Chaat
asked, as yet another possibility abruptly occurred
to him.

"Unstable, sir," answered a nearby controller.
Chaat sensed his sister's shoulders tense as she saw
the same danger.

"That I could guess," Chaat said dryly, and saw
the controller flinch from his tone. "Display a curve
on the upper board."

He and Ai-lan studied the time-power display
above their heads.

"Analyzing for pattern," Ai-lan murmured, her
hands moving quickly over her controls. "But her
ship is closer to the star—suicide?"

"I doubt it. She has less mass, more momentum:
she might ride it out from that position. We haven't
so good a . . . There!" He jabbed a finger towards
the end of the tracing. The dwarf in-collapsed a quarter of its face, and sent its shock-wave hurtling into
the system's well. Before Ai-lan could react, *Ngoh
Ge* staggered under the impact, then slipped sideways, back toward the primary pair.

"Abort course!" Chaat shouted. "Take us out of
the orbital plane!"

Ai-lan punched several buttons on her controls,
then swung her head towards the Eschoni across the
room. "Abort course!" she snarled, her voice high
with panic and rage. The crab-man cringed at her
tone and gibbered impotently, then jerked its claws
away from the controls, wailing, as the programmed

unishment struck through its collar. It shrieked its protest, tearing insanely at its chains, oblivious to the alarm lights rippling across its monitor boards. Ai-lan threw herself towards the floor controls, but too late. . . .

Ngoh Ge blundered into a deep hole in the gravity well and was wrenched violently aside by a giant invisible hand. Ai-lan sprawled on her face, and Chaat kept his feet only by clinging to the back of her chair. The deck tipped sideways, spilling the guards off their feet, tumbling controllers from their chairs. Chaat's feet skittered from beneath him as he clung to the chair's support.

"Correct our course!" he yelled.

A half-dozen alarms shrieked their warning as the ship trembled under the massive stresses of the well. The primary pair in the observation screen seemed to leap towards *Ngoh Ge* as the ship spiraled backwards, falling helplessly into the gravity well.

"Correct our course!" Chaat shouted again.

"We don't have the ship-power!" cried a panicked controller.

Chaat grabbed the controller and pulled him to the monitor station, kicking aside the Eschoni. The controller looked up, furious at his humiliation.

Chaat sketched a quick gesture of apology, unsuited to Command caste but which bespoke an equal. "I would take it myself," he said, "if I could. You must save us."

The controller bowed his crested head a moment, then knelt at the floor controls. "Sire," he murmured. Ai-lan joined him and together they assumed the functions, bringing *Ngoh Ge*'s wild fall under some control. Chaat strode to the Control board and assumed Ai-lan's seat.

"There," he said coolly, his finger tracing the plot

of the forces which surrounded them. "We will ri
this line of the well up-system."

The other controllers obeyed, their panic stilled
by his calm assumption of authority. For such crises,
Chaat had been bred, and he felt a fierce satisfaction
as Control resumed its competent operations. The
ship steadied as it accelerated into the well on a long
parabolic orbit.

The ship swept through the inner system in a long
curve, barely under control, and was finally thrown
clear far above the orbital plane. To the left in the
screens, now far distant, the tiny light-trace of *Ariel*
slowly rounded the singleton dwarf, then launched
itself for the dwarf pair far down-system. Chaat
watched her light-trace with a cold fury that boded
poorly for that Guildswoman: he'd not fall into her
baited trap again.

He restored order to the bridge with a few sharp
commands, then directed Ai-lan to bring a replacement Eschoni. She responded quickly, admiration
present in every line of her body. When the creature
arrived from the pens and was bolted into place,
Chaat raised the other controller with his own hands
and honored him before all of Command.

Then *Ngoh Ge* began the long process of nosing
its way back into the system, wary of its complicated
well.

At the edge of the system, *Ariel*'s small messenger
capsule hurtled through the emptiness of space, lost
in its far orbit around the system. The shock-wave
of the singleton dwarf propagated itself outward at
the speed of light, touching the primary pair within
minutes, its companion dwarfs within an hour, then
rippled beyond, its energy fading as it spent itself
against the unyielding fabric of space.

The pulse-wave reached the capsule and the slender statuette within, tugging at it slightly: Madringa pulsed with the brief surge of energy, then quieted as the wave-front passed in its decreasing force. The small tug was enough: slowly, inevitably, the capsule shifted its course and began falling towards the nearest star, accelerating steadily.

The in-fall collapse of the dwarf gave Jennan a series of very busy moments. The star seemed to grab at *Ariel*, seeking to pull her into its gravity maw, but the ship's momentum carried her through a close orbit and whipped her away down-system, still on course. Jennan ran a quick check of hull temperatures and *Ariel*'s particle damage, then sank backward in her chair.

"Whew!" she said.

"It's working!" Vaughn shouted a moment later. The three humans watched the trace-light of the Li Fawn ship waver, then slip backward towards the primary pair, struggling against the gravity forces released by the dwarf. For a time, it looked like Xi might solve *Ariel*'s problem, but the Li Fawn managed to extricate themselves and rode the gravity wave out of danger.

"Smart piloting," Jennan said, impressed. She doubted if even a Vang could have done better, and knew all too well her own efforts would have put the ship smack into the nearest primary.

"Luck, probably," Vaughn argued, his mouth drawn down in disappointment. Jennan looked at him coolly.

"It's only a reprieve," she remarked. "I didn't expect anything more."

"Of course," Tanner said. "But it yanked a few tail-feathers, that's for sure. Great work, Jennan." He smiled at her in open approval, but she shrugged him off impatiently.

"I don't program the stars to suit me." She studied their orbit trace. "Computer, can you track the Light's capsule?"

"Negative. Capsule is too small to distinguish within the solar wind."

"What's the problem?" Lume asked.

"That in-fall shook the whole system. I'm hoping it didn't warp the capsule's orbit."

"You mean it might fall into one of the suns?"

"Exactly. What'll happen then is your guess as well as mine. The Light was activated by warp-drive, and warp-drive is mainly modified gravity. The Light's half-awake already; infalling to a star might set it off again."

"Great," Lume said, scowling.

"And we're heading straight towards it?" Tanner said.

"You got it, Vaughn. Everybody should get to the same place about two hours from now—us, the Light, and Chaat. It should be a most interesting party. Computer, what's our engine performance?"

"With orbit acceleration, sixty-two percent of normal in-system drive."

"Let's hope it's enough. I don't expect to get away again, gentlemen, but at least we can give the Li Fawn a good chase, time enough for the Light to destroy itself, if it does."

"And maybe us."

"That accomplishes the same purpose," Jennan said flatly. "It's a long jump from Naberr: a Guild ship can't get here in time, not with the delay of the message-capsule transit. Hmmm."

"Computer," she said a moment later.

"Acknowledged."

"Load all data of the Light transit into a message capsule. Include a transcript of all conversations and computer readings aboard this ship since we left hann, including the visitape of Maleto's ship." She paused. "Include plotting trace of our orbit through Xi Scorpii, all engine readings, and all other data with twenty percent relevancy to the Light."

"Acknowledged." The computer paused. "Data loaded."

"Send to the personal attention of the Guildmaster at Naberr, with same salutation as the earlier capsule."

"Acknowledged."

"Launch."

"Acknowledged."

Tanner looked at her quizzically. "You think they can make sense of the data?"

"Maybe. At least it will put an end to the Li Fawn's supposed neutrality if *Ngoh Ge* gets away. I can't think of anything else." She rubbed her temples tiredly, feeling the dull throb of her returning headache. The room tightened momentarily, then grayed out. A mocking feverish eye watched her from a distance, and she felt the gravity waves of the system ripple through her body.

"*I AM THE LIGHT!*" Madringa shrieked.

"Yay," Jennan muttered.

"What did you say?" Vaughn asked.

"Nothing."

She watched the Li Fawn ship pass nearly out of range of her sensors, flung out of the system by the gravity well . . . then slow at the apex of its curve. Gracefully, *Ngoh Ge* turned towards them, then settled into a long orbit around the outskirts of the Xi system. Jennan bit her lip, considering possibilities but found little of hope. Even if Xi cooperated again with another infall, she doubted the Li Fawn would make the same mistake again. *Ariel* was finally running out of options.

"Computer, time of exact intersection by Li Fawn ship on that course."

"One point eight hours."

"Time of *Ariel*'s arrival at dwarf pair?"

"One point seven hours."

"Great," she said dryly and leaned back in her chair. "I'm hungry," she announced. "Anybody want to eat?"

"Eat!" Tanner protested.

"Why not?" she said. "Consider it our last meal, maybe." She stood up and put her hands on her hips, then stretched her shoulders upward to unkink tired muscles. "Though only 'maybe.' I'm still considering our options."

"Oh, sure." Tanner waved a despairing hand at the viewscreen. "Lots of options there."

"Can it, Vaughn," she suggested sweetly, all too conscious of her own bravado but unwilling—for the moment—to concede anything, at least to Vaughn Tanner.

They ate dinner on the flight deck, watching the slow approach of the Li Fawn ship towards the intersection point a few AU from the dwarf pair. They discussed the various possibilities, limited as they were. Lume again adamantly refused capture, and give pointed details of the lives they could expect in the Li Fawn pens. They'd have no opportunity for another escape: Li Fawn technology was too alien to hope to manage a Li Fawn craft, and *Ariel* presently had no out-system capacity without extensive engine repairs.

Tanner favored a shoot-em-up with the Li Fawn, but admitted that meteor wards had little impact on a cruiser of *Ngoh Ge*'s size. Gradually both men reached Jennan's own conclusion, one she had accepted hours earlier in the engine room when Shavanda's cry had echoed through her mind. The only uestion was whether *Ariel*'s self-destruction could wreak enough damage on the Li Fawn to cripple *Ngoh Ge*—and then whether Madringa might somehow complete that destruction.

Options. Possibilities.

"Computer, any trace of the Light capsule?" she asked.

"Negative. Assuming any of several possible orbits, the capsule would now be behind the dwarf pair. Impossible to scan through the particle interference."

"Very well." Jennan looked around the flight deck sadly, then began programming the engine overload into the computer controls. She painstakingly removed the safety dampers in the programming, explaining her intention to the computer itself to gain its help in dismantling the safety programming. It complied, emotionless about its own destruction.

"Can you think of anything we've overlooked?" she asked the others. They looked at her soberly and said nothing.

"Compute distance at which explosion will cause maximum damage to Li Fawn cruiser." She took a deep breath. "Engage new program at that proximity."

"Acknowledged."

Ariel slipped closer to the dwarfs, and both suns seemed to stretch out tentacles of flame towards her tiny ship, reaching to consume that small spark of life—as a goddess might stoop to destroy her own worshippers. Jennan leaned back in her control chair and wrapped her arms around herself, then focused on older memories, before the Light, before the Taki trade.

Morgen, my friend, I love you. She imaged his face, and hoped he would not grieve too deeply—only remember her with honor.

Honor . . . or mock heroism, Bartlett? But some-

times the heroine label might fit, even if othe[r]
might call it stupidity and second-guess her options[,]
conveniently ignoring the details which forced a single conclusion. *Chandra, my ferocious friend . . .*
Chandra would know the balance.

She thought of forest spaces and the gentle dap-
pling of sunlight on humid earth and living things,
of chiming laugh-notes within her mind. *Ah, sweet
T'wing, my beloved. Remember me, if you can survive the loss, if it is your nature to survive.*

She pulled up still other faces, other memories,
from her store-house and assembled them in front of
her. Last of all, she summoned the Guildmaster's
face.

Master, I promise. . . . echoed a younger voice in
her mind, her own voice of five years before. *. . . I
promise to uphold and protect . . .*

Yes. Perhaps there was heroism in that, though
she would be content with propriety. The Daruma
understood many things very well.

Resigned, she watched *Ngoh Ge* hurtle down
towards them.

Chapter 22

Ngoh Ge grew steadily closer, and the three humans watched its approach, each in his own way. Tanner shifted uneasily in his chair and he chewed on the side of his thumb, neatly pinching off the spare skin with his teeth. Lume sat with his head propped comfortably backward, his expression enclosed and distant, his dark eyes fixed on the moving light-trace. Jennan watched their faces for a time, her eyes straying more to Lume.

Curious, how much we are alike, she thought. *No time to know him now, no time. . . . but still I wonder . . .*

"Jennan," Tanner said hoarsely. "Surely there's another way . . ."

She looked at him sadly. "No options, Vaughn. I'm sorry."

Tanner returned to his restless anxiety, and the cabin was again filled with silence. *Ngoh Ge* grew still nearer, and Jennan heard a sharp click from the control board as the Li Fawn approach activated the proximity sequence. One by one the engine telltales

shifted to danger-alert as *Ariel* opened her engi
chambers to the central reactor.

No time. . . .

Then, at the edge of the viewscreen, another light
winked into sight. Jennan stared at the ship-marker,
at first unable to comprehend.

"*Ariel*," the comm crackled. "Acknowledge."

She hurriedly snapped open the circuit. "*Ariel*
acknowledging. Do you show my position?"

"Yes," a second voice said calmly. "This is Guild
Captain Landoni. Are the Li Fawn in pursuit?"

"Yes. Can you warn them off?"

"If they'll listen—which they may not." Over the
comm, Jennan heard a voice in the background send
a challenge to the Li Fawn ship.

"Li Fawn ship, state your intention. . . ."

Ngoh Ge persisted in its steady approach to Jennan's ship, dangerously close now.

"The self-destruct!" Tanner cried.

"Yes." Jennan lunged forward for the controls. The
first key of the last bank of indicators snapped down
as *Ariel* still obeyed its self-destruct sequence.
"Computer! Abort self-destruct sequence!" Desperately, Jennan pressed key after key, trying to abort
manually, then lifted her hands a moment later when
the computer swept across the controls with light-
ning speed.

"Acknowledged," it said. "Destruct sequence halted.
Restoring damper controls."

"Whew," Lume said behind her, and Jennan
shared the relief, her skin prickling with the close-
ness of disaster.

"Give me a read-out on the engines," she said.

A schematic displayed on the pilot's side-monitor.
"At critical mass. Analyzing additional damage to
warp-drive, reactor systems. Four sensors burned
out: substituting other monitors."

"Jennan," came Morgen's voice over the comm, "are you all right?"

She grimaced. "Yes, Morgen, but I have engine damage. Any response from the Li Fawn cruiser?"

"No," Landoni said shortly. "Your engine damage is noted, Guildswoman: we will compensate." She heard the low mutter of voices as new orders were given, then saw the Guild light-trace visibly leap forward as Landoni dangerously risked more speed inside the system.

In response, *Ngoh Ge* also swung inward to shorten its interception course. Jennan in turn increased power to *Ariel's* engines, hoping they held together. She turned *Ariel* away from the dwarf suns, trying to use as much of their momentum as possible to escape their gravity pull. As the ship changed its attitude, one of the dwarfs swam into view in the screen, a glowing orange ball diseased with the darker blotches of collapsing matter. High-arcing gas plumes flickered on its edges. *Ariel* struggled away from it, slowed by the forces of the gravity well.

Lume abruptly leaned forward in his chair, his finger stabbing at the screen.

"Jennan! Look!"

On the dwarf's surface, an unseen force stirred the very fabric of the star and lifted up a kilometers-tall pylon of gas, its peak surmounted by a blazing reddish eye. The figure rose still higher, drawing more and more of the star's substance to herself. She raised her arms in the exultation of her creation.

"*I AM THE ENDLESS LIGHT,*" Madringa cried to the void. She swayed in her mad joy, reaching upward, stretching her sinuous body until she stood thousands of kilometers high. And still she reached upward, fueled by the power of the sun upon which she fed.

I AM THE LIGHT!

Madringa's fiery head bent downward and s̶
looked at Jennan, striking through her with a rub̶
gaze. A glowing hand of incandescent gas reached̶
outward for *Ariel*.

Jennan leaped to her feet. "No! No!" she shouted
and pointed towards *Ngoh Ge*. "Take them, if you
must!"

I will take all, Madringa replied, stretching outward. *The order of the taking does not matter.*

"Not my ship!" Jennan cried.

As a tendril of gas flickered on *Ariel's* hull, Jennan
slammed her hand down on the warp control, sending *Ariel* on a reckless plunge into hyper-space. Jennan immediately felt the wrongness of the warp as
the ship turned itself inside out. She screamed, and
dimly heard the hoarse shouts of terror from her two
companions.

I AM THE LIGHT! Madringa cried, pursuing
them into non-space.

"No! No!"

Jennan fell into the void, spinning helplessly
downward, as the Light again splintered her body
into a dozen vaporous shapes. A rushing wind
accompanied her, bearing the voices of a dying
planet, struck unforewarned by catastrophe.

"No, no, no! *I AM THE LIGHT*," Jennan cried
and spent one of her selves on the unresisting fabric
of *Ariel*, throwing her ship outward in desperate
flight. Behind her, a goddess shrieked her rage and
snatched vainly at the ship as it slipped through her
fingers, then pulled back her hand. With another
cry, Madringa pulled the substance of five suns to
herself, and, caught forever in her destiny,
destroyed herself.

"*I AM THE LIGHT*," Madringa cried one last
time, and took all within her grasp into oblivion.

"I AM THE LIGHT!" Jennan cried, and enclosed Morgen's ship in another of her vaporous selves, uniting it with *Ariel*. Together the two ships plunged through non-space, directed by Jennan's half-conscious will, then fell through an interface into normality.

The flight deck steadied around her, its familiar sounds penetrating through the roaring in her ears. Jennan blinked and looked blankly at the viewscreen, now alight with dozens of light-traces. Where?

A tall vapor flickered against the wall of the flight deck, distracting her attention. Its mad gaze locked with Jennan's for a long moment; then it faded out. *My sister*, it whispered from the walls, its ghostly voice echoing in the enclosed space of the flight deck. *You understand.*

Jennan sat down heavily in her flight chair. "Yes, I understand." She closed her eyes wearily, her senses thrumming with the after-effects of the Light. She sensed the wraith moving easily through the walls, slipping between atoms, outward toward the emptiness which surrounded the ship.

I will return, Jennan Bartlett, it said as it launched itself away from *Ariel*. *You are the Life-Bringer*.

"What?" Jennan said, confused. The wraith's presence flickered out like an extinguished flame.

"Where are we?" Tanner asked weakly, his head lolling. "What happened?" Jennan shook her head at him, then chuckled as the comm crackled into life.

"Naberr Control to approaching Guild ships. You are in violation of traffic patterns. Warn off! Take proper orbit!" The Guildsman was nearly apoplectic.

"This is Guild Captain Landoni," a voice replied. "We will comply. Uh, sorry."

Jennan snapped a toggle and said: "*Ariel* acknowledging." Then she laughed, tears starting in her

eyes. Options. She laughed again, and heard th'
slightly hysterical edge in her own voice.

"Jennan?" Lume asked, his concern visible in his
pale face.

"It's nothing." She sobered to watch the light-
traces, multiplied a hundredfold with Naberr's intra-
system traffic, that displayed on her screen. Near
her was the Guild cruiser, moving in simultaneous
orbit with *Ariel* as the two ships spiraled in-system.

"We're home," she said with deep satisfaction.

From a prudent distance of half a light-year, Lord-
Son Chaat watched Xi Scorpii collapse upon itself.
Long streamers of gas fell into a central core centered on the now-vanished dwarf, as the matter of
the system fell inward in a great spiral to an
unknown oblivion.

"Time for the effect to absorb the star system?"
he asked.

Ai-lan turned her crested head towards him, her
expression awed. "At this rate, Lord, perhaps three
hours," she said. "It may then begin on nearby
space-time, but the effect must be self-limiting. No
force could absorb the entire universe."

"Perhaps," Chaat said, thinking of Possibility that
could blight hopes. He fell silent as he wished with
Ai-lan against such possibility, for all that wishes
might do against a Power of that magnitude. He felt
awed, again one with Ai-lan, and felt the prick of
ambition to possess that Power. The Light . . . what
was it? And where might he find another?

He watched the viewscreen soberly, his long fingers stroking the arm of his chair. The control room
became uncommonly silent, awaiting what? His
explosion of rage? His slinking away into failure? He
looked at his controllers, none of whom dared meet
his gaze.

Sometimes Command could be lonely. For a moment, Chaat thought of Chaat-lama and her beauty, wished that she . . . But Chaat had been bred to his rank, and already his mind seethed with new plans.

"Ai-lan . . ." he said.

"Yes, Lord."

"Plot a course back to Shann."

"Sire?" Ai-lan sounded astonished. "For what purpose?"

Her question enraged him. "Must I repeat my order, Ai-lan?" he said in silky threat. Ai-lan glanced at him, cowed.

"No, Lord."

"Activate warp," he commanded. *Ngoh Ge* jumped into the embracing arms of non-space.

Alone, Xi Scorpii whispered its energy winds, falling inward into infinity. Fueled by the matter of five suns, Madringa penetrated another Reality and found new strength in the worlds she consumed there. Again and again, new worshippers warily approached her, their energy-shapes fluctuating with emotions of alarm, awe, confusion—then terror as she absorbed them.

I AM THE LIGHT! she cried as an entire universe lent itself to her purpose. Then, flickering, empty, she fractured herself into a thousand selves, a thousand universes.

I AM THE LIGHT! the thousand cried, and fractured again and again and again in a mad ecstasy of self-destruction, fading at last into the lostness of Infinity.

THE MANY WORLDS OF
MELISSA SCOTT

*Winner of the John W. Campbell Award
for Best New Writer, 1986*

THE KINDLY ONES: "An ambitious novel of the world Orestes. This large, inhabited moon is governed by five Kinships whose society operates on a code of honor so strict that transgressors are declared legally 'dead' and are prevented from having any contact with the 'living.' . . . Scott is a writer to watch."—*Publishers Weekly*. A Main Selection of the Science Fiction Book Club.
65351-2 • 384 pp. • $2.95

The "Silence Leigh" Trilogy

FIVE-TWELFTHS OF HEAVEN (Book I): "Melissa Scott postulates a universe where technology interferes with magic. . . . The whole plot is one of space ships, space wars, and alien planets—not a unicorn or a dragon to be seen anywhere. Scott's space drive and description of space piloting alone would mark her as an expert in the melding of the [SF and fantasy] genres; this is the stuff of which 'sense of wonder' is made."—*Locus*
55952-4 • 352 pp. • $2.95

SILENCE IN SOLITUDE (Book II): "[Scott is] a voice you should seek out and read at every opportunity."
—*OtherRealms*.   65699-7 • 324 pp. • $2.95

THE EMPRESS OF EARTH (Book III):
65364-4 • 352 pp. • $3.50

AN OFFER HE COULDN'T REFUSE

They were functional fangs, not just decorative, set i.
protruding jaw, with long lips and a wide mouth; yet the to
effect was lupine rather than simian. Hair a dark matted mess
And yes, fully eight feet tall, a rangy, tense-muscled body.

She clawed her wild hair away from her face and stared
at him with renewed fierceness. Her eyes were a strange
light hazel, adding to the wolfish effect. "What are you
really doing here?"

"I came for you. I'd heard of you. I'm . . . recruiting.
Or I was. Things went wrong and now I'm escaping. But
if you came with me, you could join the Dendarii
Mercenaries. A top outfit—always looking for a few good
men, or whatever. I have this master-sergeant who . . .
who *needs* a recruit like you." Sgt. Dyeb was infamous for
his sour attitude about women soldiers, insisting that they
were too soft . . .

"Very funny," she said coldly. "But I'm not even human.
Or hadn't you heard?"

"Human is as human does." He forced himself to reach
out and touch her damp cheek. "Animals don't weep."

She jerked, as from an electric shock. "Animals don't
lie. Humans do. All the time."

"Not *all* the time."

"Prove it." She tilted her head as she sat cross-legged.
"Take off your clothes."

". . . what?"

"Take off your clothes and lie down with me as *humans* do.
Men and women." Her hand reached out to touch his throat.

The pressing claws made little wells in his flesh. "Blrp?"
choked Miles. His eyes felt wide as saucers. A little more
pressure, and those wells would spring forth red fountains.
I am about to die. . . .

*I can't believe this. Trapped on Jackson's Whole with a
sex-starved teenage werewolf. There was nothing about
this in any of my Imperial Academy training manuals. . . .*

**BORDERS OF INFINITY by LOIS McMASTER
BUJOLD**
69841-9 • $3.95